Revved
to the Maxx

NEW YORK TIMES AND USA TODAY BESTSELLING AUTHOR
MELANIE MORELAND

Dear Reader,

Thank you for selecting Revved To The Maxx to read. Be sure to sign up for my newsletter for up to date information on new releases, exclusive content and sales. You can find the form here: https://bit.ly/MMorelandNewsletter

Before you sign up, add melanie@melaniemoreland.com to your contacts to make sure the email comes right to your inbox!
Always fun - never spam!

My books are available in paperback and audiobook! You can see all my books available and upcoming preorders at my website.

The Perfect Recipe For **LOVE**
xoxo,
Melanie

ALSO BY MELANIE MORELAND D2D

The Contract Series

The Contract (Contract #1)

The Baby Clause (Contract #2)

The Amendment (Contract #3)

The Addendum Coming to Radish 2022 - Wide Release 2023

Vested Interest Series

BAM - The Beginning (Prequel)

Bentley (Vested Interest #1)

Aiden (Vested Interest #2)

Maddox (Vested Interest #3)

Reid (Vested Interest #4)

Van (Vested Interest #5)

Halton (Vested Interest #6)

Sandy (Vested Interest #7)

Vested Interest/ABC Crossover

A Merry Vested Wedding

ABC Corp Series

My Saving Grace (Vested Interest: ABC Corp #1)

Finding Ronan's Heart (Vested Interest: ABC Corp #2)

Loved By Liam (Vested Interest: ABC Corp #3)

Age of Ava (Vested Interest: ABC Corp #4)

Happily Ever After Collection

Heart Strings

MORELAND
BOOKS INC.

Edited by Lisa Hollett of Silently Correcting Your Grammar
Cover design by Melissa Ringuette, Monark Design Services
Cover Photography by Eric D Battershell
Cover Model Nelson Lopes
Cover content is for illustrative purposes only and any person depicted on the
cover is a model.

DEDICATION

Love comes in all forms, shapes, and packages.
But it is still love.
The greatest gift we can share is our hearts.
This one is for you.
To love in all its glory.
And to my Matthew who epitomizes it.

CHAPTER 1

MAXX

The night was pitch black, and outside, the wind blew hot and strong. The only other sound was the low beat of the rock music playing in the background. I took a long draw on the bottle of beer I had grabbed from the small fridge in the garage and finished the sandwich I had thrown together. I stared at the computer, then opened a new document. I scrubbed my face in vexation. I had no idea how to do this, nor did I particularly want to, but at this point, it was something I had to try, like it or not.

Wanted:

~~Helper~~

~~Errand boy~~

~~Errand girl~~

~~Assistant~~

~~Personal Assistant~~

~~Housekeeper~~

~~Bookkeeper~~

~~Sidekick~~

I sat and mulled over the list. None of the descriptions seemed right. A memory floated through my head of my dad and mom in the office. He always called her his Girl Friday, saying there wasn't a task she couldn't do. He always insisted she was better at everything in the office than he was and he'd be lost without her. *That* was the sort of person I needed. I typed it into the ad.

Girl Friday
Duties:
~~Running mechanic shop plus~~
Housekeeping, Grocery shopping, Laundry, Cooking meals
Must also be proficient at bookkeeping, invoicing, ~~other various duties~~

I looked over the list with a frown. Mary, my neighbor, had told me to place an ad on this site and be very specific about what I was looking for. I reread the list and started typing again. When it was done, I checked it, deciding it was specific enough.

Wanted: Girl Friday
Duties:
Housekeeping, Grocery shopping, Laundry, Cooking meals
Must also be proficient at bookkeeping, invoicing, banking, inventory control, and website upkeep for business.
Must be able to drive, be highly organized, and able to work without supervision.
Must like living in the country, with limited access to major towns.
Must like dogs.
Ability to make pies an asset.
Work – Monday to Friday 8 a.m. to 6 p.m. Saturday 8 a.m. to 12 p.m.
Saturday afternoons and Sundays are free
Room with private bath. Board plus salary.

Only serious applicants need apply.

I looked around the shop. I needed help. Since Shannon had taken off, things had gotten worse. They'd been slipping for a long time, but somehow, I had never noticed. I snorted and drained my beer.

I hadn't noticed a lot of things.

I paused. Was the pie thing a bit over the top? I knew pie making was a lost art and probably not done by people under the age of fifty. I decided to leave it. Maybe it would weed out the non-serious applicants.

I loaded up the document on Solutions for You and double-checked it for errors. I liked the fact that with this website, you could "chat" with interested parties and get a feel for them before hiring. I had tried a couple of other job sites but didn't like them. This one had simpler guidelines and was not only for jobs. You could buy and sell things. Trade. Post for lost articles. In the past, I had only used it to find parts, but Mary had found her last two helpers there and encouraged me to try. It seemed like a good idea. I had nothing to lose at this point. I wasn't really holding out much hope on this idea, although I had to try something.

You could choose the reach of your ad, and I purposely set this one for outside my region, but within the province. I had to hire from outside the small town where I lived. I didn't want to see the pitying looks or give the gossips anything new to yak about by having them here in my shop and, especially, my home. I needed a stranger with no connections to this place or me.

Someone I didn't know or care about and who felt the same way about me.

It was simple. I needed a job done, and I was sure there was someone out there looking for a job to do.

Satisfied, I hit submit.

Now, all I had to do was wait for the applicants to fly in.

Who could resist such a great job offer?

CHARLYNN

I stared at the piece of paper in my hand, horrified. I was certain I had to be reading this wrong.

"Eviction notice," I whispered. I looked up at my landlord. "Eviction notice?" I repeated, my voice louder. "But I'm only behind by a month!"

Terry leaned on the doorjamb, not at all concerned. He looked me over with one of his long leers that I hated. I backed up a step, not liking his close proximity.

"Nope. Including this one, you owe me three months."

"Three?" I squeaked. "But I gave Trish my share of the rent —I don't understand. She told me the rent was paid—I have the receipts!"

"Let me see them."

I hurried into the small kitchen and yanked open the drawer. I pulled out the envelope and grabbed the slips of paper. I turned, startled when I realized Terry had followed me into the kitchen. I didn't like him very much—he gave me the creeps. I tamped down my nervousness and thrust out the papers. "Here."

He looked at them and shook his head, pushing them back at me. "Fakes."

I looked down at the slips. When Trish had told me the rent was paid, I never looked at the slips. She put them in the drawer with the others. Now, as I studied them, I could see Terry wasn't lying. These were copies.

"Where did the money go?" I mumbled.

He shrugged. "She gave it to someone else."

I fought down my sense of panic. "There has to be something

I can do." I swallowed my revulsion at asking Terry for anything, but I had no choice. "Trish screwed me over, Terry. She took off with everything I owned and cleaned me out. Plus, I lost my job. Surely, you can give me a little time to figure things out."

A predatory light sparked in his eyes and he came closer, his eyes traveling up and down my body, this time not bothering to disguise his interest. "I could let you pay off what you owe the same way your roomie did."

"Wh-what?"

"She paid your rent the last couple of months on her back." He winked lewdly. "And her knees."

I took a step back, shaking my head wildly. "No."

He smiled. It was cold and cruel. "I bet you're a hellcat in bed, aren't you?" He reached out and grabbed a piece of my hair, pulling on it sharply. "Redheads are known for their tempers. I'd like to see you all riled up and fighting me." He paused, licking his lips. "I like it when they fight."

My stomach turned at his words. I slapped away his hand, disgusted. "Unless you want your balls in your throat, I suggest you step back. I said no. Get out."

His expression never faded—if anything, it got colder. "Give me what I want, and you get to keep your apartment for another month." He sneered at me. "If you're good, maybe longer."

I wanted to gag. But instead, I tilted my head and studied him as if considering his generous "offer." I stepped forward and laid my hand on top of his, casting my eyes downward. His grunt of satisfaction became a howl of pain as I roughly bent back his fingers. I took advantage of his discomfort and gripped his arm upward, bending it at an awkward angle I knew would be painful. I frog-marched him over to my door, pushing him out.

"I'd rather be homeless."

I slammed the door shut and locked it, fuming. I slid the

chain in place with a loud snap. I could hear him cursing and muttering on the other side of the closed door.

I walked away, only to swing around when the door unlocked and Terry's ugly face appeared through the opening allowed by the chain.

"You forget, bitch. I have a key that gets me in anytime I want."

He slammed the door before I could move.

For a moment, I stood, anxiety sinking into my chest. He was right. He could get in anytime. There had been times after my first roommate, Rhonda, moved out, I thought someone had been in the apartment while I wasn't home, but I could never prove it. My next roommate, Trish, worked from home, and she denied he'd ever bothered her.

Terry lifted the mail slot of the old-fashioned door. "You have until the end of the month. Either pay up what you owe plus an extra month, or you're out of here."

The mail slot slammed with a loud metallic noise, and his heavy footsteps echoed in the hall.

The end of the month was in a week. I owed three-months' worth of back rent now. I slid down the wall, pulling on my hair in worry.

I looked around the small apartment. I had lived here for two years. When Rhonda had gotten married, I had advertised and found a new person to split the bills. Trish seemed great at first. She liked to cook, she was fun to be around, and I felt as if I had found a new friend. When I confessed to finding the landlord a little unnerving, and that Rhonda had always dealt with him, Trish insisted she be the one to pay the rent every month, saying she "didn't want me uncomfortable," and she "could handle him." She'd made a point of showing me she put the receipt in the drawer the first month, and I never gave it a second thought after that.

Until I came home one day two weeks ago to find she'd hacked in to my accounts, stolen all my money, racked up some charges on my credit card, taken anything of value I owned, and disappeared.

Literally.

It was as if she had never existed. Which, it turned out, she hadn't. When I went to the police to file a report, I discovered I had been scammed. There was no such person as Trish Gordon. She was good. The numbers I had called to check out her references no longer existed. The names on her application were all fake. She was a pro, and I had fallen for her friendly, helpful act —hook, line, and sinker.

The same week, I lost my job. The industrial company I worked for simply closed their doors with no warning. I hadn't been able to find another full-time job, and the part-time ones I could find barely covered basic necessities, never mind rent. I had been further horrified when I found out the money I had put aside for this month's rent, Trish took along with everything else.

And now I found she had taken the other rent money and traded it off for blow jobs and sex.

I was screwed. Completely screwed.

Kelly looked at me over her glass. "What can I do, Char?"

I sipped my wine. Kelly was almost as broke as I was, so there was no point in asking her for a loan. "Nothing. I have to move and find a job in a week. Easy peasy, right?"

"You can sleep on my couch," she offered halfheartedly.

I patted her hand. "You sleep on your couch already." Kelly's apartment was tiny—one room in a boarding house. She loved it, but the one time we had tried to live together, it almost destroyed our friendship. We were two very different people.

"We could figure it out."

"Thanks." I hated to think it might come down to that, but the truth was, it might.

"Where have you applied?"

"Everywhere. Coffee shops, temp services, businesses. I've put my resume online on a bunch of those job sites. Nothing."

"Let me see."

I handed her my laptop and filled up my wine. It was one of the few things Trish had left behind—the box too awkward to carry, I supposed. That and ramen made a great dinner. The first time. By the tenth, it was barely palatable. Now, the wine was almost gone, and so was the ramen.

"You've covered a lot."

"I know."

"What is Solutions for You?" she asked with a frown.

"Oh, it's like Craigslist—a little less formal than some other job sites," I explained. "You can find a job or a new dresser if you want. It's sort of a catchall of ads. I heard about it and figured nothing ventured, nothing gained."

"I suppose." She scanned the screen. "Oh look, here's a new listing." She snickered. "It looks…interesting."

I peered over her shoulder, squinting a little to see the screen. Between the wine, and not knowing where my glasses were, it was hard to concentrate.

Wanted: Girl Friday
Duties:
Housekeeping, Grocery shopping, Laundry, Cooking meals
Must also be proficient at bookkeeping, invoicing, banking, inventory control,
and website upkeep for business.

Must be able to drive, be highly organized, and able to work without supervision.
Must like living in the country, with limited access to major towns.
Must like dogs.
Ability to make pies an asset.
Work – Monday to Friday 8 a.m. to 6 p.m. Saturday 8 a.m. to 12 p.m.
Saturday afternoons and Sundays are free
Room with private bath. Board plus salary.
Only serious applicants need apply.

I started to laugh. "Seriously? Girl Friday? Who uses that expression these days? Old farts?"

Kelly snickered. "That's quite a list."

"Wow, it certainly is," I muttered, reading.

"You are a great baker. You make an awesome lemon pie. Your blueberry is pretty stellar too," she joked.

I giggled and nudged her with my elbow. "Definitely an old guy. They like pies."

I skimmed it again, looking at his user name and snorted. "Cycleman has a lot of 'musts.' The guy must be a control freak. Is he looking for an employee or a wife? Holy moly, the only thing not listed is bearing children and missionary sex."

She winked. "Maybe he likes anal. No babies that way."

I snorted in amusement. "I can't believe anyone would post something like that." I looked at the stats. "It has four replies! Oh my god!"

"People." She shook her head. "They are weird."

I shut the laptop and drained my glass. "That they are."

CHAPTER 2

CHARLYNN

K elly left, and I locked the door, staring at the mainly empty apartment. The old sofa and a battered table were all that remained. Anything Trish had been able to lift and carry was gone. In the bedroom, my bed sat on the floor since she'd dismantled the frame and took that. The dresser that held my clothes was still there—no doubt she thought it was too old and ugly to bother with. She'd taken everything from the room she had stayed in.

I was grateful that we weren't the same size. Otherwise, I was certain all my clothes would be gone as well. Luckily, she hadn't touched my closet, which meant the photo albums that belonged to my parents were safe. At least I still had those. I'd had my laptop with me that day. If I hadn't, I knew it, too, would have been gone.

With a sigh, I decided to take a shower. I was exhausted. I changed into my robe, stopping at the sound of a knock at my door. Laughing, I went to open it, wondering what Kelly had forgotten. She was scatterbrained and left her keys or phone behind all the time.

But it wasn't Kelly's smiling face that greeted me. Terry was standing there, swaying slightly, the smell of liquor rolling off him. He leered at me openly.

I pushed the door, leaving it ajar a few inches. "What do you want?"

He eyed me through the narrow opening. "Wanted to see if you changed your mind."

"No." I tried to push the door closed, but he shoved his foot in, stopping me.

His voice was low and angry. "You think you're too good for me?"

"I am not trading sexual favors for rent. Get away from my door or I'll call the cops," I snapped.

He leaned on the door, and I let it go. Unprepared, he fell into the apartment, and I jumped on his back, bending his arm. "How many times are we going to do this, you asshole? I said no."

I stood. "Get out."

He stumbled to his feet, fury in his expression. I dared him to do something. With the door open, there would be witnesses —I could scream with the best of them. He staggered closer, his stale breath making me want to gag. "I can get in your apartment anytime I want, you little whore. Think about that while you're calling the cops." He snorted. "My word against yours." But he turned and stumbled away. "Bitch," he muttered.

I shut the door and locked it, then stared at the wood. He could get in. He had master keys to every door. There was only the one lock, plus the silly little chain I could slide across and use to peek out the door if I wanted. It gave me zero protection against someone like Terry. And I wasn't sure the cops would do anything. I'd had enough trouble convincing them about Trish. It was only when another cop overheard me and knew of an additional complaint that they took me seriously enough to file a report.

I shivered, deciding to forgo the shower, and sat down on the sofa. I opened my laptop, googling ideas for added protection for a door. Ten minutes later, I stepped back and admired my handiwork. I had slid the blade of a butter knife under the loose door trim, with the handle resting on the door, adding a small layer of protection. I added two more knives along the frame to be sure. Terry could unlock the door, but the knives would stop him from opening the door unless he broke it down. He would never draw that sort of attention to himself. It was a small thing, but perhaps with them in place, I would sleep a little.

Rattled, I drank the last of the wine, the buzz catching up with me. Pissed off, angry at the world, and needing to stay busy, I clicked on the Solutions for You site, shaking my head in disbelief at how many people had contacted Cycleman about his fabulous job.

Unable to resist, I sent him a message

Charly: *Is this a posting for a job or a wife?*
Cycleman: *What kind of question is that? It's a job. The duties are listed.*
Charly: *Sexist. Girl Friday? Duties? How old are you? Get with the times.*
Cycleman: *Forgive me for the insult. What would you suggest? Person Friday? You interested?*

I snorted.

Charly: *Person Friday would at least be better. But I don't work for sexists. In this day and age, you need to be respectful. The position would be Assistant. Aide. Office Manager. Dude—get with the times.*

Cycleman: *Not sexist—never done this before. I will change the wording, if I can figure out how.*

I laughed again. As I suspected, he was older.

Charly: *Good luck with finding someone to do all that for you. I suppose you had best add maid to the listing.*
Cycleman: *If you are applying, your attitude needs some adjusting.*
Charly: *I'm not the right type for the job.*
Cycleman: *Because you're male? I'd hire a guy. In fact, I would prefer it. Less trouble.*

I furrowed my brow. Why did he think I was a guy? Another burst of laughter left my lips. Charly was short for Charlynn. My friends called me Char or Charly. I always used a shorter version online. I shrugged since it didn't matter.

Charly: *Guys can be trouble too. I should know. And few can bake pies.*
Cycleman: *Now who's sexist?*
Charly: *Just keeping it real, unlike your posting.*
Cycleman: *I'm too busy to keep chatting. If you aren't interested, goodnight.*

I flipped the monitor the finger and closed the window.

Interested? Not likely. Good luck to whoever went to work for him.

I felt better after giving him a hard time, though.

Not better enough to sleep well. I napped on the sofa, my cell phone and a kitchen knife close at hand. Morning took forever to arrive.

I had to go out the next morning since I had a job interview lined up. I dressed carefully, checked to make sure the hallway was empty, and headed out. I was exhausted and still unsure what I was going to do but holding on to hope that if I got a job today, I could sleep on Kelly's floor for a while and find a new place while I saved up for the first and last month's rent. I certainly couldn't stay at my place anymore. Even if I got this job today, I didn't have the money to pay the back rent, and there was no way I was going near Terry.

I arrived at the building ten minutes early, stopped at the washroom to make sure I was tidy, and headed up to the office number I'd been given. I smiled at the receptionist, giving her my name. She frowned at me.

"I'm sorry, there's been some confusion."

My heart dropped. "I beg your pardon?"

"The position was filled yesterday. You were supposed to have been contacted."

I swallowed, my throat dry. "I didn't get a call."

She huffed out a sigh. "I apologize for wasting your time."

"Is there anything else? Another position?" I asked, desperate. "I can do anything."

"No." Her face softened. "I'm really sorry. I know it's hard out there. Good luck."

I hurried away before she saw the tears gathering in my eyes. I returned to the bathroom I'd been in earlier and shut myself into a stall. I let the tears I was holding in go, sobbing into my hands. I had been counting on this—on something—to go right. This was the last interview I had lined up.

I let myself cry, then wiped my eyes, and used the sink to wash my hands and splash cold water on my face. I walked aimlessly around downtown Toronto. I'd had such high hopes when I came here, the lure of the big city fascinating me. Now, it seemed cold and scary. I had never felt as alone as I did right now, sitting on a bench, watching people bustle around, hurrying to and from work, busy living their lives.

My dad's face came to mind. *"Keep your head up, girl. Tomorrow is always a new day."*

I blew out a long breath. I had to figure this out and I had no one left to turn to for help. My mom had died when I was ten from a brain aneurysm. My dad passed two years ago, and the little money he'd left was now gone, thanks to that bitch Trish. Kelly didn't have two dimes to rub together, and I was about to lose my apartment.

Unless I whored myself out to Terry.

Simply the thought of that made my skin crawl.

I looked up at the sky.

When had my life become this tragedy?

I checked my wallet. I had twenty-seven dollars to my name. That was it. At the apartment, there was some ramen, the empty box of wine, some crackers, and a jar of instant coffee. Trish had taken the coffeemaker.

I spent the day wandering around, applying for jobs, finally giving up when I ran out of resumes and smiles. I went to the store and bought a loaf of bread and the cheapest jar of peanut butter they had. At least I could eat sandwiches for a few days. Back at the apartment, I opened the fridge door to put the bread inside and froze. Sitting there on the empty shelf was a bottle of beer.

I didn't drink beer.

Terry did. I recognized the brand from the bottles I had seen dangling often from his hand.

Terry had been in here. He had left the bottle as a reminder he could get in whenever he wanted.

Terrified, I grabbed the knife and searched the apartment to make sure he wasn't still there. Once satisfied, I slipped the knives into the door trim and sat on the old sofa, drawing my knees up to my chest.

I wasn't safe here, and I had to go.

The question was, where?

I picked up my laptop, scanning the sites I had been on, hoping maybe there would be a message waiting, but there was nothing. I checked all my stats, but there had been zero new views anywhere. I had hoped for a call to fill in at a waitressing job, do some bartending, a temp job, but I had nothing.

I wondered if I would qualify for welfare. Then I shook my head. I needed to find a job.

Any job.

My gaze fell to the tab I had open for Solutions for You, and I reread the posting I had made fun of last night. I chewed on my fingernail, staring at it. After last night, I was certain whoever posted this was a grumpy old curmudgeon.

Girl Friday. Cycleman. How ridiculous.

Something caught my eye, and glancing toward the door, I could see the shadows of feet outside the door at the bottom, and the handle was turning. Slowly. Silently. I watched, scared, as my lock turned, the metal glinting in the hall light. The door moved a fraction and stopped, the metal of the knives I had slid in stopping it. It moved again, then once more. The lock reversed back into place, the handle spinning back. There was a low curse, and the feet disappeared.

But I knew he'd be back.

My gaze went back to the screen. A grumpy curmudgeon was far preferable to a would-be rapist.

Recalling what he'd said about my attitude, I was certain he wouldn't even accept my chat request.

Swallowing my pride, I clicked on the post and opened a chat window.

Charly: *Is the job still available?*

CHAPTER 3

MAXX

I sat at the old desk, running a hand through my hair. It had been another busy day—another day of falling behind on all the things that needed to be done. I grabbed a bottle of water and drained it, tossing it into the recycle bin.

I clicked the mouse, checking the computer. I needed to order some parts and get to the bank. I needed to do a lot of things that I never seemed to have the time or energy for these days.

I clicked on the job site, scanning through the messages. I'd had a dozen replies to the ad, all of which I dismissed quickly. Four were bogus, and one shared far too much personal information. A few wanted way more money than I offered. A couple frightened me, the women responding too old to be working. They were looking for a place to live, not a job. I didn't have time to look after anyone. The others weren't serious, which pissed me off. I didn't have time to deal with idiots. The guy who had sent me a message last night had been a bit of a surprise. He certainly had an attitude and told me what he thought of my posting. He'd made me laugh, to be honest. It was a little sexist when I reread it, but I hadn't had time to change it today. I disliked technology, mostly because I didn't understand most of it. When I was younger, I was far more interested in the mechanics of an engine and spent all my time in the garage with my dad. I could use technology I was trained on for mechanics—the rest I found overwhelming and, frankly, annoying. Facebook, Instagram, websites—all of it. I used what I had to, but I also knew I needed someone with more experience to help me figure it out.

I was surprised to see a new message from Charly. Even more surprised when I saw he was asking if the job was available. At least, I thought that was his question—part of me wondered if he just wanted to spar again. Before responding, I checked his profile, seeing it gave little information, except he had experience in office management and was seeking a job immediately. Both of those pieces of information were welcome. Otherwise, it was set to private with no picture or other personal details.

> **Cycleman:** *Is this a general inquiry so you can criticize or a real question?*
> **Charly:** *It's a real question. It is a job, right? I need to be clear on that.*
> **Cycleman:** *What else would it be?*
> **Charly:** *Your post makes it sound like you're looking for a spouse. If so I'm not the right one for you. I mean, Girl Friday—a little outdated.*

He was right. It was outdated. But I didn't want to waste any more time since I already knew his opinion.

> **Cycleman:** *You made that clear last night. My first time posting. I need someone to look after my shop and the house. The title was something I was familiar with.*

Charly: *Maid/Go-fer might be the best description.*
Cycleman: *Okay, fine. I am not looking for a spouse. At all. How about Assistant? Can you work with that description? Are you interested? I'm a busy man.*
Charly: *Busy—so you've said before. Keep your shirt on. I'm interested. I have a lot of experience in running an office and keeping a house clean. Been on my own for years. I can do both. Not a fancy cook, but you won't starve. And I can bake a pie. How big is your dog?*

I pursed my lips. At least he was asking questions now. I replied.

Cycleman: *He's a Golden Lab. Big but friendly.*
Charly: *Okay. I like Labs.*
Cycleman: *Do you have a resume?*
Charly: *attached*

I opened and scanned it. It told me very little about the person, although I could see he had been working for over five years. The name on the top said C.L. Hooper and a phone number, but there was no address. The date of birth gave me pause. He was only twenty-five—twelve years younger than me. I rubbed my chin, deciding that didn't matter. As long as he worked hard, I didn't care. He was going to be an employee, not a friend. I was pleased to see a mechanic shop listed under past employment. I hated to admit it, but so far, he was the only viable candidate.

Cycleman: *You worked in a garage? You know engines?*
Charly: *I get by. Not an expert. I was in the office more than under the hood.*

I grunted in satisfaction. I didn't want a mechanic, but someone who understood what I did was a bonus.

Charly: *There is a reference from my last boss attached.*

I scanned the document from Peter Phelps. Loyal, hardworking, honest, bondable were the keywords I picked up on. Those were important traits to me—especially now. The fact that he stated he would hire C.L. Hooper again in a heartbeat spoke well. There was a phone number to call for further details, so I could check that this was legitimate. As soon as I had time.

Cycleman: *Why did you leave your job?*
Charly: *Company folded.*

I paused, then made a decision. I needed someone, and Charly needed a job. He seemed like an okay kid. A little mouthy, but we could work on that.

Cycleman: *The hours are long, and I expect you to work hard.*
Charly: *Hard work doesn't bother me. You said board was included?*
Cycleman: *Yes.*
Charly: *Does the door lock?*

That seemed a strange question, but I supposed a valid one.

Cycleman: *Yes.*
Charly: *Okay.*
Cycleman: *You will have to drive to get groceries and pick up supplies.*
Charly: *Heavy lifting?*
Cycleman: *Is that a problem?*

Charly: *Yes, I have a disc problem.*

I paused. I didn't want some idiot I was going to have to baby.

Cycleman: *Okay, we can work around that.*
Charly: *Where are you located?*
Cycleman: *Outside of Lomand. A small town.*
Charly: *Lomand is a small town.*
Cycleman: *This one is even smaller. Not much around.*
Charly: *No problem.*

I sat back and studied the screen. He seemed like a decent guy. He asked fairly intelligent questions and his profile had a good ranking. He'd never given anyone a problem, and the people he'd connected with had scored him high on ratings.

Cycleman: *Are you interested? Pay is $1000/month plus board. One-month trial.*

I waited a few moments as the screen remained blank, then the reply appeared. I was prepared to go a little higher but waited to see his reaction.

Charly: *When do I start?*

I glanced at the calendar on the wall. It was Wednesday. I was booked solid tomorrow and Friday.

Cycleman: *Are you driving here?*
Charly: *Bus. Coming from Toronto.*

I scratched my chin. Toronto was about three hours from

here. Far enough away, they probably had no connections to anyone here. That was a plus.

Cycleman: *But do you drive? Stick a problem?*
Charly: *No problem. I can drive standard. Having a car in Toronto is too expensive.*

That made sense. I checked the bus schedule then replied.

Cycleman: *I looked at the schedule. There's a bus that gets you here at ten Saturday. You get off at Littleburn. It's the stop after Lomand. Tell the driver to let you out, or he'll just go past it.*
Charly: *Okay.*
Cycleman: *I will be waiting by the general store.*
Charly: *Okay. See you then.*

He signed off.

I sat back, feeling pleased. Having a guy made the accommodations decision easier. If it had been a woman, I was worried I might have to give them a room in the house, but I really didn't want to. The space at the back of the garage wasn't much, but it was private, had a comfortable enough bed and a decent bathroom. There was even a chair and a TV and a small storage area. The kid could use the fridge here in the office to store cold drinks if he wanted. He could keep some snacks around, although I would have to warn him about mice. Leaving unsealed food around was a written invitation for the little buggers. Even in the house, I kept stuff in sealed containers.

I stood and stretched, calling for Rufus. He appeared from the back, his tongue already out and his tail wagging. It was dinnertime, and he knew it.

I locked up and headed back to the house, wondering what

frozen entrée I would heat up tonight. The kid said he could cook well enough. I hoped that meant it was better than mine.

I regarded the contents of the freezer and threw another tasteless meal into the microwave.

It certainly couldn't be worse.

CHAPTER 4

CHARLYNN

I stared at the computer screen, not really believing what I had just done. Taken a job I had mocked the other night. Hired by a stranger to basically be a maid and go-fer.

He seemed very straightforward, asking the basic questions. I supposed that came with age. He didn't care about my background or anything, only that I filled the requirements and could do the job.

I shut the laptop, pushing it away. This was not how I'd planned my life to be. I shut my eyes, refusing to cry. It was only temporary. My dad always said you had to make do with what you were given. I had a chance at a job. It would get me out of this apartment, and I could save money. I would work hard and show this Cycleman what I was made of. Once I'd saved enough, I could come back to Toronto and find another job. If it was terrible, at least I'd have a thousand bucks in my pocket and be somewhere other than here. I loved working as an assistant in a fast-paced office. I was great at organizing, details, and keeping people in line. I had a talent for websites and social media. I could handle multiple tasks at once, I never lost my cool, and I rocked the sassy assistant look. I got along well with coworkers and my superiors.

I was certain I would get along fine with Cycleman.

As long as he got over the fact that I was a woman and not a guy. Once I showed him what I could do, he'd adjust. I had always been good at charming older people.

Curious, I grabbed my laptop and googled garages in the Littleburn area. Four came up, and I examined the information I could find. They all looked reasonably okay. One of them specialized in motorcycles and restorations, and they were the only one with a website, but it was very outdated. There were some pictures of bikes that had been restored, and I studied them carefully. They were all well done. My dad loved motorcycles and had worked around them his whole life. He'd had a small shop, which was where I spent my summers until I was old enough to know I preferred dresses to jumpsuits and makeup to grease. Still, I answered the phones and did invoicing and ordering for him in the summers to help defer the cost of hiring someone. When my brother died, my dad's enthusiasm for the shop, and for life, died with him, and he sold it.

I shook off those memories and looked at the computer again. I was at least honest with Cycleman about that. I could name engine parts and knew how to do an oil change or switch out a tire, but I was better acquainted with the workings of an office.

I had no idea which of the shops it was I was now going to be working for. One picture caught my eye of an older man, standing beside a Harley, obviously ill at ease in front of the camera. He scowled at the lens, and behind him, the shop was chaotic and messy. I had a feeling that was the one. It certainly looked as if he needed help. I peered at the grainy picture. If that was Cycleman, he didn't look mean, just a bit grumpy.

I could work with that.

A sudden thought occurred to me, and I pulled up the bus information, found the bus Cycleman had mentioned, then swallowed when I looked at a one-way fare.

It was forty-two dollars. I now had twenty-one dollars in my purse. It was all I had. I would have to borrow the money from Kelly. She was the only one I could ask. It wasn't much, so I had a chance at least. I shot her off a text, asking where she was. Her reply made me groan.

Kelly: *Had a chance to fly to Jamaica for a shoot. Back in a week! You okay?*

Kelly was an assistant to a photographer. The pay was terrible but the fringe benefits great for her, plus she was learning a ton. If she was out of town, I couldn't borrow from her. She was a little leery of online banking and did everything in cash. I sent back a fast reply, not wanting to upset her.

Charlynn: *Found a job, things looking up. It's out of town—will be in touch when settled.*

All I got back was a smiley face, so I knew she was busy. I sighed, wondering how I was going to get the rest of the money for the bus fare. I wondered about sending Cycleman a message and asking him to forward me a little cash, but I had a feeling he wouldn't like that, so I decided to use that as my last resort. I was about to get up when I saw it again. The shadows of feet outside my door. The handle turning slowly.

I crept to the door, knowing Terry was on the other side. I could hear him breathing, cursing low under his breath. I wanted to peek through the peephole then suddenly remembered seeing a show where the person on the other side had a piece of equipment that let them see inside using the peephole. I tiptoed to the kitchen and found some masking tape and a black marker. I soaked the tape with the ink, then snuck back and covered the peephole.

"I hear you," he muttered. "I know you're in there."

I held my breath and lowered myself to the floor, picking up the sawed-off hockey stick I usually used to prop open the window.

He jeered. "You can't stay in there forever. I'll be back. You have a debt to pay."

Carefully, I opened the mail chute. As I suspected, Terry was in front of the door. I flattened myself and peeked under the doorframe, lining up the stick with his feet.

He loved to go barefoot around the building. I thought it was disgusting to walk in other people's homes with your bare feet and asked him to wear shoes once. He had laughed in my face.

"Should have listened, asshole," I muttered, then drew back my arm as if I were holding a pool cue and let it thrust forward fast.

His howl of pain was loud. I pushed back away from the door, holding my breath.

"You are going to pay for that, bitch," he hissed and stormed away.

I began to shake. Maybe I needed to simply ignore him. Except it pissed me off. This, for all intents and purposes, was my home, and I wasn't safe here. But where was I going to go? I had no money, no place to crash, and I was stuck. I had no one to turn to anymore. I was really alone.

I felt better once I shoved a chair under the door handle. I couldn't get out, but between the knives and the chair, he couldn't get in either. I made sure my windows were shut and locked, although, being on the third floor, I was sure I was safe that way. I did draw my curtains closed in case he was looking in from downstairs.

I walked down the hall to my bedroom. I needed to stay busy, or I was going to go crazy. I was leaving here in two days and there was nothing I had to leave the apartment for until then, so he wouldn't have a chance to get in. I could handle it. In the meantime, I would get organized.

I pulled out my suitcase from under the bed and turned to the closet. The bag had been a gift from my dad—the bright flowers on it hard to miss. I could only take what I could carry, so it would only be personal things. The first items that went into the suitcase were my photo albums. The rest of the possessions I got after my dad's death were in a small storage locker up north. One day when I had a place for them, I would collect them. Luckily, I was prepaid for another little while, so I didn't have to worry about that bill right now, or not being able to pay it. I didn't want to lose the items in storage.

I added my favorite clothes, then went into the kitchen and made a sandwich. I ate it while scouring the drawers for loose change. On occasion, I used to leave a five-dollar bill in places for emergencies, but Trish must have found them all. All I came up with was a buck-fifty in coins.

In vain, I ran my hands under the sofa cushions and through the drawers in the mostly empty bathroom vanity. The bitch had even taken my makeup. But it was all for nothing.

I sat on my bed, noting my suitcase was mostly full but pleased I had most of the things I wanted packed. I brought my laptop into the bedroom and figured out how far I could go for $22.50. I would be about an hour from Lomand. I wondered if I could hitchhike.

My head fell back to the wall as my father's voice ranted in my head about the danger of hitchhiking. Growing up in a small town, a lot of kids did hitchhike. Often, they were picked up by neighbors or friends. It didn't work that way closer to the big city, and I knew no one out Lomand way. But what choice did I have?

MELANIE MORELAND

I turned my head, wiping away a tear. A glint caught my eye, and I recalled the box I had stuffed in the back of the closet. I dragged the stool over and climbed up, pulling out the shoe box and carrying it to the bed. I stared at the contents, smiling and crying at the same time. For years, my father had given me the same gift at Christmas. Every year, he gave me a new wallet. But not a regular, usable wallet. It was as if he went out of his way to buy me the ugliest wallet made. Bright colors, patchwork, fringed, bedazzled—if a wallet could be jazzed up, my father found it. The funny part was, he thought I loved them, and I never had the heart to disabuse him of that fact. Even after I moved here, the wallets appeared. I laid them on the bed, staring at them. Ten in all, each one provoking a memory. Happier times when my brother was alive. The three of us on Christmas morning, opening presents, drinking hot cocoa. There was never a lot of money, but there was love. The gifts were simple, but every year, both my brother and I got a wallet. The biggest difference was Sean's were simple, black or brown, double folded, normal wallets. Mine were anything but plain. We bought my dad one as well since he felt each new year deserved a new wallet. It was our tradition.

Inside each one there would be a quarter in the change purse and a ten-dollar bill tucked away.

Sadly, both the quarters and the ten dollars were long gone. I ran my fingers over the ones my dad had given me once I moved. They were even more outrageous than the rest—his thinking, no doubt, now I was in the city, I needed an even wilder wallet. His sense of style was pretty bad. To him, the louder the plaid, the dressier the shirt. I had to laugh, thinking of some of his "dress shirts" that I now used on occasion to throw over the top of T-shirts.

I picked up a wallet, smiling at the number of zippers and pockets it contained.

I looked at them scattered on my bed, an idea forming. I wondered if I could sell them to a pawn shop. Surely ten wallets would give me enough cash to get a bus ticket? I hated the thought of selling them since my dad had given them to me, but it made sense. Besides, if I pawned them, I could come back to the city and buy them back once I had some cash.

I swallowed at the emotion I was feeling. My dad would understand, I assured myself. He would want me to sell them.

Idly, I picked up another wallet, opening the zipper, remembering how my brother would keep his quarter and ten dollars in the lining of his wallet for emergencies. That was where my dad kept his too. For years, I'd kept the quarter, but eventually it, too, was spent. I was about to close the wallet when I felt a small thickening in the lining. Curious, I ran my finger over it again. There was something inside. I slid my finger around, finding a loose edge, and delved under the satin interface. A folded bill fell out, and I stared down in shock at the fifty lying on the bed. With shaking fingers, I picked it up, recognizing my dad's handwriting on the Post-it note attached.

If you found it, I hope it helps. Love you.

Fifty dollars. He had slipped fifty dollars into the lining. I looked at the wallet again. It was the last one he had given me. Scrambling, I placed all the wallets in order, then I examined them all. The ones he'd given me before I left home were empty, but the three I'd gotten after I moved each contained hidden cash and a little note.

I began to weep. I had one hundred and fifty dollars. In the grand scheme of life, nothing, but right now, a fortune.

Enough to escape from this city and start again. It also meant I could keep these silly little wallets with me.

I checked the bus schedule, noting there was another bus

Friday to Lomand. It left at ten in the morning. I only had to make it through tomorrow, and I could leave on Friday. That meant I just had to get through one more day. I had enough cash to get a motel room overnight once I got there and to buy something to eat. Saturday, I could catch the bus as it went through Lomand and get off in Littleburn. Once I was there, Cycleman would pick me up.

I racked my brain, trying to recall Terry's schedule. He was always in the basement early on Friday morning, getting the garbage ready for the truck. As soon as I saw him leave, I could go. He would never know.

I'd be gone before he figured it out and wait at the bus station.

I'd be safe.

I cast my gaze upward. "Thanks, Daddy."

CHAPTER 5

CHARLYNN

I stayed up well into the early morning on Thursday, making sure I had everything packed I wanted to take with me. I had Friday planned—as soon as I heard Terry go past my door and the stairwell door shut, I would head in the other direction. He would be busy for at least an hour—usually more. I had certainly heard him complaining about the amount of time it took him to "take out the trash." I wished he would add himself to the pile.

By the time he finished and came back upstairs, I'd be long gone.

I fell asleep for a while, waking up when I heard my door rattling. Angry, I got up and went down the hall.

"Get away from my door, or I'm calling the cops, asshole. I am not interested in your offer," I shouted, getting my stuff ready.

"Then you owe me rent."

"It's not the end of the month. I have until next week. Leave me alone, or I'm serious, I will call the cops. I'll tell them you're attempting to break in to my apartment."

His answer was low and threatening. "You think they'd

believe you? The girl who claimed she was ripped off by an unknown roommate? A girl I was simply checking on since she hasn't paid her rent in three months and I've been so nice to let it slide?" He barked out a laugh that made me shiver. "Good luck with that."

Part of me was afraid if I called the police, they wouldn't believe me. And since I didn't plan on sticking around, there seemed to be little point. "I will never sink to fucking you."

"Oh, you're going to sink all right. Right on my cock. You'll be begging by then. In more ways than one. I look forward to next week."

I delivered a fast jab to his knee with my stick through the mail slot. I grabbed the beer bottle beside me, popping off the top and shaking it hard. As I suspected, he cursed and bent down, opening the mail chute and meeting my eyes.

"You are going to pay for that."

"So you've said before. I think you're the one going to pay." Then I shoved the neck of the beer bottle in the chute and lifted my finger. He yelled as the beer hit him in the face, no doubt stinging as it splashed in his eyes.

I rolled away from the door, trying not to laugh but failing. I covered my mouth, holding in my guffaws. He was furious, thumping on my door.

"You bitch," he growled into the mail chute, keeping his voice down. "Now you have to clean it up."

"Nope," I responded. "It's outside my apartment. That's the custodian's job. Oh, that's you. Get to it."

"You are going to regret this."

He finally walked away, dragging his sore leg, and I sagged against the door.

"Good luck with that, asshole," I whispered.

34

I spent the rest of the day worried and anxious. I napped fitfully, showered in the middle of the night, and by six on Friday morning, I was ready. My bag was packed, my knapsack strapped on my back, and I stood by the door, listening. I heard the click of Terry's door opening around quarter to seven, and his footsteps echoed in the hall in the early morning stillness. The rasp of his low chuckle as he passed my door made me want to throw up, but I remained still and silent by the door. The noise of the stairwell door shutting at the other end of the hall seemed to take forever. I waited five minutes, then I moved as quickly as I could.

Late last night, I had discovered a mouse in the trap under the cupboard. I always trapped them then freed them outside. I hated killing them. At first, I thought I would simply release it back into the apartment, then I had a better idea. I knew Terry detested mice. I had heard him scream once when he thought he saw one in his apartment.

I grabbed the trap and hurried to Terry's door. Taking in a deep breath for bravery, I reached in and lifted out the mouse by his tail, then quickly slid him through the mail chute, repressing a shudder. I didn't mind them, but I didn't like to touch them either.

"Run, little guy. Wreak havoc."

I addressed the door sarcastically, "Thanks for being such a great human, asshole."

Then, I grabbed my suitcase and knapsack, hurrying down the steps holding up the suitcase, the weight of it making me clumsy and slow. But I made it down the steps, and I was out the door and into the dim light. I set down the suitcase, pulling it behind me, and began to run. I went as fast as I could until I turned the corner, pausing to catch my breath. I peeked behind me, but there was no one around. I took a moment to collect myself, then I hurried down the street, determined to get as far away as possible, as quickly as I could.

I wouldn't relax until I was out of this city.

An hour later, I was at the bus station, ticket in hand. I sat in the corner, watching the busy crowds, willing time to go faster. I had locked my apartment door and left things the way they looked on Wednesday. The bread on the counter, a scarf I rarely used draped over the chair, the bedding still there. If the asshole went in again, he would simply think I was out. I doubted he would be going into my closet. He had no reason to suspect I was gone and zero idea I was at the bus station. Still, I couldn't relax. I tapped out an uneven rhythm with my toes, sipped a cup of coffee, and used my laptop to check the news. I had sent Cycleman a message confirming Saturday again, and his reply had been short but affirmative. I had also asked him his name, and his reply was one word.

Maxx

I was glad he had never confirmed I was a guy, but I would deal with that tomorrow. I was glad to have confirmation he wasn't backing out. Part of me whispered I was being stupid doing this. Jumping from the proverbial frying pan into the fire— but at this point, I felt I had nothing to lose. I couldn't stay, so leaving was my only option. If he was an asshole, I would find something else.

Finally, my bus was announced, my suitcase stowed underneath, and we were on our way. When the door closed and we began to move, I felt a long tremor of relief flood me, and I had to cover my eyes with my hand as a wave of emotion hit me.

"Okay there, dear?" the elderly woman sitting beside me asked. With her gray hair and twinkling blue eyes, she looked like a picture postcard for a grandmother.

I wiped my eyes. "Left a bad situation," I murmured.

"Oh. Well, best out, then." She agreed. She reached into her bag, pulling out a sack of apples. She chose one, then offered me the bag. Unable to resist, I accepted one and bit into the crisp, sweet flesh.

Monica, it turned out, was going to a town just before Lomand. She spent the first hour of the trip telling me about the area and all her grandkids. It was a good distraction, and I appreciated it. She gave me her number, insisted on taking mine, and told me to come and visit, then advised me if my new job didn't work out to come to her and she would make sure I was looked after. I sputtered out my thanks, but she waved me off.

"You remind me of my Julie. She's a ginger, too. Takes after my own father with that coloring and all those freckles. I'd like to think if she were in trouble, someone would help her. Just passing it on."

She hugged me before she got off the bus. "I'll be checking on you, child."

"I look forward to it."

When we arrived in Lomand, the bus driver told me he was doing the same route the next day and instructed me to be at the same corner tomorrow and he'd take me on to Littleburn. I thanked him, marveling at the kindness I'd experienced so far today. It made me feel better than I had in a long time.

I found a small motel I'd seen online the night before. The rooms were cheap and the place was deserted, so they let me in right away. I shut the door, sank onto the bed, and was asleep in five minutes, exhausted from the past few days of stress.

I woke up confused, hungry, and thirsty, shocked to see I had slept for almost six hours. I grabbed my stuff and had a shower, then changed into fresh clothes. I brushed out my hair, feeling the positive effects of the long nap and the easing of the stress being in that apartment had caused me. I felt more like myself, not a scared girl. Briefly, I wondered if Terry had realized yet I was gone or was lying in wait for me.

Satisfied, I headed out, stopping at the office to ask about a place to eat. The woman pointed to the left, telling me there was a restaurant and bar about two blocks down. I walked that way, stopping to peek into a few windows. There were some nice little shops in town, and once I had some money, I would come back and look around.

I found the restaurant, the neon sign, Zeke's Bar and Grill, hanging over the sidewalk, the arrow pointing to the door. I hesitated before entering. I hated going into bars or restaurants on my own, but I was starving and needed to eat. Summoning my courage, I opened the door and stepped inside. The place was bustling, and the smell of the grill hit me, the air heavy with the scent of meat cooking. My mouth watered, and I looked around for a place to sit. The tables were all occupied, but I spotted an empty stool at the end of the bar and headed that way. A woman was busy wiping down the counter, and I plucked a small menu from the holder in front of me. When she came over, offering me a friendly greeting, I ordered a cheeseburger and fries, and a glass of red wine, deciding I could treat myself tonight. I also asked for a glass of water, and I sipped the icy cold liquid as I looked around the place. It was obviously a gathering place for locals, the people in the crowd greeting one another, conversations happening between tables. The walls were thick planks of wood, scarred and worn, with a lot of posters and farm implements hung on them. The floor was buffed to a high gloss, but you could see the years of wear. Simple tables, sturdy chairs, and a well-stocked bar spoke of a place you could sit, have a meal, a drink, and relax. I noticed a few looks I was getting, but they didn't make me uncomfortable. I was a new face in a sea of familiarity. I met a couple of gazes, then took out my phone and started a game of FreeCell. My dad had got me addicted to it years ago, and I still loved playing it. It would keep me busy until dinner came. I was grateful at that moment that my cell phone number had never been listed on the lease. At least Terry had no way of getting ahold of me. I was safe.

The hum of the bar and the music playing was a great background as I ate my dinner and sipped my wine. I wasn't in a hurry and took my time. People around me came and went, dinner morphing into drinks and relaxation, the music becoming louder as time went on. I stayed in the corner, watching and enjoying the atmosphere. I chatted with the woman tending bar who introduced herself as Vanessa. I told her my name, but it seemed all she caught was Lynn, and I let it go. She assured me this last seat was rarely taken and I could stay as long as I wanted. I ordered another glass of wine and slipped off the stool to go use the washroom. Vanessa assured me she would keep my drink behind the bar until I returned. Rounding the bar, I collided with what felt like a wall, but as I lifted my hands to steady myself, I realized what I was touching was a taut, firm chest. I raised my eyes, meeting the amused gaze of an incredibly fine specimen of a man. Tall, broad, with eyes so dark they were almost black, he looked startled, then frowned and stepped back. "Sorry," he muttered, running a hand through his hair.

I shook my head. "My bad," I managed to utter before I hurried to the washroom, suddenly feeling overheated. I glanced over my shoulder, our eyes meeting again. He was massive, towering over the crowd, easy to spot. He was dressed in a black T-shirt that hugged his torso and showed off his arms, and his gaze was intense. His jeans hugged his thick thighs, and his large feet were encased in black shitkickers. I loved a man who wore heavy boots. It suggested strength. Durability.

I fanned myself as I closed the door behind me. "Wow," I muttered. He certainly stood out in a crowd. You couldn't help but look at him. I barely came up to his chest, and I was average height. He was at least six foot five.

I finished, washed my hands, fluffed my hair, and went back

to the bar, sliding up onto my stool. I took a sip of wine and lifted my gaze, my eyes instantly falling on the stranger now sitting at the other end of the bar. Seated, he seemed even bigger. He called over to Vanessa, who waved and told him to keep his shirt on, referring to him as Reynolds. It was an odd name, but it suited him. As she brought him a large glass of beer, the foam dripping over the edge, and stood talking to him, I took the chance to study him. He was in his late thirties, I judged, his dark hair short on the sides, longer on top, shot with silver. His tightly trimmed beard had the same silver in it, but more of it. He was rugged, rough, and extremely sexy—masculine. There was something about him that suggested controlled power. It was in the way he moved, the tilt of his head. His rigid posture as he sat at the bar. The stern expression on his face. The way his gaze swept the room. I watched, fascinated, as he wrapped his huge hand around the glass and lifted it to his full lips, taking a long sip. Idly, I wondered what his touch would be like. Rough and demanding? Soft and teasing? Both? I swallowed heavily at the thought of him touching me. I wondered how it would feel to have his full mouth brush against my skin. How those hands would feel wrapped around my hips as he rocked into me. I gripped my thigh at the tremor of pure lust that ran through me with the mere thought, shocked at the intense sensation simply staring at this man caused me. I blinked and refocused my gaze.

That was when I realized he was now staring back at me—watching him. I didn't think it was possible, but his frown deepened, his eyebrows pulling down in a glare. Flushing, I grabbed my phone and opened a book on my Kindle app, embarrassed at being caught.

MAXX

I smirked into my beer when, across the bar, I met the frank gaze of the pretty girl I had bumped into a few moments ago. She dropped her eyes fast, but not before I saw the flare of heat, directed at me. I glared at her, wondering why she'd be checking me out. I was by far the oldest guy in the place. She picked up her phone, giving me the opportunity to look back at her. She was unusual and striking. Deep copper hair fell in long waves down her back. I recalled the unusual color of her eyes—a soft green, muted and gentle. They had been startled when she'd walked into me, lifting in apology. The sight of her pretty face, a liberal dusting of freckles scattered over her cheeks and a faint blush diffusing her skin, caught me off guard. The warmth of her hands resting on my chest before she snatched them away felt odd, but good. She was unexpected.

Sitting in the corner, trying not to look my way, she was sexy and sweet. A combination I usually ignored. But something about her called to me.

"Who's the ginger?" I asked Vanessa as she wiped the bar beside me.

"Name's Lynn. Just passing through."

"Ah," I muttered.

"Seems nice. Likes red wine. Maybe if you smiled at her instead of scowling, you'd have a shot."

I narrowed my eyes. "Not interested, just a question. I'll have a burger when you have a moment. Make it a double. Onion rings on the side."

She shrugged and moved away.

I sipped my beer, enjoying the cold beverage. I'd had to come into town to get a part I required to finish a job. I was swamped, but luckily, Wally had stayed open late so I could grab it. I would finish the car in the morning, then pick up Charly and get him settled. I had been so busy, I hadn't even had time to get in touch with the kid. He'd confirmed he was arriving tomorrow and asked me my name. I meant to write him back and give him more information about the place, but time had gotten away from me. I would explain everything to him tomorrow.

Since I was here, I'd popped in for a beer and a burger. My gaze roamed back to the redhead in the corner. She was unexpected eye candy, and I couldn't seem to stop staring.

My burger arrived, and I ate it with gusto. Zeke's Bar and Grill was solid for a good meal. Simple, but tasty. I ordered another beer, relaxing on the padded stool and sipping the icy cold liquid. A few people dropped by to say hi, but otherwise, I enjoyed the sounds around me, keeping to myself. My gaze kept wandering over to the girl. She appeared to be engrossed in something on her phone, occasionally picking up her wine for a sip. Our eyes met across the bar a few times, and once she offered me a small smile before dipping her head back down, no doubt, as Vanessa stated, put off by my scowl.

I had to admit, she was intriguing. Oddly sensual with her coloring, poise, and demeanor. She didn't draw attention to herself, but it happened, regardless. She stood out from the locals.

Internally, I rolled my eyes. Intriguing or not, I wasn't looking. I had learned my lesson the hard way, and I was still recovering from the betrayal I had suffered months ago. I had to admit, though, if I were looking, the pretty girl across the bar was as opposite from Shannon as you could get. That was a huge plus in my book.

But I wasn't looking. Or interested.

Until movement caught my eye, and I glanced up to see the pretty girl looking uncomfortable. I cursed low in my throat when I saw the reason. Standing beside her, far too close, was Wes Donner. He was one of the Donner brothers, a bane to many in town. Rich, entitled, and far too full of himself, he thought he was god's gift to women. Both brothers did. The younger one, Chase, had been a good kid at one time, but his brother's influence changed that. The truth was, they were rude, obnoxious, and immature. I'd dealt with them many times and had zero patience for either of them.

Especially now, as I watched the girl shake her head and politely turn her face as she lifted up her phone again.

The asshole had the gumption to loom over her, invade her personal space, and grab at her phone. I tried not to snicker as she snatched it back, jabbed her finger into his chest and mouthed off to him.

He didn't get the message, grasping her wrist, and pushing closer.

She tried to yank her hand back, but he refused to let go. I heard her voice over the din of the bar.

"Unless you want to speak in a higher octave, asshole, *back off*."

Those words only seemed to entice him, and he cornered her. The girl grimaced and moved her arm, and suddenly, Wes was bent over the bar, his face twisted in pain.

Without a thought, I was out of my seat and by her side of the bar in a flash. Once close, I could see she had twisted his little finger, holding it at an odd angle. He was acting like a child, almost howling in pain.

"I believe the lady said no."

Wes grimaced but refused to back down. "I'm not talking to you, Reynolds."

"Neither, it seems, is the lady. You gonna leave her alone if I tell her to let you go?"

He huffed and cursed. "Fine."

I turned to the girl. "I think he's done."

"Gosh dang right, he is," she grumbled. "This keeps happening. Holy moly, I'm sick of men like this idiot."

I held back my amusement. "Let him go, Red."

She released him, and he dropped to the bar with a groan before straightening up.

"You bitch," he muttered.

I grabbed his arm, yanking him close. "What did you just say?"

"Nothing."

"That's what I thought." I glared at him. "It's time you were leaving, Wes."

"Why don't you fuck off and mind your own business, Reynolds? I was just talking."

I turned my head, meeting the wide gaze of the girl. "You interested in hearing him talk?"

"Unless it's an apology before he leaves, no."

I turned back to him with a smirk. I liked her sass. "You have your answer." I leaned forward, dropping my voice. "Leave now, while you can still walk."

He cursed and spun on his heel, shoving through the crowd. My eyes followed his path until he stormed out of the door, slamming it behind him.

I turned and smiled at the girl. "Sorry about that. A few idiots around here have no manners. You should be fine now."

I began to move away, and her hand shot out, landing on my arm. "Wait."

I glanced down where her fingers lingered on my skin. Pale against the tanned color of my forearm. Surprisingly delicate, given the punishment they'd just inflicted on Wes. I was taken aback at her touching me since most people steered clear of doing so.

"Thank you."

I nodded. "Sure."

"Can I—" She cleared her throat. "Can I buy you a drink?"

"Not needed."

"Please."

I couldn't say no to her pleading eyes, and frankly, I really didn't want to. She had yet to remove her hand from my arm, and I had to admit, I liked how it felt when she touched me. I sat beside her, and Vanessa came over, sliding a beer my way.

"On the house. Thanks for taking out the garbage."

I picked up my glass. "He took himself out."

Vanessa placed a glass of wine in front of the girl. "On the house for you too. I like your style."

The girl picked up her wine with a shaking hand. "That's the second time in as many days I've had to rely on my self-defense class. I've never used it until now…" She trailed off.

I lifted my glass in a toast. "Always a first time."

She was quiet, seemingly in thought.

I sensed a story there. I assumed she'd been hassled already this week, but I stayed quiet.

She turned to me, holding out her hand. "Thank you, Reynolds, for coming over. I appreciate it."

I looked at her hand, then had to tease her. "Is that safe?"

She laughed, the sound light. "Yes."

I shook her hand. "You're welcome." Then I furrowed my brow. "I think Vanessa said your name was Lynn?"

She shrugged and muttered something about it being close enough. Then she grinned, making two deep dimples in her face appear. They were right by the corners of her full lips, making her expression mischievous. "You asked her my name?"

"You remembered mine," I responded drolly.

She chuckled. "Vanessa missed part of my name. It's *Char*lynn."

"Pretty."

She shrugged. "A mouthful."

"Maybe I'll stick to Red. It's easier."

She didn't say anything or object. We studied each other, our gazes locked in silence. Up close, she was even prettier than I'd thought. Her wide eyes were intelligent and warm. Her lips full and pink. Kissable. She was dressed casually, but her green T-shirt set off her hair and eyes. It pulled tight across her high breasts, dipping low in the front to show her cleavage. The freckles on her face were more than a small smattering, extending down her neck and arms, little trails of cinnamon over her ivory skin. She was extremely sexy, and I felt an odd draw to her. I had to admit, I had felt it the moment she ran into me.

And now, she was flirting with me.

"You gonna give me my hand back?" she asked.

I looked down, shocked to realize I was still holding it.

"You gonna tell me why these hands need to be registered as a lethal weapon this week?" I responded, then mentally kicked myself.

Why did I want to know that? And why was I flirting back?

She looked down at our hands, slowly pulling hers away. She sighed, taking a drink of wine. "It's been a bad week."

"Sorry, I wasn't getting personal."

She glanced to the side, her eyes dancing. "No, I don't mind telling you. I'm just not sure how you're going to take it."

I leaned one elbow on the bar, facing her. "Try me."

Ten minutes later, I was laughing so hard, I could barely sit on my stool. Her story about her asshole of a landlord and how she handled him was brilliant. When she got to the part about the beer, then the mouse, I lost it. I couldn't remember the last time I'd laughed that hard. She didn't tell me what led up to the altercation, and I knew she wasn't giving me the entire story, but what she had shared was priceless. I had a feeling this was a girl who would keep a man on his toes.

I wiped my eyes. "So, now what?"

She shrugged. "I have a new job. A new beginning, far away from Toronto and that creep."

I sipped my beer, still chuckling. "Good plan. Anything interesting?"

Her eyes danced. "I'm going to take care of an elderly gentleman. He needs a lot of help." She leaned close, her voice dropping, those dimples deepening as she beamed. "He's a bit grumpy, a curmudgeon, I think, but I can handle him. Easy peasy."

"I bet you can." I paused. "You like older men, Red?"

"You mean like you?" she responded, teasing. "What are you —thirty-five?"

"Close. Thirty-seven."

She shrugged. "Age is a number. That doesn't bother me."

I had no idea why that news pleased me.

"I'm twenty-five," she offered. "I feel older most days. Like I said, just a number."

I asked her some questions about Toronto, and she responded with witty comments, making me chuckle more. She asked about the area, and I told her what I knew. I resisted asking her if she would be returning.

I wasn't looking to start anything. I pushed aside the fact that I found her pretty, intelligent, and funny. I liked the way she spoke, meeting my eyes directly, using her hands to emphasize something. On occasion, I would catch a whiff of her perfume when she moved her head or pushed back her hair. It was light and citrusy—not overpowering or heavy. Her eyes fascinated me; the odd shade of green seemed to deepen to almost gray at times, depending on her emotion. I had never seen eyes like that.

Often, our knees pressed together, the warmth seeping into my skin. She was a toucher. My arm, hand, shoulder. Once, she brushed my cheek, showing me a small spot of ketchup I had missed earlier. My skin felt as if it were on fire where her fingers touched me.

She suddenly yawned, covering her mouth, her eyes wide.

"Holy moly, I should get back to the motel. I have a long day ahead of me tomorrow."

I didn't ask where she was going. It was none of my business. But I stood. "I'm parked by the motel. I'll walk you."

"I don't need protection."

Eyeing her diminutive stature, I lifted an eyebrow. She was tiny in my eyes. "Maybe I was hoping you'd protect me."

She tossed her red hair, the color catching the light. "That makes more sense."

I waved to Vanessa and followed Red from the bar. Outside, it was quiet, the streets mostly deserted. I was surprised to see it was past ten. I had been sitting talking to her for over two hours. We turned in the direction of the motel, neither of us in a hurry.

"Wow, you really see the stars out here."

I glanced up with a nod. "Yeah, it's clear."

She sighed. "Not in Toronto. Sometimes the smog is easier to see through, but they are never like that."

We were close to the motel when it happened. She was so busy staring up, she missed a small divot, and with a gasp, fell forward. I bent fast, grabbing her around the waist and stopping her from hitting the pavement. I yanked her up tight to my chest.

"Okay there, Red?"

She stared up at me, her eyes wide. Her cheeks were flushed —from the wine or the scare of almost falling, I wasn't sure. But for some reason, I loosened one arm and ran my fingers down her cheek. The skin was soft and supple. The air around us became warm. Heated. My heart rate picked up. Charlynn's breathing became deeper, her chest pressing into mine.

"You are beautiful," I murmured.

"You're really tall," she breathed out.

I couldn't help my chuckle. "I am."

"And so sexy."

I lifted one eyebrow. "Is that so?"

"Yes."

Like magnets, our heads were drawn together. I bent as she lifted up on her toes, our mouths hovering, tasting each other through our heavy breathing.

My lips ghosted over hers, feeling the full lushness of her mouth tremble.

Hers pressed up, seeking, warm, and tender.

I slid my tongue along her bottom lip, teasing, light. Testing.

She whimpered, reaching up her hand to fist my T-shirt, bringing me in closer.

Our mouths fused together.

And the rest of the world ceased to exist.

CHAPTER 6

CHARLYNN

His mouth. His wicked, talented, sexy mouth. I had been staring at it all night. When he smiled, Reynolds was the sexiest man I had ever seen. He had a stern, frosty air about him. But when he relaxed, his entire countenance changed, and the sexy, dangerous edge melted away, leaving only a charismatic, intriguing man behind. The way he had laughed when I told him my story, his eyes wide, teeth gleaming white against the tan of his face, he had taken my breath away.

When he had appeared by my side while that idiot had been hassling me, I was annoyed since I had the situation well in hand. But he let me lead, assisting me, and adding only his quiet strength. Sitting beside him after, sharing a drink and talking, I felt as if he was really listening. His gaze was focused entirely on me, and he asked the right questions, letting me know he wasn't simply putting in time. I felt strangely safe next to him, his massive frame blocking out the people behind him. I was fascinated watching the way his muscles flexed as he moved. How his biceps bunched and rippled when he lifted his glass or used his hands to make a point as he spoke. Up close, I could see the richness of his dark eyes, but I noticed that, even relaxed, they were wary. He held himself tense, his shoulders ramrod straight, his expression guarded at times. When he had spoken to that asshole Wes, his low voice, growly and rough, had sparked something primitive inside me. Not usually drawn to broody men, I was surprised.

But now, wrapped in his strong embrace, his lips on mine, there was no wariness. He held me tight, his arms a cage around me, pressing me into his hard, muscular chest. He slanted his lips, going deeper, a possessive, dangerous edge to his kisses that somehow turned me on even more than I thought possible. His tongue stroked along mine, seeking, exploring. He lifted me into his arms, and I wrapped my legs around his hips. I felt the cold metal of the truck we'd been standing beside hit my back as his kisses deepened, and I drowned in the sensations he brought forth in me. My nipples hardened against the rough feel of his chest; my body felt as if it was on fire, aching with desire. My clit strummed against the fabric of my jeans, desperate to feel him, and I felt myself growing wet for him. I slid my fingers into his short hair, pulling at the silky strands and playing with the nape of his neck.

He dragged his mouth from mine, his beard scratching my skin as he moved to my ear. "Tell me to stop."

I gripped him tighter. "No."

"Then take me to your room."

I tipped up my head, meeting his dark stare. His gaze was riveting, passionate. His lips were wet from mine.

"I don't do this."

"Neither do I," he retorted. "This is not my style. But I want you." He rolled his hips, leaving me no doubt as to his want. His erection was huge, pressing against me, cranking me higher.

He was right. I wanted him as well. It was only one night. Then I would leave this town and go find a new life.

Why not?

"It's the last room on the corner."

I tried not to giggle as he stepped away from the truck and headed to the motel, keeping me wrapped around him. Teasing, I bit his ear, licking the shell. I grinned as he shivered, liking his reaction to me. "I'm on the pill," I whispered.

"I have condoms."

"Always prepared, like a Boy Scout?" I murmured, tamping down the pang of jealousy that flashed through me at the thought of him using a condom with another woman.

"Habit, I suppose," he replied. "Haven't used one in a long time."

I liked that response and rewarded him by licking his neck and nibbling on his skin. He groaned low, smacking my ass as he carried me across the parking lot, sticking to the shadows. "Get your key ready, woman. We need to get inside your room." He paused. "So I can get inside you."

I had my key out by the time we reached the door. Inside, he stepped around my flower-covered suitcase and tossed me on the bed. He stood over me, his chest heaving, his eyes dark and intense.

"Lose the shirt," I whispered.

He tossed it over his head, sliding his hand down his torso and flipping open the button of his jeans. His erection strained against the material, hard and massive. I slid closer, running my hands up his stomach and chest. He was taut, firm, chiseled. Every muscle defined, his jeans hanging low enough to show me the start of that sexy V. I slid my fingers over his bulge, hefting it in my hand.

"This all for me?"

His eyes rolled back in his head, and he sank his fingers into my hair, drawing me close. Teasingly, I nudged at him with my nose. "Maybe I need an introduction."

He stepped back, tugging down his zipper, the sound of the teeth opening a low metallic growl in the room. With a push, his jeans fell to the floor, his erection springing free. It hit his stomach, hard, long, and perfect.

"Holy moly," I whimpered. "Good thing you have condoms, because the ones I left behind never would have fit."

For a moment, he stared, then threw back his head in laughter. I giggled as he yanked me to my feet, kissing me, tugging off my clothes, throwing them behind him. He teased me with his hands, caressed my skin as he uncovered it, moaning.

"I wondered how many of these little dots you had all over your skin," he murmured, licking his way down the path of freckles on my arm. "So sexy."

"They're everywhere," I groaned.

He met my gaze, lifting his eyebrow. "Is that a fact? I look forward to finding them all."

He had me back on the bed before I could blink. We became a mass of writhing limbs, seeking hands, and hot, wet mouths. He liked having his nipples sucked. He moaned low when I brushed my mouth over his stomach and wrapped my hand around his erection. He shouted when I licked the crown, teasing him with my tongue. He rolled me over.

"Later," he promised.

I swore he discovered every one of my freckles. Licked and kissed them all. Nibbled on my neck, laved my breasts, cupping them in his hands and teasing the nipples with his tongue until they were hard and aching. He slipped his hand between my legs, circling my clit, groaning in my ear.

"You're so wet for me, Red. I love it."

He slid on a condom and hovered over me. There was a glint in his dark gaze, a hesitation I didn't expect. I lifted my face to his and kissed him. "Please."

He stared at me, the most profound expression on his face.

He was a study in contrasts. His mouth curled into a wicked smile, his facial expression filled with desire, but his eyes were unsure, almost vulnerable. An odd thought flashed through my mind.

This man has been hurt. Badly.

A wave of tenderness ran through me.

"Please," I whispered again. "I want you so much."

He sank inside me, his gaze never wavering. His eyes lost that vulnerable look, becoming darker, sexier as he slid in inch by inch until we were flush. He dropped his forehead to mine.

"Jesus," he moaned.

"God needs to wait," I begged. "Move, Reynolds. *Take me.*"

And he did.

He drove into me powerfully, the feeling of him immense and satisfying. He braced one hand on the headboard, the other on my hip, gripping me tightly. The bed creaked under his aggression, the headboard slamming against the wall repeatedly. I came almost immediately, and he hissed in pleasure as I gripped him, my muscles fluttering in pleasure.

"Yes, choke my cock, baby. Take it. There's going to be more —I promise."

His dirty words only made me hotter. He captured my mouth, kissing me deeply, his tongue thrusting in time with his hips. He sat up, lifting my hips, pulling me tight as he continued to pound into me. I gripped the sheets, trying to find purchase before he drove me right into the headboard.

He pulled out, and I whimpered, then gasped as he flipped me as easily as if he were lifting a feather. He dragged me up to my knees and sank back inside me. I groaned at the sensation of being claimed. Possessed. He was buried so deep inside me, I was stretched full. Still, he moved, groaning and powerful. He bent over my back, his body hard and pressing, but welcome. He cupped my breasts, stroking my stomach, whispering in my ear.

Dirty words, sweet endearments, pleading gasps, all fell from his mouth.

"*You are so beautiful.*"

"*I love how you strangle my cock.*"

"*Jesus, you feel as if you were made for me.*"

He kissed my neck, licked my ear, bit gently at the juncture of my shoulder, then slipped his fingers down and stroked my clit.

"Come for me again, Red. Let me hear you." He pressed harder. "Let me feel you."

I cried out, my body exploding in ecstasy. I gripped the pillow under me, screaming into it, pushing back against him. He thrust again, then stilled, sitting back and taking me with him as he moaned and cursed. He wrapped his arms around my waist, pulling me tight to his chest, burying his face in my shoulder. Weakly, I lifted my arm, wrapping it around his head, stroking the sweat-soaked skin on his neck.

Moments passed with him holding me, not speaking. He turned his face, kissing my neck, his voice low in the room.

"Are you all right, Red?"

I drew in a shaky breath. "I'm good."

"I lost myself with you. Was I too rough?"

I shook my head. He had been forceful and in control, but I never felt threatened or hurt. Even when he was at the height of his passion, his touches had been controlled, even gentle at times. "No," I replied. "You were perfect."

His arms tightened, and I felt his smile against my skin. "You were the perfect one."

Carefully, he laid me down, and we separated. I rolled onto my side, and after discarding the condom, he did the same, facing me. He pulled me close, then laid his heavy arm over my waist, holding me. I liked the feeling. He made me feel…protected.

I wasn't sure what to say. I didn't have any experience to draw on. I'd never met someone and had sex with them the same night. A giggle burst from my lips, and Reynolds frowned.

"What?"

I decided to be honest. "I've never done this before—ever. I'm not sure what's supposed to happen next."

His chuckle made me smile. "I'm your first pickup, Red? I'm honored."

I slapped his chest, and he caught my hand and kissed it. "This isn't my usual style either, but—" he sighed and pushed back my hair "—I don't think you're a usual sort of woman. At least, not mine."

"Is that a good thing?"

"Yes."

I wanted to ask him about the pain in his eyes. But somehow, I knew he'd shut down.

"So, ah, what happens next?"

He rolled, keeping me close and bending his other arm under his head as he stared at the ceiling. "You can tell me to leave. You can ask me to stay. It's up to you."

I knew what I wanted. I hoped he wanted the same thing. I traced my finger down his chest, stroking it across his flat, hard nipples, then descending lower to his stomach. I teased the muscles, slowly drifting lower. "If you stayed, then what?"

"I'd fuck you again. A few times."

"You can do that at your age?" I teased.

"Not a problem," he growled. "You want more? It's yours."

"Well, that settles it. You're staying, big man."

His chest rumbled, and for the second time that night, I found myself trapped under his heavy body.

"Good choice, Red. Good choice."

I woke up alone. Slowly, I sat up, squinting at the clock on the night table. It was almost seven. The last time Reynolds had woken me up, it had been five. He had taken me differently that time—slow and gentle, rocking into me from behind, his voice low and gruff as he brought me to a powerful climax. He had kissed me for a long time after, then slipped from bed. Exhausted, I had fallen back asleep, assuming he would return. I recalled the sound of a door closing in my sleep-addled mind—and I realized he had probably never returned to the bed, but left quietly, saving us both the awkwardness of a long goodbye in the morning.

That's what he'd been doing earlier—saying goodbye with his body instead of words. I ran a hand through my hair and stretched, feeling aching muscles from last night protest as I moved. I looked around the room, feeling a strange sense of loneliness. I realized I was leaving this morning to start a new job, but it wasn't that far away. I thought I had felt a connection with Reynolds, and he with me. I had hoped he would want to exchange numbers, perhaps get together once I was settled.

I sighed and flung back the blanket. Obviously, I thought wrong. It was a one-night stand. The closeness I felt with him was just sex. He was experienced enough to know that and had left. He was right to have gone. I had liked him—really liked him. He was intelligent and funny. The sexiest man I had ever met—or slept with. He had been an incredible lover—giving, in control, and his kisses left me breathless. I had even liked the way he called me Red—drawing it out a little as if he was caressing the word with his tongue. He made me feel safe, cared for, and even sexy. All with a touch and some softly spoken words.

My heart ached a little, as if it felt it had lost something.

I stood, shaking my head. What an odd thought.

CHAPTER 7

MAXX

I finished the job I had been working on and wiped my greasy hands on the cloth. For the millionth time that morning, I tried not to think of the way my hands had felt against the soft skin of Red's body. I shook my head. *Charlynn.* Nicknames suggested familiarity. A relationship. I had never been one for nicknames, so why that one came so easily, I had no idea, but I had to stop thinking about Charlynn as Red.

In fact, I had to stop thinking about her altogether.

I had hated to leave her this morning, fighting an odd sensation that pulled me toward her once I was dressed and getting ready to walk out the motel room door.

She was beautiful in the dull morning light, her brilliant hair spread over the pillow, her body supple and relaxed under the blankets.

I smiled as I recalled one of our murmured conversations in the night.

"Tell me a secret," she whispered against my throat.

"I don't do secrets," I replied.

She ignored me. "I hate the wind."

I frowned. "The wind? You'll hate living around here, then. There is always a breeze."

"No," she replied, snuggling closer, my arms pulling her tighter, seemingly of a mind of their own when it came to her. "Wind. Like during the storm when it drives itself against the window, making it shudder, trying to get inside."

"Ah. Any reason why?"

"No, just always have. I don't tell people because they think I'm weird."

There was silence. I could feel her waiting, hoping.

"I idolized my father," I said quietly. "I miss him every day—and sometimes I talk to him like he is still there."

"When did he die?"

"Two years ago. My mother died in January, and he followed about six months later. He couldn't bear to live without her."

"That's beautiful. Two souls so tightly connected they need each other to survive." She paused. "I'm sorry you lost them."

I didn't say anything but pressed a kiss to her head. She was almost too sweet to be true. I could feel her empathy in her sincere words, and it made me feel oddly vulnerable. I cut off any more conversation by kissing her.

Even now, standing in my garage, I could feel the warmth of her against me.

I had watched her for a few moments, the urge to wake her and ask for her information nagging at me. But I resisted. There would be no more relationships for me. I had learned my lesson.

Instead, I'd lifted one of her curls, and rubbed the silky tress between my fingers.

"I hope the wind never blows where you're going, Red. Thank you for last night. It was a gift I can never repay."

Then I walked out of her life and headed back to mine. She was starting down a new road, and I sincerely hoped she found what she was looking for.

I shut the hood, then backed out the car, leaving the keys under the seat. John would be around to pick it up later, and I would get the new kid to call him for payment next week. My passion was motorcycle restorations, but the bread and butter of the shop was the mechanical work. I needed to do one in order to pursue the love of the other. I grimaced as I thought of how many people needed to be called. My bank account was getting pretty low, yet I couldn't bring myself to contact people and get payment. That meant talking. Which led to questions and the offer of sympathy or outrage on my behalf. Neither of which I wanted. I simply didn't want to talk about it.

I headed inside, throwing off my clothes to have a shower. I hesitated as my shirt tore over my head, and I sniffed the material. I could smell *her*.

Light, citrusy, and lovely. Her scent was seeped into my shirt. For some reason, I was loath to toss it in the hamper, then with a muffled curse, I did. I stepped in the shower, almost growling when the heat lifted her scent to my nose again. I grabbed the soap and scrubbed.

I had to stop thinking about her. It was a one-night stand, and it was over. I needed to get my head back in the game, pick up the kid, and move ahead.

I ignored the little ache in my chest as I thought about never seeing Red again. It was stupid, and the bottom line was, it didn't matter. She was gone and the chances of me ever seeing her again, slim.

I pulled up in front of the general store about ten minutes late. Sitting on the bench was a lanky kid who looked much younger than twenty-five. He lazed back on the bench, his sunglasses covering his face, feet crossed at the ankles, beat-up sneakers on his feet. He looked relaxed with his arms crossed behind his head. Beside him sat a wild, flower-covered suitcase, and I frowned. Had I hired some runaway? He barely looked old enough to be out of school. Had he lied on his resume? I looked again, wondering why the suitcase looked vaguely familiar. Maybe my mother had had one like it at one time.

I waited a moment, then tapped the gas, gunning the engine. He didn't stir or change his position, and I muttered under my breath. He was going to be a lazy one.

Angry, I got out of the truck and slammed the door. I stalked over to him, standing by the bench. I cleared my throat, noticing too late he had earbuds in and couldn't hear me.

I hunched down and plucked out a bud. He sat up, startled. "What the hell, man?"

I bent close. "We're going to be talking about this."

He frowned, glancing around. "What?"

"Get your stuff, and let's go."

"I'm not going anywhere with you, mister. And that's not my stuff. I'm just watching it."

I felt a small sliver of relief flow through me, even as a voice spoke up behind me. A voice I knew far too well, for all the wrong reasons.

"It's mine."

I spun on my heel, meeting the wide green eyes of Charlynn.

"What are you doing here?" I snapped. "Did you follow me earlier?"

"Me?" she responded. "I'm here for my job."

I narrowed my eyes. "Your job?"

The owner of the general store came out, holding up a slip of paper. "Miss, you left this!" She approached and handed Charlynn something and lifted a hand in greeting. "Maxx."

I tilted my chin at her in greeting, and Charlynn gasped. "You-you're *Maxx*?"

I crossed my arms. "I am."

Her wide eyes became huge. She laid a hand over her throat, her stare confused. "But last night, they called you Reynolds."

"My name is Maxx Reynolds." A nagging thought entered my head. "Charlynn? Is that your real name?"

"Yes." She paused and swallowed. "But I go by Charly."

I blinked. Looked at the kid on the bench who was watching us as if we were on some sort of reality show. He had pulled off his glasses, and his gaze was filled with curiosity.

I was dumbstruck. Charlynn was Charly. I had hired Charly and slept with Charlynn.

They were the same person.

I spun on my heel and headed to my truck.

I was out of there.

CHARLY

Maxx strode to his truck, anger rolling off of him. I was taken aback when I realized the man I slept with last night and my new boss were one and the same. His reaction was far more vehement.

I raced behind him, grabbing the door before he could slam it and drive away.

"Wait!" I pleaded. "Where are you going?"

"Home."

"I need to get my suitcase before we go!"

"You," he growled, "are *not* coming with me. I don't know what games you're playing, girl, but I'm not having any of it."

My heart sank. "I'm not playing any games," I insisted. "You hired me—you promised me a month's trial."

He got out of the truck, looming over me. His eyes were dark and stormy, his shoulders tense. "I hired a kid named Charly."

I thrust out my chin, refusing to let him see how scared I was. "You hired *me*. Nothing has changed about my qualifications. I can do the job."

"How many other lies have you told me?"

"I haven't told you any lies. You never asked if I was male or female—you just assumed. In fact, you stated you didn't care. I'd say you're the one who lied," I responded, slamming my hands on my hips.

He ran a hand over his face. "Go back to wherever you came from Charlynn—or Charly. Whoever you are." He began to turn away, and I grabbed at his arm. If he drove away, I had no idea what I was going to do. I had enough money to get back to Toronto, but the next bus wasn't until Thursday. I didn't have enough money to live on until then. And once I got back to town, I had nowhere to go. He couldn't abandon me here.

"Please," I begged, my voice low. "I can't go back. I-I have nothing there."

He dropped his head, cursing under his breath. I kept talking.

"I can do all the things you need. Give me a chance. Two weeks. Give me two weeks at least to prove I can do the job. I'll —" my voice broke, and I swallowed "—I'll even work for free. Just board."

He didn't say anything for a moment. When he spoke, his voice was cold. "Last night never happened. I don't know you, and you sure the hell don't know me."

"All right," I agreed, desperate. Once he calmed down, I was certain we could talk and clear the air. But I had to get him to agree to let me stay.

"You want a two-week trial?"

"Yes."

He still didn't look at me. "Then *Charly* gets one. I was expecting a guy. You get treated exactly like one. There are no concessions because you're a girl. You do what I say, when I say it. You work hard, and you don't complain." He turned and looked me in the eye, his gaze stony and removed. "I never saw you before today, do you understand?"

I tamped down my odd feeling of hurt. "Yes."

"Know one thing, *Charly*. I hate liars. I hate deceit and subterfuge. I catch you, even suspect you're doing anything underhanded, and you're gone. I don't care if you have to walk back to Toronto, you're out of my place. You hear what I'm saying?"

His voice was even, his tone commanding. His gaze never wavered from mine. Still, I heard it—the underlying pain of something that had hurt him. Something that caused this reaction. I didn't like this cold man in front of me. Especially not compared to the warm, passionate lover I'd had last night, But I needed the job, and I needed to prove to him he could trust me.

"I hear you."

"Then get your suitcase and get in." He swung himself into the truck and slammed the door. He started the engine and rolled down his window. "Move it, Charly. I don't have all day."

I grabbed my case and headed to the truck.

"Good luck, lady," the kid called from the bench. "I think you're going to need it."

He was right.

I hauled my case up and over the liftgate and scampered up into the truck. Maxx didn't wait until I was buckled in to reverse. He gunned the engine and drove like a bat out of hell down the dirt road toward his place.

I held on and didn't say a word.

MAXX

I drove like a madman, my anger burning a hole in my gut. The last thing I expected was to find Charlynn at the general store. The one fleeting second of pleasure had been eclipsed by fury when I realized that the beautiful, sexy woman who had been haunting my thoughts all morning was the person I had hired to help me straighten out my world.

She wasn't going to straighten it; she was going to blow it the fuck to smithereens. How was I supposed to work with her, live with her, after what we shared last night?

How was I ever going to trust her?

I tried not to groan out loud when I realized perhaps part of my anger was due to the fact that I wasn't sure I could trust myself. This morning, in the clear light of day, without a bit of makeup on and wearing a pair of jeans and a girly blouse, she was stunning. Her hair caught the light, a burnished cascade of curls down her back. When I had turned around and seen her, my first instinct had been to yank her close, bury my hands in that gorgeous hair and kiss her.

Until her words registered.

It was true. She never said she was a guy. I assumed from her username that she was. Something she said last night ran through my mind, and I spoke without looking at her.

"Why did you think I was an old man?"

"What?" she asked, looking startled.

"Last night. You said you were going to look after an old man. A curmudgeon, I think were your exact words."

"Oh. You sounded like it. Your ad. The way you responded. The duties you listed. Like you needed help but didn't want to ask. My dad was that way." Out of the corner of my eye, I saw her lift one shoulder. "I guess we both thought wrong."

"No shit," I snapped. "We're both disappointed."

"I never said I was disappointed," was her reply. I risked a glance, but I saw she was staring out the window. I grunted and she spoke again.

"I'll do a good job, Maxx." She paused. "Or do you prefer *Reynolds?*" Sarcasm dripped from her voice.

I didn't bother to explain. "Sir will do."

"I am not calling you sir," she sniped back at me, trying to sound tough. If I weren't so angry, I would have chuckled at her. She kept going.

"In fact, let me tell you a thing or two."

I didn't say anything, figuring at least what she said would be interesting.

"You plan on treating me like the kid you think you hired? Fine. But I expect you to be polite, courteous, and fair. I don't expect to be punished because I have breasts instead of a dick. I'll do my work, and I will show you the respect you deserve as my boss as long as you show me the respect I deserve as an employee and a human being." She drew in a much-needed breath. "You understand me, *Maxx?*"

I pulled into the driveway and brought us to a lurching stop. I climbed out of the truck and looked at her across the bench. Her cheeks were flushed, and her hair tousled from the open windows. She was as angry as I was right now, her little fists clenched, and her brows drawn down in a frown. She was fucking adorable, and it made me angrier than ever.

"I hear you, Charly. You sure about that dick? Your balls are certainly big enough. Now, get your suitcase and follow me."

I slammed the door, ignoring the screech of rage I cut off. I was glad I was walking away, because this time, I couldn't stop my amusement.

And that pissed me off even more.

CHAPTER 8

CHARLY

Holding my tongue, I followed Maxx as fast as I could. Entering the garage, I barely looked around as he headed swiftly toward the back. My suitcase bounced on the floor, one wheel spinning off and flying across the room.

"Shit," I muttered, half carrying, half dragging it the rest of the way. I went through the office and down a short hall, trying not to shudder at the chaos the office contained. Papers were everywhere. Files piled up, boxes on every surface.

I knew where I was going to start.

I entered a room, trying not to look as horrified as I was feeling. This was where I would be staying. A room in the back of a garage.

I looked at Maxx, keeping my expression neutral, knowing he was waiting for a negative reaction and refusing to give it to him. I flung my knapsack on the bed. He glowered at me, indicating the room. His voice was laced with sarcasm as he gestured with his arm, pointing to the bed. "Your bedroom." His finger moved to the single chair and the small TV on top of it. "Your entertainment area." Another point to the corner, where an old but serviceable dresser stood. The wall had a few hooks drilled into it next to the wooden chest. "Your dressing area." Then he opened the only other door in the room with a flourish. "Your spa."

I didn't even look, unsure if I could hide my reaction. I made a show of turning and inspecting the door. There was a lock on it, but not much better than I'd had at the apartment. The door felt solid, though, and I could shove the chair under the knob if I needed to. I crossed the small room and opened the curtain covering the window, and I couldn't help my smile. Nothing but trees and grass as far as I could see. It was, at least, a pretty view —and private. And I was safe here. No matter how angry Maxx was, he wouldn't hurt me—I knew this for sure. He had protected me before he even knew me, and I had discovered the gentler side of him last night.

Even if, as he insisted, it never happened.

I turned, crossing my arms. "Okay. I'll unpack later. Next."

His mouth tightened, and I wanted to stick out my tongue at him. He had hoped I would see where I was going to stay and want to leave. But he didn't know how stubborn I could be—nor did he realize I had literally nowhere to go and no way to get there, even if I did. Once I paid for the bus ticket, my meal, and motel room, I had less than fifty bucks. I had to make this work.

He brushed past me, and I tried hard not to inhale his intoxicating scent. He might be acting like a bastard, but he certainly smelled good.

I followed him back through the garage, noting the contrast to the office. Everything was in its place, and it was meticulous. Large, with three bays, it was well-laid-out. I would have to investigate it later as I hurried to keep up with Maxx. We walked about fifty feet, him not saying anything until we got closer to a two-story house.

"Rufus will barrel out the door. He doesn't bite, but let him come to you," he said, his voice warmer as he spoke about his dog, but still removed.

"Sure."

I stood back and waited as he opened the door, and a large dog loped out. He pushed against Maxx, happy to see him. Maxx, in turn, stroked his great head, murmuring low to him, and the dog gazed up at him adoringly. Then he spotted me and trotted over. I remained still, holding out my hand. He sniffed me, then lifted his head and let me stroke him. He was affectionate and happy, his tail wagging. I liked him.

"Enough," Maxx snapped. "Rufus, heel."

Immediately, Rufus returned to Maxx's side, and I heard him mutter "traitor" under his breath before pushing open the side door and letting it shut behind him. I rolled my eyes but followed, walking into a large mudroom. I stepped into the next room, taking it in. The kitchen was huge, with white cupboards, pretty trim, and well-worn butcher-block counters. There were a few dirty dishes in the sink. Otherwise, it had a neglected look to it. Dusty, unused, and needing attention. There was a dining room, with a huge farm table piled high with more boxes on top and around it, one space cleared where Maxx obviously ate. Ahead was a living room, a big fireplace in the center. It was a well-proportioned room, but sparse. There were plain white walls, no pictures or anything personal around. A TV hung on the wall, one chair in front of it, and a sofa pushed against the far wall. It needed attention.

Maxx let me wander, not saying anything, leaning against the counter in the kitchen. Rufus kept me company as I explored. The stairs divided the house, the central hall the focal point. There was a nice bathroom off the kitchen, and opposite it, behind the living room, was a bedroom—unused and piled with more boxes. I trailed my fingers over them, noting these were of a more personal nature, labeled and stacked neatly. Looking at the fading wallpaper and the old-fashioned bed frame dismantled and resting against the wall, I had the impression this room stored Maxx's parents' most prized possessions. Feeling as if I were intruding, I left the room, shutting the door behind me.

I hesitated at the bottom of the stairs, looking up. I glanced to the left, where Maxx was now leaning against the doorframe, watching me in silence. I tilted my head toward the stairs, and he pushed off the door and went ahead of me. At the head of the stairs was a set of barn doors which he bypassed and showed me the other two bedrooms. Both had a bed and dresser but were obviously unused. There was another bathroom, this one with a claw-foot tub, and I wondered if I might be allowed to use it. If, that was, I made it past my trial period.

Maxx hesitated then opened the barn doors. I stepped inside, knowing it was his room. His scent saturated it. Manly, woodsy, and warm. He had a huge bed made from rough wood, and the oak floors were stripped and wide. Through the open doors, I could see one side of the room had a closet and the other a bathroom. It was tidy, but like the rest of the house, neglected and sterile. All the walls were white, and there was little in the way of pictures or personal touches.

It felt as if Maxx was existing, not living.

"Seen enough?" he asked.

"Lots of work to be done," I replied lightly.

"Sort of the reason for my ad," he responded, walking ahead of me down the stairs.

"Easy peasy." I sniffed. "I look forward to it."

In the kitchen, I opened the fridge and the cupboards, growing more confused at the empty shelves. There were some staples—sugar, peanut butter, coffee, and the fridge held a large selection of condiments, but there was little in the way of groceries, aside from some canned goods.

I turned to look at him, aghast. "Where is your food?"

He shrugged. "I don't cook well. I buy enough food for a week. I usually shop on Saturday afternoons." He smirked. "Which is now your job, Charly. Get to it."

I placed a hand on my hip and arched one eyebrow. I held up my phone, showing him the ad he had placed. "Huh. Would ya look at that? The ad said Saturday afternoons and Sundays are free."

He glowered. God, he was handsome when he did that. It really should be illegal. I shouldn't enjoy it as much as I did, but there was a little flutter in my chest, regardless.

"It's either shopping today, or we both go hungry this week. Your choice."

"Fine." Then I paused. "How will I pay for the food?"

He snorted. "A, if you think I'm going to hand over the keys and a pile of cash and let you leave, you're crazier than I think you are. I'm not that stupid, Red—" he paused, flustered, color creeping up on his neck "—I mean, *Charly*. I'm driving you into town, and I'll pay for the groceries. And B, I think you lied about being able to drive my truck. I doubt you can even see over the dashboard."

"I can so," I protested, even though I wondered if he was right. The thing was massive. "I've driven a truck before."

"Not this one."

We glared at each other, and I tried not to notice the way his eyes looked in the bright light of the kitchen. Dark and deadly, the small lines around them only emphasizing the sexiness of his stare. If only he wouldn't ruin the image by talking. But that was impossible.

"It's your job to make the list, plan whatever you need, and do the cooking." He glanced at his watch, a chunky silver one that showed off his tanned forearms. I noticed a woven leather strap above the metal and a set of smooth beads. "You have twenty minutes."

I looked around, spying a cup with some pens. I found an old envelope and began to write. Lists, I excelled at.

"Bring your debit card, buddy. You need a lot of shit."

He strode from the room. "I have a feeling you are going to enjoy being the person to give me that shit."

"Gosh dang right, I am," I called after him, scribbling furiously.

Before we left, Maxx made me get behind the wheel of his truck. He lifted the seat as high as it would go, pushing it forward. I felt like a child behind the steering wheel, but I refused to show him my fear. "It's fine. I can drive this."

He laughed, actually sounding amused instead of angry. "You can barely reach the pedals. There is no way you can work the clutch and shift." He moved the seat back into the position he used. I could barely climb out of the truck, and he didn't offer to help. I almost fell trying, and with a curse, he caught me, setting me on my feet and shaking his head. "Yep. Good job, Charly. You are never driving this truck."

I wanted to stamp my feet. "Holy moly, that isn't fair. You haven't even let me try. I can learn. Otherwise, I can't do your errands, and you'll use it as an excuse to fire me."

He waved his hand. "We'll call a draw on this one. I'll figure out an alternative." He glanced toward a barn sitting behind the house, rubbing at his scruff, thinking.

"What?" I asked.

"Get in the truck," he replied, shaking his head.

I crossed to the other side, scrambling in.

"Not exactly graceful there, *Charly*," he mocked.

"Yowsers. Running boards would help," I muttered.

"What did you say?"

"I said running boards would help." I threw up my hands in frustration. "Look, I can't help it if I'm only five feet four. Or a girl. I know you hate it, but I'm here. I'm sorry, all right? Your truck was obviously built for a freaking giant. Stop finding things to find fault with. Save your breath. You can't growl and bitch me out of here, so stop chapping my ass. You're stuck with me for the next two weeks, so shut up, drive us to the store so I can get groceries and go home to start doing the job you hired me for." I crossed my arms, staring out the window. The truck was silent, and I wondered if I had said too much. Pushed him too far. Maybe he was going to tell me to go get my suitcase and get out. But I couldn't waver.

There was an odd sound, almost a begrudging chuckle, then he started the truck. "Fine, Charly. Let's go get groceries."

I considered that my first victory.

In the store, Maxx followed me around like a silent shadow. More like a growly grizzly bear at times, but he didn't say much or protest as I filled the cart, but he made some odd noises. He added a few things that I assumed he liked. I made notes to keep apples, pears, and bananas on hand. He also seemed to like fresh veggies, so the cart was loaded with lots of those. It made up for the horrid "healthy choice" meals his freezer contained. I stocked up on staples, meat, and other items—including the makings of my lemon pie. Maybe that would soften him up a little.

He paid the bill, helped load the groceries, and even unloaded at the other end. He answered my questions as I thought of them on the drive back, keeping his replies short.

"What hours is the shop open?"

"Eight to four. Monday to Friday. Appointments after hours and Saturday."

"Do you only do restorations?"

"No."

"So, you're a full-service garage?"

"Yes."

"How many mechanics?"

His hands tightened on the wheel before he responded to that question.

"Me."

I frowned. That seemed unusual.

"I saw your website. It needs updating." I didn't mention the picture. That was obviously not Maxx. Maybe his dad?

He grunted. "Hence the job, Charly. Keep up."

I looked out the window. "I can keep up no problem, grump. Easy peasy."

I felt his glower, but I didn't look at him.

"Anything you don't like?"

"We covered that at the bus stop."

I rolled my eyes and huffed. "Holy moly, you're a hard nut to crack. I meant food-wise, buddy."

"A little late to ask since you just spent all my money on food."

"Yowsers, you were right there, big boy. And obviously, you have a voice that you like to use to berate me."

He huffed.

"And," I continued, "since you're not paying me, consider that part of the payment."

He shocked me when he pulled the truck into his driveway and parked it.

"You do your job, you'll get paid, Charly." He swung himself out of the vehicle, staring at me across the seat. "You have two weeks. Impress me."

He shut the door, and I had to smile. I planned on impressing him, all right. In two weeks, he'd be lost without me.

After we got back, Maxx disappeared. I assumed he went to the shop, but I didn't ask. I relaxed a little without him watching me. Envious, I watched Rufus out in the sun, rolling on the grass. I had no time for fun today. I got busy, quickly dusting out shelves and loading them up with groceries. The fridge was clean, and by the time I finished, full. I had no idea what to do about dinner. Did I make it and we would eat together? Leave it for Maxx to eat when he wanted? Too tired of fighting and knowing I had a lot of long days ahead of me, I made a simple dinner of baked chicken and rice, threw together a salad, then ate alone, standing at the counter. The kitchen already looked better, the counters gleaming, the cupboards full and clean. I stretched my tired muscles and left dinner in the oven, then headed to the garage. I bumped into Maxx partway across the grass. He and Rufus looked windblown and relaxed, although Rufus looked happier to see me than Maxx did.

"How do I get to the room?" I asked. "Does the side door lock as well?"

For the first time since I arrived, he didn't snap at me or behave rudely. "Yes. And there is an alarm. Come, and I'll show you."

I followed him, and he took me through the simple steps.

"So, will it go off in the morning if I walk through the garage?"

"No. Only if the windows or doors are opened. The alarm sounds inside the house, so I would hear it." He handed me three keys. "One for the side door, one for the room, one for the house."

I took the keys, trying to ignore the heat I felt as his fingers brushed against mine.

"You're sure I won't sneak in and murder you in your sleep?"

"Tempted, Charly?"

"There are moments," I replied. I swore I saw his lips quirk, but I must have imagined it. He stared at me, and I cleared my throat.

"Okay. Your dinner is in the oven. Salad in the fridge."

"What about you?"

I couldn't resist. "Oh, the big man cares."

He rolled his eyes, glaring at me again. "I don't want you dropping from hunger. I don't have time to look after you." He stomped to the door.

"I ate already," I informed him.

"Fine." He yanked open the door, pausing to enter the code on the alarm. "Charly," he called over his shoulder.

I turned, expecting another rebuke about not setting off the alarm or something. Instead, he surprised me. "You'll be perfectly safe here."

He shut the door before I could respond.

CHAPTER 9

MAXX

I walked into the house, the scent of dinner filling my head. I couldn't recall the last time I had walked in to such a homey smell. Shannon hadn't been a great cook and I sucked at it, so meals had been either from a box, the one pizza place in town, or the barbecue. I did a good job on the grill, when I bothered to try. Since she left, I hadn't bothered once.

I opened the oven and took out the casserole, inhaling. My mouth watered at the aroma, and I filled my plate, carrying it to the table, surprised to see the spot I usually sat in tidy, with a place mat and cutlery waiting.

I tried the chicken and rice, almost moaning at the flavor. It was simple but delicious, and I was starving. As I ate, I glanced out the window, wondering what Red was doing.

I shook my head.

Charly. She was Charly, and I had to think of her that way.

I had to admit, as I'd suspected, she was a feisty one. She hadn't shrunk from me once today, no matter how much I snarled or sniped at her. In fact, she gave as good as she got, at times making me want to laugh. There were moments I had to look away in order not to do so. Her facial expressions were amusing—she would make a horrible poker player—she was far too expressive to keep her emotions hidden. In the store, she was efficient, loading the cart, muttering to herself. At times, it was as if she was checking off a recipe in her head, adding the ingredients. She used odd expressions. Gosh dang it. Easy peasy. Holy moly. Would ya look at that. Yowsers. Chap my ass. They dotted her mutterings and entered her conversation. If she didn't annoy me so much, I might find them, and her, adorable.

But I didn't.

I filled my plate again and opened the fridge to get the salad. I stopped and looked inside. It was clean, organized, and full. The counters were spotless. She had certainly been busy.

I sat back down and polished off another plateful. If this was how she cooked, I was okay with it. I glanced out the window again, feeling somewhat guilty. Would she be okay in the garage? I had expected her to throw a fit. Inform me she wouldn't be sleeping in a room at the back of the garage. I had to admit, I had only taken her there to punish her. She'd told me to treat her the way I would the kid I had been expecting to show up, so I did. I fully anticipated giving in and carrying her broken suitcase into the house and giving her one of the other bedrooms, but she refused to rise to the bait. Instead, she was calm and surveyed the room, then asked to see the house.

It was for the best. It was hard enough, knowing she was across the yard. If she had been down the hall, I wasn't sure I could resist her. That goddamn gorgeous hair, her expressive eyes, and her smart mouth.

What a mouth it was. Simply thinking about what it did to me last night made me hard.

Never mind what her scent did to me. As I followed in her wake at the grocery store, she was all I could smell. Citrusy, musky, light, and feminine. I wasn't sure if it was entirely the fragrance she wore, or if that combined with the essence of her made it so irresistible. More than once, I wanted to take her down right there and bury my face in her neck while I fucked her. I had no idea how she had such a hold over me. I barely knew her. I didn't want to know her.

I wasn't in the market for a relationship. Especially with a smart-mouthed, redheaded, little snippet who liked to try to put me in my place. And she wasn't the type for a sexual relationship without ties. I'd figured that out last night—it was a one-off for her. Her whispered little secrets and the way she wanted to be snuggled after. I refused to admit how good she had felt in my arms, or that I had succumbed to her whispers. I had nothing left emotionally to give anyone, so we would never work.

She was an employee. Simple as that.

I scrubbed my face, then rested my head in my hands, knowing my words were full of shit.

I wanted her. And I was pretty sure she wanted me.

Which one of us, I wondered, would break first?

The next while would, at least, prove to be interesting.

CHARLY

I slept surprisingly well considering I was in a new place. When I got to my room the night before, I had been shocked to discover a new lock on the door. It was a simple metal slider, but with the other lock on the door handle, it gave me a measure of safety. Obviously, Maxx had added it and simply not said anything. He must have remembered what I told him about Terry and installed it for me. Despite his gruffness, he cared.

Checking my new space, I decided, as far as rooms went, it was fine. I unpacked my clothes, used the few hooks in the wall to hang my skirts, and slid my suitcase under the bed. I texted Kelly to let her know I was okay, knowing if she didn't hear from me, she'd get worried, then I took a shower, grimacing when I was done as I realized there were no towels. I used the shirt I'd worn that day and made a mental note to find some in the morning. The sheets were scratchy and old, but they would do until I discovered where all the linens were in the house.

I sat in the bed, surveying the room. With a small reconfiguration, it would work better. I would do that later today, but I wanted to get a start on the office in the garage. I got dressed, wearing a pair of jeans and a long shirt, unsure what to expect today but knowing I had a lot of work ahead of me. I bundled my hair into a bun to keep it out of my eyes, found my glasses, and headed to the office.

I stood in the chaos, unsure where to start. Files were everywhere. Piles of paper. Parts, notes, discarded coffee cups. I wasn't even certain there was a desk under the mounds of stuff. I blew out a long breath and decided to simply start.

Half an hour later, I had scrubbed the coffeemaker, had a pot brewing, and tidied up the little kitchen area. The only things in the old refrigerator were some bottles of water, beer, and creamers for coffee. I was grateful to find they were still usable. I checked the storeroom and discovered a few new banker boxes which I carried to the office. I peeked in the ones on the shelf, noticing how tidy the paperwork inside was. Everything seemed to be in order up until the last year or so, and then it stopped. It was all there, but not in any order. I pursed my lips as I wondered what had occurred then that caused the sudden shift.

Back in the office, a cup of coffee in hand, I sat in front of the desk and decided swift action was best. I unfolded three boxes, and carefully piled everything off the desk and into the boxes, sorting as I went. As I went through the files, I noticed there was a system of sorts. One file contained a multitude of pieces of paper with jobs done, prices scribbled, and names. On the front of the file, written in a bold script, was the word INVOICE. I lifted my eyebrows in shock at the vast amount of money outstanding to Maxx. That would be my number one priority. "Yowsers," I muttered, keeping that file on the desk.

It took me an hour to clear away the top of the desk, adding more papers to the invoice pile, finding unopened mail, bills to be paid, and a lot of junk. Once the desk was clear, I cleaned it, organized the top, and sat back, sipping my third cup of coffee. I glanced at the clock, noting it was almost seven thirty, and wondered if Maxx would want breakfast. We hadn't discussed that last night—the fact was that we hadn't talked at all. I pulled a piece of paper toward me and made yet another list.

The sound of the side door opening and the alarm switching off made my shoulders stiffen. I shook my head, preparing myself to face Maxx. Would he be friendlier today? I was determined to start the day off right and show him what I was capable of. I fixed a smile to my face and waited for him to walk in.

I wasn't prepared for him, though. Freshly showered, his hair still damp, and smelling so good I wanted to lick him, he strode in. His T-shirt was stretched tight across his muscular chest, his biceps bulging in the short sleeves. The jeans he wore hugged his thighs, and I could only imagine how good they looked from the back. I had to swallow to clear my dry throat and force a neutral expression on my face.

"Morning, boss."

He stopped in the doorway, clutching the frame. For a moment, he stared, his eyes narrowed, his frown deepening, then without a word, he spun on his heel and went back the way he came, leaving me staring at the door.

Holy moly, he was rude. He could at least say good morning. I scrubbed my face in vexation, refusing to give him the satisfaction of seeing me upset. I returned to the task at hand, not bothering to look up when he walked back in ten minutes later.

"Charly."

I cursed the way he made my name sound like a caress without even trying. It rolled off his tongue like an endearment, even though I was certain he wasn't trying to do so.

I glanced up, attempting to appear casual.

"Oh, you can speak."

He had the grace to look abashed. "Sorry. I realized I forgot my cell in the house."

I rolled my eyes, not believing him for a moment.

"You don't have to work Sundays."

"I'd rather get a head start."

"What have you done to the office?"

"I'm organizing it." I lifted a file as proof.

"It was organized," he huffed. "I knew where everything was."

"Gosh dang it," I muttered. "Already, Maxx? You're going to chap my ass already? You said you needed help. I am trying to help."

"There were parts there I need. How will I find them?"

"I took every part and placed it on the workbench. Every screw, every wire, every little mechanical piece that you left on the desk is out there." I indicated the boxes. "All the paperwork is in these boxes. I will go through each box and organize it. Then I will invoice all these jobs and get some capital flowing in." I waved my hand at the old computer sitting on the desk. "That needs updating."

"It works," he protested, crossing his arms.

"It's ancient. Does it still run on Windows98?"

"I have no idea," he admitted. "I'm not one for technology of that sort."

"I do and I am. A nice laptop would work well. And a new

printer. You want a decent website, I need the tools to do so." I pushed a piece of hair over my ear. "I'll use mine until we get one. Until then, I need the password for this one."

"Cycle."

"Original."

"Stop busting my chops."

"Stop being a dick."

We were locked in a battle of glares. I gave in and shook my head. "Coffee is made. Do you want breakfast?"

"No."

"Fine. I'm going to work in here this morning unless you want something else done?"

"No."

He was obviously going to be difficult no matter what I said or did.

"I assume tomorrow you have appointments? Do I answer the phone? How do you want them booked?"

He blinked, for the first time looking unsure. "However they come." He paused and ran a hand through his hair. "Why don't you look after this, and I'll look after the front. I sort of have my own system."

I looked around the office. "I'll say. Holy moly, what a mess."

I swore his lips quirked. Then he schooled his features. "Do your job, Charly."

"Trying."

He turned, and I called out, "Wait."

"What?"

"No breakfast, but I assume you want lunch and dinner?"

"Yes. I have a job I'm working on. So just a sandwich at some point. Dinner..." His voice trailed off, and a real, honest smile lit his face. "Whatever that was you made last night, I approve."

"You liked it?" I asked, suddenly feeling shy.

"I polished it off. All of it."

"Oh. Okay. I'm glad you liked it."

"I did."

For a moment, something warm and real passed between us. I caught a glimpse of the man from Friday night, and it made my heart jump in my chest.

"Thank you for the lock."

He lifted a shoulder, then paused, as if wanting to say something.

"Yes?" I asked

"Nothing. I have work to do. Since I'm paying you, I suggest you get back to yours."

I sniffed. "Been at it since six, so you know. And as you pointed out, it is my day off."

"Nice to see some initiative," he shot back, heading to the coffeemaker. "Stop brownnosing the boss." He poured a cup of coffee and took a long sip. "Just because you're working today, don't be late tomorrow. I will drag you out of bed and kick your ass to get you to work."

"I'd like to *kick* your ass," I muttered.

He appeared by my elbow. "What was that?"

"I said I have gas," I deadpanned. "You might want to leave the room."

He blinked, stepped back, then walked away.

But I heard him laughing, and I hugged myself. Another small victory.

Midafternoon, I stood and stretched. The desk was now organized and tidy. Tomorrow, I planned on tackling the huge pile of outstanding payments. That would take me a while, but it needed to be done.

I walked through the garage, Maxx busy under the hood of a

car. I couldn't help staring at his ass as I walked. Bent over, his jeans pulled tight, it was spectacular. Sculpted, round, and I recalled, firm. Not looking where I was going, I tripped over a piece of equipment, ending up on the hard cement floor, muttering in pain and exasperation.

"Holy moly, crap on a cracker…" I cursed, holding my hand.

Maxx pulled himself up, hurrying over. "What happened?" Concern colored his voice. "Are you hurt?"

Up close, under the bright lights, his dark eyes had flecks of gold and green, and they were mesmerizing, rendering me unable to speak.

He grabbed my shoulders, shaking me a little. "Charly!"

I blinked and flushed, realizing how silly I must look. "I'm fine."

He tugged on my hand. "Let me see."

I uncurled my fist, and he cursed. The skin was torn and bleeding, having taken the brunt of my weight as I fell. He stood, taking me with him. I yelped in shock, pushing on his shoulder.

"What are you doing?"

"I need to bandage your hand."

"I can walk."

"Apparently not well. How the hell did you trip over a creeper? It was right there!"

My cheeks became hotter. "Um, I was distracted." I wiggled a little. "Let me down."

"No."

He headed down the hall and into the small bathroom off the office. He held my hand under the water, ignoring my gasp of pain as the water hit the torn flesh.

"We need to make sure it's clean."

He opened the small cupboard and took out a first aid box.

"I can do that."

He shook his head, looking around. "Where's a towel?"

"I don't think there is one. You didn't give me one either. Good thing I had my own soap. Otherwise, the shower would have been a total wash." I waggled my eyebrows, trying to get him to lighten up. He looked far too serious.

He ignored my humor. "I forgot. Sorry."

Before I could recover from his apology, he whipped his shirt over his head, standing in front of me bare-chested. He wrapped my hand in the shirt, still warm from his body, then rummaged in the first aid box. I tried not to gape. I had seen him naked in the motel room, but the lights were low. That view hadn't done him justice. He was sculpted and firm, his muscles rippling as he moved. He had a six-pack, maybe even an eight-pack. I couldn't count, my head was so muddled. He crouched in front of me, saying something, and I blinked.

"What?"

"I said, this is going to sting." Then he dabbed at the torn skin with alcohol, and I yelped.

He blew on my hand, and my breath caught. It was highly erotic watching his mouth work to cool my skin. His closeness was having the opposite effect on the rest of me. My body felt heavy and warm. The desire to drape my arms over his shoulders and have him lift and carry me to the small bed down the hall was prevalent. He bent his head as he added some ointment, then covered the skin with a large bandage.

"We'll check it tomorrow," he said, looking up and freezing.

Our eyes locked in a heated, silent exchange. His hands tightened on mine, gripping them with an intensity that was thrilling. His pupils dilated, his breathing picking up to match mine. Memories of the night we shared came alive, swirling around us. I licked my lips, and his gaze flicked to my mouth, then back to my eyes.

We drifted closer, like magnets unable to stop the pull. His mouth was almost touching mine, and I whispered his name.

"Maxx."

He released my hands and stood so fast, I almost toppled over. He stepped back, his eyes wild.

"I have to go and do some errands. Try to be more careful in the garage, Charly."

Then he turned and almost ran, as if the hounds of hell were pursuing him.

I drew in a shuddering breath, hearing the sound of the garage door closing and his truck starting.

I dropped my head into my hands, wincing at the pain.

What just happened?

CHAPTER 10

MAXX

I pulled out of the driveway so fast, my tires kicked up a cloud of dust and pebbles, shooting them all over the road.

I didn't care. I had to get out. Get away from *her*.

A short distance away, I steered to the side of the road and hung my head.

Twice.

That was twice in one day I couldn't stop my reaction to her.

When I walked in the office this morning, the sight of her sitting at my desk, her legs folded under her as she worked, caught me off guard. I thought I was prepared to see her. I wasn't.

Her hair was piled high with tendrils escaping in little corkscrew curls around her face. Her shirt hung off her shoulder, exposing the creamy flesh I remembered kissing. Tasting. And the kicker? The sexy, come-fuck-me librarian glasses perched on her nose. My cock hardened instantly.

I wanted to drag her off the chair, pull those glasses off her face, and take her. Right there on the desk. I had to turn around and leave before I did. Give myself a chance to collect my thoughts and brace myself to go back and pretend nothing was amiss. Treat her the way I had the day before—with barely concealed annoyance.

Except, I was finding it hard to do so for some reason. She had been working hard, for how long, I wasn't sure. But she was obviously determined to make the best of the job I hired her for. I hassled her a little, but this morning, my barbs were off and my comebacks weak.

Then when she fell, the sense of needing to look after her shocked me. Cleaning her hand, being that close to her was a mistake. The heat between us was undeniable. The urge to kiss her, yank her to my chest, and lose myself to her was intense. To carry her over to the little bed in the back and spend the rest of the day inside her, palpable and strong.

I had to physically remove myself. I hadn't even put a shirt on. I grabbed a spare one from the back seat and yanked it over my head, then banged my hand on the steering wheel in frustration.

How the hell was this going to work?

I hung my head again in resignation. I was being a fool. It wasn't going to work. One of us was going to break, and when we did, the entire fragile bomb we were dancing around was going to explode.

Somehow, something told me it would make the last explosion that rocked my world look like nothing.

A truck came up behind me, stopping. The passenger side window rolled down, and Mary tilted her head, studying me.

"What the hell are you doing?"

I sighed. There was no point lying. She'd figure it out. "Hiding."

"From?"

"My new assistant."

I had sent Mary a message, telling her I had hired someone.

She'd been away, so it was the first time I had seen her since she convinced me to place the ad. She had given me an earful about the contents of my ad, much the same way Red had, and was shocked anyone had replied.

"The kid just got here. More trouble than he's worth already?" She chuckled. "Give him a chance."

I met her gaze. "He's not a kid, and he's not a he."

Her eyebrows rose. "This I gotta hear. Follow me home, Maxx." Her tone left no room for argument.

I sighed and put the truck in gear.

Mary puttered around her homey kitchen, making coffee, relaxed and at ease. I sat stewing—and fidgeting.

"Should I put a splash of brandy in that coffee? Calm you down some?"

"I'm fine," I growled.

"Brandy, it is."

A mug thumped down in front of me. Mary sat down across the table. "Now, spill."

"The kid isn't really a kid."

"How old is, ah, your new assistant?"

"Twenty-five."

"Twenty-five isn't usually considered a child, Maxx," she stated mildly.

I sipped the coffee. "Everyone seems like a kid to me these days."

She laughed. "Wait until you get to be my age. Keep going."

"So, Charly is short for Charlynn. He is a she."

"Oh. So, your Girl Friday turned out to be exactly that. A girl. You never checked?"

"Her resume said C.L. Hooper. Her username was Charly. I never even thought."

"A natural assumption, I suppose," Mary murmured, her tone telling me she thought I was full of bullshit.

"When I found out, I almost left her at the bus stop. But she begged me for a trial."

"I assume she needs the job."

"Yeah." I ran a hand through my hair. "Anyway, she's a pain in the ass."

"Oh, pot meet kettle sort of thing?"

I glared at her. "She's a redheaded, back-talking little snippet. She keeps forgetting I'm the boss."

Mary's lips quirked. "I see. And she's doing a lousy job in the twenty-four hours she's been here?"

I leaned back in the chair, looking at the ceiling. "No. Hell, she did the grocery shopping, organized the kitchen, and I found her neck-deep in paperwork this morning."

"Wow. What a slacker. You should fire her."

I chuckled at her dry comment.

"So, you're angry that she's a woman?"

I scrubbed my face. "Not really. I had thought I would be hiring one, so him being a her isn't a bad thing."

"And she is trying?"

"Yes."

"I don't understand. It's a personality thing? You dislike her?"

I drained my coffee. "Not exactly."

She studied me. "What aren't you telling me, Maxx?"

I met her frank gaze. Mary and I had a solid, if slightly odd, friendship. She was older, widowed, and moved here about ten years ago. She and my mother had become friends, and when I lost my parents, she became almost a surrogate mother to me. I helped her around this place, fixing things. I kept her small truck in perfect running order. She fussed over me, and I allowed it.

We were also brutally honest with each other.

"We met Friday night. She came to town early, and I was in the bar having a bite, and we, ah, connected…"

"Oh, my god. You slept with her."

"Yes."

"And then you found out the he you thought you hired was a she, and you had already bedded her."

"In a nutshell."

Mary stared at me, tilting her head. Then she began to laugh. Long peals of laughter that echoed in the kitchen. I glowered at her, not finding this situation funny at all.

She calmed down, wiping her eyes. "I should have known," she muttered. "As soon as I saw that asinine ad you placed, it was asking for trouble."

"Trouble with a head full of red curls and a smart mouth," I agreed.

She studied me. "You like her," she stated.

"No, I don't."

"Yes, you do. That's why you're reacting this way. You actually like her."

"I'm not in the market for a relationship."

She reached across the table and clasped my hand. "Maxx, I know what happened shook you. Destroyed your trust. But not everyone is them. Not everyone is out to take from you."

"Leave it alone, Mary."

She sat back, crossing her legs. "I'm going to come and meet this girl that has you tied up in knots."

"No, she doesn't. She's just a pain."

"Then send her away."

"She has nowhere to go. She just got out of a bad situation. I can't do that to her."

She smirked. "Good thing you don't like her. You might care about her welfare, then."

"Okay, fine. I liked *Charlynn*. She was funny and droll. Sexy. I wouldn't have slept with her if I didn't like her."

"Aren't Charlynn and Charly the same person?"

"No. Charly chaps my ass. She does all these crazy things, and she has the weirdest little expressions." I waved my hands, fluttering them in the air, raising my voice. "Easy peasy. Holy moly. Chap my…" I let my voice trail off when I realized I had used one of her expressions. Dammit.

Mary bit her lip to stop from laughing again. "She gets under your skin."

"She annoys me."

"So, how do you solve it?"

"I ignore her. She can do her job, I'll do mine."

"How is that working for you so far?"

"It will be fine."

"What room is she in?"

I squirmed a little in my seat. "She told me to treat her like the guy I thought I hired. So, I'm doing exactly that."

Aside from wanting to kiss her all the time. I didn't share that piece of information. It was a passing phase. Once we put aside the night we shared, I'd be able to ignore her and only see her as Charly. I was convinced of that.

Mary narrowed her eyes at me, waiting for my response.

"She's in the room behind the garage."

"You put her in the *garage?*"

"That's where I planned on putting Charly, so that's where she stays."

Mary struggled to keep her amusement in but failed. "This is better than reality TV. You hire a stranger you thought was a guy, sleep with a pretty girl who turns out to be said guy, and you stick her in the garage to avoid temptation. You refuse to admit you like her, regardless of her name, and she's been here less than twenty-four hours and has you tied up in knots and running from your own place." She wiped her eyes. "Yep. I definitely need to come and meet this girl. Soon."

I stood. "I'm leaving. I'll show myself out. Thanks for nothing, Mary."

Her laughter followed me out the door.

I arrived back at the house a few hours later. I was calmer and my head clear. Charly was unexpected. We'd had amazing sex, and I was still reacting to the memories. It was as simple as that. I would put that aside, treat her as an employee, and give her a shot. She was obviously a hard worker, and I needed that. She could concentrate on the business, and I would concentrate on the customers. Once money was flowing again, maybe I would find the enthusiasm to start a new project. One to replace the one I had lost. I tried not to dwell on that.

Except as I rounded the truck and saw what was waiting for me, all my clarity disappeared. Lying on a blanket on the grass, Rufus stretched out beside her, was Charly. Her legs were bare, a T-shirt hanging off her shoulder. She was on her stomach, knees bent, legs crossed at the ankle as she typed on her keyboard, enjoying the sun. I had to stop and take a few deep breaths before I went over, pushed away her laptop, and mounted her like a dog in heat.

Jesus, she was sexy.

I waited a moment then walked over, and she sat up, looking leery. "Hi."

"Hi. How's the hand?"

"It's fine."

"What are you doing?"

She crossed her legs and pulled her laptop onto her knees.

"Looking at the website. Coming up with ideas. How attached are you to your, ah, logo?"

I sat down across from her, imitating her crossed legs. She was trying, so I could do the same. "It's old and outdated, I suppose. There used to be a sign." I indicated the pole at the end of the driveway.

"So, it was your dad's shop?"

"Yes, he ran it. He worked on cars, motorcycles, anything with an engine." I smiled as I remembered being young and hanging around his garage. "When I was a kid, people even brought their lawn mowers here to be fixed."

"So, the house…"

"…was my parents," I finished for her. "I grew up there. I moved to Lomand when I was older, then when my dad wanted to retire and they needed a smaller place, I bought the shop and house." I plucked a blade of grass, twirling it in my fingers. "I grew up in that shop. Being a mechanic was in my blood, and it was all I ever wanted to do."

She shut the laptop, pulled off her glasses, and leaned forward. "Your dad taught you?"

"Yeah. He started me on those lawn mowers, then we moved to cars. It was a long time before he allowed me to touch his precious motorcycles. Those were his babies."

"My dad's too. He and my brother Sean worked on them for hours."

"Does your dad still own the shop?"

She drew her knees up to her chest, wrapping her arms around them. Her voice was low and sad when she spoke. "No. My dad sold the shop after my brother died." She looked away. "Then my dad died a couple of years ago."

Without thinking, I reached out and touched her hands. "I'm sorry."

She nodded, not speaking.

"How?" I asked quietly.

"Sean was on his bike. A car cut him off, and he rolled and was struck by another car coming in the opposite direction. He died at the scene."

"Fuck."

"My dad blamed himself—needlessly, of course—and he never got over it. He sold the shop, and not long after, he got cancer. I don't think he had the strength to fight it, and I lost him too." She met my sympathetic gaze. "So, I know what you mean when you say you miss your dad, Maxx. I miss them both every day."

A moment of kinship passed between us. A shared feeling of total understanding and clarity. We'd both lost people we loved, and we knew that pain.

Still, I didn't want to get too personal. Too involved. I couldn't risk that.

Despite what Mary said, it would be a long time before I could trust anyone new again.

I cleared my throat. "In answer to your question, no, I'm not attached to the logo. It's pretty old-fashioned."

"Like your ad," she teased, but it was without malice.

I chuckled. "I told you, I come by it honestly. My dad was old-fashioned, and I guess I am too in some ways."

"Holy moly, Maxx. Did you just agree with me on something?"

"Don't get used to it."

She laughed. The sound was sultry and rich. She tilted her head back, her hair tumbling down past her shoulders as she let out her amusement. She was breathtaking in the sun, the brightness of her hair, her profile delicate and pale. I had to look away.

"Got it, boss."

She slipped her glasses back on and pulled her laptop back on her knees. "Okay. Once I catch up on paperwork and invoices,

I'll start designing a new one and work on the website. I already have some ideas."

"I need to approve them."

She peered over her frames, shaking her head. "And we were getting along so well. Of course I'll show them to you."

"And if I don't like them, you'll change them."

"I assumed so from your tone."

"I want to be involved. It's my business, so you include me in every decision, do you understand?"

With a huff, she stood, brushing her hands along the back of her shapely legs. She picked up her laptop. "Yowsers. And you say I have big balls. I'm going to check on dinner."

Rufus followed her, giving me the eye as he trailed behind her. She must have charmed him with treats. That was the only explanation.

I watched her walk away, her ass spectacular in those shorts. She was rather touchy about the logo thing. It was my business; of course I would want to check it. The balls remark was really uncalled-for.

I stood and grabbed the blanket, shaking it out. I followed her into the house, stopping as the scent of whatever she was cooking hit me. It was rich and hearty, and there was a trace of sweet lingering in the air.

I set down the blanket, wandering into the kitchen. "Something smells awesome," I offered in way of apology, although I wasn't sure what I needed to apologize for. I didn't want to jeopardize dinner, though.

She lifted the lid off a roaster and stirred the contents.

"It's ready whenever you're hungry." She took a bowl, filling it, then busied herself at the counter. She turned, and my eyes widened at the sight of the piece of pie on the plate she had placed over the bowl. Lemon meringue. My absolute favorite.

"You made pie?"

"Yes, Captain Obvious, I made pie."

"What's for dinner?"

"Short ribs."

She grabbed some cutlery, tucked her laptop under her arm, and sidled around me. "Make sure you clean up."

"Wait, where are you going?"

"To my room. Sundays are supposed to be a day off, and I'm done. You're on your own, unless you tell me you need to be spoon-fed too."

"You're going to eat in your room?"

She waved toward the crowded, messy dining table. "Unless I sit in your lap, there is nowhere for me to eat, and besides, I want to enjoy my dinner. And with you glowering at me, barking orders, I doubt that will happen. I'll see you in the morning."

Then she was gone.

I stood, perplexed. Part of me wanted to go after her and tell her she could sit on my lap and eat. Then after, we could figure out how to work off the food. The other part of me was annoyed over her glowering remark. We'd had an amicable time chatting outside—until the website talk.

I stomped to the cupboard and grabbed a plate. I didn't glower. Or bark orders.

I dished out the meal she'd made. The pot had short ribs, potatoes, and carrots—like a whole meal in one pot, and once I had a taste, I moaned out loud. Again, it was simple, but amazing. I had a feeling the pie was going to be even better.

I ate until I was full, enjoying everything she had made. Oddly enough, I felt almost lonely while I polished off my meal. It might have been nice to share it with someone.

Even someone with a smart mouth, who would, no doubt, "chap my ass" while sitting across from me.

I might have to do something about that. Lord knew what would happen if that occurred, though.

CHAPTER 11

MAXX

Charly was already at the desk when I walked into the garage the next morning. I was determined today would be better. A fresh start. Officially, she was now an employee, and I would treat her as such. I rolled my shoulders, shook my head, and headed toward the office, plastering a smile on my face.

"Morning, Charly."

She lifted her head from the mess of papers on her desk, smirked, then intoned in a deep voice, "Morning, Angel."

Then she burst out laughing at her own joke, the sound echoing off the walls. I rolled my eyes and filled a clean mug with coffee, noting the office was even tidier today than it had been yesterday.

"What time did you start?" I asked, curious.

She shrugged, sorting papers, not bothering to look up. "About five."

"Are you not comfortable in your room?"

She stopped, lifting her gaze to mine. Behind her glasses, her green eyes were bright, although I thought she looked a little tired. I knew better than to say that, though. I had enough experience with women to know they didn't like comments on their appearance unless they were complimentary.

"It's fine. I've always been an early riser." She waved a hand filled with papers. "Lots here to catch up on."

"Hence the job, Charly."

She rolled her eyes at me. "I know. This is my plan. I am going to sort in here this morning, then spend the afternoon sorting stuff in the house. I assume you have cleaning supplies in there?"

"I assume so."

She huffed. "I may need to go get a few things."

Right. We were back to her driving the truck. Not happening. I sighed, thinking over my schedule. "I'll have something for you to drive tomorrow. Can you make do until then?"

"Sure."

I pushed off the counter, but she held up her finger. "I need you to sign in to your bank account."

I stiffened. "I beg your pardon?"

"I'm going to be contacting people for payment. I want to offer e-transfer, so we need to set it up."

"Why?"

"So the money comes in faster, Maxx," she stated patiently.

"I'm not giving you access to the bank accounts."

She sighed, crossing her arms. "Then how am I supposed to make deposits, pull statements, and balance the accounts?"

"I'll pull the stuff and give it to you."

She shut her eyes, and I swore she counted to ten before opening them. "Look, Maxx, obviously you don't know me. I get it. But how about this. You sit here, open the banking info, I'll tell you how I am going to set it up, and we will turn on alerts. Every time I send out an invoice, pay a bill, deposit money, your phone will get an alert."

"Every time?" I asked suspiciously.

"Yes. You can even put a second password on it so you know everything I'm doing."

Still, I hesitated. She frowned but let me think. In order for her to do her job, I had to offer her some sort of trust. It didn't come easily to me now, though. She must have sensed my unease, because she made another suggestion.

"How about this," she suggested. "We'll set up the e-transfer part and the alerts. We'll do the rest another time, once you decide you're more comfortable with the arrangements. We can sit down once a week, and you can sign checks for bills, pull me any statements I need and so forth."

"Fine."

"Okay."

She stood, and I took her seat, signing in to the banking site. She was true to her word and waited to the side until I was signed in. I stood, giving her back the chair and watched as she set things up, explaining as she did.

"How does e-transfer work?"

"Instead of sending in a check or giving you a credit card, they transfer the money directly to the account. I, or you, will get an alert when the payment comes in. Simple and faster. No fees either."

That made sense. She was right; I needed to get the cash flowing again. One look at the balance and I cringed. I filled my cup and headed to the garage, turning as I paused in the door.

"Thanks."

She smiled at me. A real, honest smile that almost knocked my socks off. She was breathtaking when she did that.

"You're welcome."

"And dinner last night was delicious. Again."

She leaned back, lifting her arms over her head and locking her hands in place. "Did you like your pie?"

I tried not to notice how high her breasts lifted in the light, frilly blouse she was wearing. How they rippled and pulled at the material as she moved. How the swell of her breasts peeked out from the low vee in her shirt.

I tried to ignore how my dick got hard at the sensual pose and the huskiness of her voice.

My efforts failed.

I swallowed, gripping the edge of the doorframe, almost snarling at her. "Yep. It was good. Really good."

Then I turned and hurried to the garage, slamming down my mug, frustrated at how easily she could affect me. I needed to think of car engines, parts, oil changes. Not making her purr, stroking her parts, and how slick she would be if I did.

I groaned as I ran a hand over my face.

Today was going to be a long-ass day.

And I had a feeling it was just the start.

I thought things would be normal in the garage. I would work on the vehicles, and she would stay out of my way.

I thought wrong.

She wandered in all morning, bringing with her the scent of her skin, the brightness of her smile, and the fucking sexy office girl look. She asked me endless questions. Part numbers, more descriptions on the notes I had for invoices, dollar amounts, phone numbers.

Every customer, every single goddamn one of them, stared at her. They watched her sashay around the place,

"Who the hell is that?" My customer Brian, asked, staring at her retreating figure.

"New assistant."

"Jesus," he muttered. "You lucky son of a bitch." He stroked his chin. "She single?"

"No," I snapped, having no idea why I said that.

"Damn."

"Trust me, be grateful. She looks like an angel, but she has a forked tongue."

"Who said I wanted to listen to her talk?" He quirked his eyebrows, which for some reason enraged me more. "Maybe I'd like that tongue somewhere."

"Show some respect."

He held up his hands. "Wow. Sorry."

I bent over the engine again, unable to explain my anger. Brian was a decent guy and I had known him a long time, but I didn't like the way he was looking at Charly.

I finished his job, shutting the hood. Before I could say anything, Charly came out of the office, her attitude brisk and businesslike. "Cash or credit?"

He blinked. "Oh. Usually, I pay whenever."

She shook her head. "New policy. You have work done, you pay today."

"Oh." He pulled out his credit card. "Okay."

"Oil change and tune-up?" Charly asked me. "List price?"

It was my turn to blink. I had a list price?

"Ah, five percent off for being a loyal customer," I muttered.

"Easy peasy. Follow me," she directed Brian.

He left a few moments later, clearly shell-shocked. I waved as he backed out the car, stopping to drink my now-cold coffee.

I brought in the next car. She strolled out, her laptop and file in one hand, a steaming cup of coffee in the other. "I'm heading to the house. How many more cars do you have today?"

"Only three. Tomorrow is booked solid."

She pursed her lips, setting down the items she was carrying. She waved toward the wall. "We need a system. Like a wipe-off board you write the schedule down on, so I know when to be around for payment. No more walking out without paying."

"They're good for it."

"Not anymore. You do the work, I take the payment."

"I appreciate what you're trying to do, but you don't make the rules here."

"Rules?" she snorted. "Yowsers—there are *no* rules! You need to pay better attention. I don't know where you've been the last while, but your mind is not focused on this place."

Her words made me see red. I stepped right in front of her. "Where I've been is *none* of your business."

"Obviously it is if you hired me to help."

"You're a pain in the ass, anyone ever tell you that?"

"You're a controlling jerk who refuses to admit he needs help."

We were so close, I could feel her warm breath on my face. See the flecks of gray in the green of her eyes. I glared at her.

"You're trying my patience, Red."

"You're pissing me off," she retorted, jabbing at my chest with her pointy finger.

I grabbed her hand, and we both stared at it. Felt the heat bubbling in the air around us. Our gazes locked, and suddenly, my mouth was on hers. Demanding. Hard. Determined.

She yanked back, her breathing hard. "You're an asshole."

"I know."

Then she flung her arms around my neck and kissed me back. She pulled me hard, yanking on my hair. I wrapped my arm around her, settling my hand on that spectacular ass, and dragging her close. Our tongues battled for dominance, neither of us giving an inch.

It was only the sound of a car door slamming out front that had us pulling apart. We faced each other, her lips swollen from our passion, her rapid breathing matching mine. My cock was hard and erect, pulsating with need.

She swallowed. "I'll order that wipe-off board."

I nodded. "Yeah, you do that."

She turned and fled.

CHARLY

I didn't run because he kissed me. I ran because I was afraid that regardless of the fact that a customer was about to walk in, I was going to drag him back to my mouth.

My god, the man—the growly, snarly bear of a man—could kiss. Considering the venom his mouth spewed, his lips were addictive and sweet. Even when he was angry. He controlled my mouth, and me, easily. Kissing him made me remember the night we shared. How he felt inside me, the sounds he made while we…

My thoughts came to a standstill.

Made love?

Fucked?

Had a fast fling?

All three?

I set down the laptop on the counter, noticing he had cleaned up after his dinner last night. I had to admit, the place was in chaos, but he, himself, was neat. He simply needed someone to sort through the destruction he'd created around himself.

I sighed, confused. We were like oil and water. He was swift to anger, and somehow, he brought out the same reaction in me. One glare from him and my hackles rose.

Holy moly. So did my temperature.

I rubbed my forehead. I came here to do a job, and I was going to do it. He could huff and puff all he wanted. I ignored the little voice in my head that whispered she hoped there'd be more kissing. Pushing that annoying little voice away, I concentrated on the tasks I wanted to accomplish.

I decided to start a simple casserole of macaroni and cheese for dinner. There were a couple of pieces of short ribs left over that Maxx could eat in addition to the casserole if he wanted to. I put the pot on to boil, then found a sharp knife, and began sorting boxes in the dining room. Most of them were empty, simply tossed to the side. I kept all the box tops so I could match them up with jobs, or where they were in the supply area of the garage. The ones that still contained parts, I piled in the mudroom to be carried to the garage. I worked happily, turning on some music, pleased when a couple of hours later, I stood back and admired my process. The table was clean, and I had polished the wood until it shone. I vacuumed the floor, admiring the heavy oak planks and the vintage scatter rug under the table. The casserole was on the counter, ready to heat, so I sat down, making more calls. Most people were shocked when I explained why I was calling, introducing myself, and the reason for my call. Many were more than happy to send an e-transfer once I gave them the amount owed. I had found a list of prices in the drawer and, after doing some checking, increased the pricing more to reflect today's rates. No one objected to the amounts. A few were hesitant about my identity, and I informed them to feel free to call Maxx to verify who I was. Some insisted on dropping off payment at the garage later this week, no doubt curious as to what was happening. I was friendly and courteous, trying to represent Maxx in a professional manner.

At least to his customers.

I glanced around, surprised to see it was only three. The sound of heavy footsteps made me look up from the pile of paperwork as Maxx walked in, Rufus trailing behind him. Rufus headed in my direction, and I stroked his large head, scratching behind his ears the way I'd discovered he liked it.

Maxx looked around, blinking. He sat across from me, silent and tense. I kept giving Rufus attention, waiting to see what Maxx would say.

Would it be rude? Demanding? Snarky?

He ran a hand through his hair and sighed. His voice was even, maybe even slightly amused. "My phone's been going off nonstop."

"Oh?"

"Customers making sure you aren't scamming them. People wanting to know who you are."

"I see. I assume you verified I work for you and they better pay their damn bills."

One of his eyebrows slowly lifted, a grin playing on his lips. "I was a little more polite, but basically, yes. There should be more of your e-bills coming."

"E-transfers."

He waved his hand. "Whatever." He eyed me with speculation. "What is this price list you referred to this morning?"

I pushed a list toward him, and he scanned it. "You increased all my prices."

"You were far too cheap. Not a single person complained when I gave them the amount they owed. You can offer your 'loyal customer' discount if they do."

He stroked his short beard, and I gazed at the movement of his long fingers, recalling how his scruff had felt against my skin.

"Fine," he agreed, pushing the list my way. "But I told you, I need to okay all changes."

I rolled my eyes. "You just did."

He opened his mouth, then shut it as if deciding not to argue with me.

That was a first.

"Maybe you can print out a list of deposits tomorrow. I'll update the books and keep calling the rest," I said, pushing forward. "And here's some quotes for a decent computer. Look them over." I tapped the top page. "This one is a great deal and is on sale. And there's a newer software package that would work well for you. It would cut down a lot of time since it will track the deposits and payments after I set it all up."

"All right." He cleared his throat and tapped the table. "Looks good."

I tilted my head. "Thanks," I stated dryly.

"You're a hard worker," he said grudgingly.

"And you're a hardhead. Period." I sniffed and got out of the chair, going into the kitchen.

With a low growl, he followed me. I spun on my heel, meeting his glare with one of my own.

"What?"

He crowded me against the counter. "I was paying you a compliment."

"You almost choked saying it. I promise I won't get a swelled head if you say something nice and mean it, Maxx."

His expression softened, just a small thaw, but I saw it.

"I did mean it," he said. "I just don't know how to do this, Charly."

I frowned.

It was his turn. "What?"

"You called me Red earlier. Just before you kissed me."

"You kissed me back."

"I like kissing you," I whispered. "I like it when you call me Red."

He shook his head, even as he lowered his mouth closer to mine. "We can't do this."

"I know," I replied, aching to feel his mouth on mine again.

His lips were right there. Barely a breath between us. All I had to do was tilt my chin and our mouths would connect.

Except the screen door in the mudroom opened and a voice called out.

"Maxx? You here?"

Maxx stepped back so quickly, I almost fell. He gripped my arms, steadying me, then moved toward the mudroom. "Hey, Walt."

"You called about helping you with the car?"

Maxx sighed, looking back over his shoulder at me, and he called for Rufus.

Then walked away.

I was too restless after Maxx walked out to stay in the house. I slid the casserole into the oven on low—Maxx could eat it whenever he wanted. Deciding I had worked long enough, I went for a walk, heading down the road. There was little traffic, the area quiet. I marveled at the sounds of nature, the sightings of birds and wild animals—things you never saw or heard in Toronto. I veered closer to the edge of the road as I heard a vehicle behind me, worried as I saw it pull up alongside me. A woman beamed at me from behind the wheel of a truck. Not as large as Maxx's monster truck, but more manageable, I assumed. She was a small woman with a head of wild gray curls. She pushed up her sunglasses onto her head.

"You *must* be Charlynn. The redheaded snippet."

There was no doubt she knew Maxx. He liked to call me that name. "I am," I responded. "And you are?"

She laughed. "The reason you're dealing with grumpy Gus down the road. Are you running away from home, too, the way he did yesterday?"

I felt a smirk pull on my lips. I knew he'd left to avoid me. "No, just out exploring."

"How about a glass of lemonade on my porch instead?"

I paused.

"I'm Mary," she said, as if that explained everything. "Maxx is like an adopted son to me." She slid on her sunglasses and peered over the top of them. "A difficult, ornery one most of the time these days."

Laughing, I stepped into the vehicle. "In that case, then yes, a glass of lemonade would be most welcome."

"Excellent."

I settled into the porch swing at Mary's, a tall glass of lemonade in one hand and a cookie in the other. I munched happily, letting the swing move, enjoying the quiet and the vista until Mary came out, carrying a steaming cup of tea. She sat down on the chair and eyed me frankly.

"You are nothing like the last one. Thank god for that."

I frowned. "Maxx's last assistant?"

She snorted, lifting her tea. "Sure, we can call that thieving backstabber an assistant. Usually, I simply refer to her as The Tramp."

I choked on my lemonade, trying not to laugh. "Yowsers." Swallowing, I cleared my throat. "I take it you know Maxx well?"

"Yes. His mother and I were great friends."

I was careful as I spoke. "I don't know much about him, to be honest. I only started working for him yesterday."

She winked at me. "You certainly arrived with a bang, didn't you?"

I gaped at her. Then, seeing the amused look on her face, I began to giggle. "That's one way of putting it."

She relaxed back in her chair. "I was the one who told Maxx to put an ad on that online site. I use it for lots of things—even hired kids to help out around here." She sighed. "I told him to be specific. I had no idea how specific he was going to be."

"I thought he was an old curmudgeon," I admitted. "But I was desperate."

"Did you know he thought you were a man?"

"Yes, but as I said, desperate."

"What's your story?"

Normally, I would brush a question like that aside, or tell a humorous rendition, the way I did to Maxx on the Friday night. But something about this woman made me feel as if I could tell her the truth. So, I did. I told her about moving to Toronto. Losing my dad. The roommate from hell. The lecherous landlord. She guffawed loudly at my antics with Terry. Frowned over Trish. Patted my hand when I spoke about my dad.

When I told her about the wallets and the money, she smiled. "Heaven looks after those in need, child. Your father was watching over you."

"I think so too."

"Did you tell Maxx all this?"

"Some. I glossed over a few details."

She pursed her lips, not speaking for a moment. "You should tell him the whole story. The two of you have a lot in common."

I lifted my eyebrows. "The, ah, Tramp?"

"Yes. She did a number on him. She and that asswipe of a friend. Billy," she spat his name. "I never liked him. He proved me right."

I nibbled another cookie. "I don't think Maxx and I will get around to sharing our life stories, Mary. I don't think he likes me that much."

Unless he was kissing me—then he seemed to like me a lot. But I refrained from adding that statement.

She waved her hand. "He's a good man. He was a good son, too—took care of his parents. He refused to allow his father to give him the shop, instead buying it. He knew they'd lost a lot of money, and he wanted them comfortable. He had no desire to live in that house, but he bought it too. Moved back from Lomand and took it over. Fixed it up nice, at least until that cow moved in and mucked it up."

I thought of the house. The differences in the various rooms. Some, like the kitchen and dining room, were warm and homey. Others, stark and out of place in the setting.

"He's been hurt and is cautious," she added, taking another sip of tea.

"And grumpy."

She agreed. "You've sent him into a tailspin, I'll say that much. He doesn't know whether he's coming or going."

"I just want to do a good job."

"Maxx was impressed by what you had done yesterday."

I told her about the invoices and Maxx getting annoyed over my bossiness. That made her laugh all over again.

"Oh, child, you are going to be good for him. Stay strong. He needs that."

"What did that other woman do to him?"

She shook her head. "That's for him to decide if he wants to tell you. I hope that he will. I think it would help both of you."

I wasn't sure Maxx would ever confide anything in me. He was too busy being grouchy all the time. Or telling me what to do. And, on occasion, that little voice reminded me, kissing me.

I shook my head to stop that little voice.

"Would you like to stay for supper? I have a pot roast in the oven. Maybe we can play cards after or something. I'll drive you home later."

I hesitated then decided I would like that. I'd left Maxx his dinner. I had worked all day. It would be nice not to eat alone in my room again.

"Sure." I smiled at Mary. "I'd love that."

Mary's pot roast was amazing, and I begged her for the recipe. It would make an easy dinner one night for Maxx. She opened a bottle of wine, and we ate on the porch, enjoying the nice evening. After, she brought out a deck of cards, and we played Fish and Crazy Eights, laughing and stealing cards like old friends. She was funny and witty. Sarcastic and sharp. I learned a few more things about Maxx, his parents, and his love of motorcycles. We ate cookies and drank tea as twilight descended.

"His father was very old-fashioned. A real gentleman. He adored Maxx's mother, and the two of them were a great couple. He believed in doing things the right way—even if they were outdated. He brought Maxx up the same way. In many ways, Maxx is just like his father." She shook her head. "I've been trying to get up to update his systems and software. He resists because he understands the old ways. I think you'll be good for him. Bring him into the twenty-first century."

I chuckled. "I'm going to try. He is certainly old-fashioned in some respects."

"Some things you will never be able to change." She met my eyes, hers serious. "Some, I would hate to see go."

I knew what she meant. His courtesy, and the manners he had when he wasn't growling at me. The way he dealt with people. He was kind and thoughtful. Under the right circumstances, tender. I had certainly experienced that part of him. Those traits were rare and special. I wouldn't want to change that part of him at all.

"Did she do that?" I asked hesitantly. "Try to change him?"

Her nod and the swinging of her foot were the only affirmation I needed. I returned her gaze, not needing to speak. We understood each other.

We sat in companionable silence, enjoying the quiet.

"I suppose I should get going," I said regretfully just as the sound of a rumbling engine broke the stillness.

Maxx's truck pulled into the driveway, his face like thunder behind the wheel.

"Uh oh," I muttered. "The bear is back."

He got out of the truck, slamming the door. He stalked up to the steps, looking at us without saying a word.

"Maxx," Mary greeted him. "Something on your mind?"

He ran a hand through his hair. By now, I realized it was one of his tells when he was upset and about to tell me off.

"Nope," he said shortly.

"You were just driving by?" Mary asked, amusement lacing her voice.

"Something like that."

"I was about to drive Charly home."

"I'll save you the trip and take her. You ready, Charly?" he asked, his voice telling me, no matter what, I *was* ready. *Now.*

I stood. "Yep." I turned and hugged Mary. "Thanks for the girls' night."

"We should do this every week," Mary insisted.

"Sounds like a plan. I'll call you."

"Oh, interesting," Maxx said in a snarky tone. "You can call *her*." He stomped to the truck. "I'm waiting."

I exchanged glances with Mary, slightly shrugging my shoulders.

I climbed into the truck, the wine making me a little uncoordinated. Maxx watched me, not helping, a scowl on his face.

He backed out of the driveway quickly, before I could even put my seat belt on. He didn't say a word, but I felt his anger rolling off of him. He turned into his driveway, pulling up in front of the house and braking hard. He slammed out of the truck, walking toward the house. Feeling angry now myself, I followed him.

"Crap on a cracker, what is your problem?" I shouted, chasing him into the house.

He whirled around. "My problem? *My problem?* You have a serious lack of communication skills, Charly."

"What are you on about?"

"I come in and find you gone. Your bag is here, your laptop on the table. No sign of you. Dinner is in the oven, so I figured you went to your room, but you never showed up to eat—even later. So, I went looking for you, but you weren't there. I had no fucking idea where you were. No way to call you since your phone was in your bag!" By the end of his diatribe, he was yelling. "I had no idea where you were!"

I stepped back at his vehemence. "I'm sorry. I went for a walk, and Mary picked me up. We were talking and enjoying each other's company, and she invited me to dinner. I-I never thought... I mean, it didn't occur to me you would even..." I trailed off.

"You were worried?" I asked. "Really?"

He sighed, his voice losing some of its edge. "Of course I was worried. I've been searching for you all over the fields. I called Mary and she never answered, so I drove over to ask if she'd seen you." He tugged on his hair again, the anger returning. "And there you were, laughing, eating, and having fun. Not the remotest bit concerned about anything else. Not the fact that I might have wondered where you were or been looking for you!"

"Why would I think that? I had no clue you'd even notice I was gone!" I responded, throwing up my hands.

"That's the problem, isn't it," he snarled. "You. Have. No. Fucking. Clue."

And then he was kissing me. He yanked me tight to his chest, and I flung my arms around his neck. He growled low and deep in his chest, lifting me into his arms, his lips never leaving mine. He carried me up the stairs, tossing me on the bed.

"Let's get something straight," he hissed, pulling off his shirt. "You tell me before you leave this property again, you understand?"

I whimpered at the sight of his muscled torso.

"I don't want you chatting to the male customers. You leave them to me." He kicked off his shitkickers and dragged his jeans down his legs. "I make the prices, you got that? I have the final decision on *everything*."

I clutched the sheets, nodding, feeling frantic.

He gripped my jeans, tearing them down my legs. "Do you have contacts?"

"Yes," I panted, desperate to feel his hands on me.

"You need to wear them."

At this point, I would agree to anything.

He gripped the bottom of my blouse. "Sorry."

Before I could ask why, he tore it. Right up the middle.

I gasped as the cool air hit my skin.

"You need to wear heavier shirts," he demanded, placing a knee on the mattress and glaring at me. "Maybe turtlenecks."

Then he was on me. Kissing, licking, biting. His mouth and hands were everywhere. He tugged my bra down, my breasts spilling over the cups. He sucked and licked them, holding them in his big hands, pinching the nipples and making me cry out. He ground his massive cock into my center, the cloth separating us only adding another layer of sensation.

"I'm going to fuck you," he promised darkly. "Rough and hard. You prepared for that, *Red?*"

I pulled his mouth down to mine, devouring him. He tasted like sin—citrus and sweet and him. He fisted my hair, tugging it in his hands, our mouths locked together.

"Take me," I pleaded.

He grabbed a condom, and then he was ready. There was no hesitancy tonight. No more foreplay. One snap of his hips and he was lodged deep inside me. I barely had time to catch my breath, and he started to move. Fast, forceful thrusts, hitting me exactly where I needed him. He gripped my hips, almost furious in his need as he took me. Sweat dotted his forehead, his arms shaking with repressed energy as he drove forward, pistoning in and out, cursing and groaning.

There was no doubt what this was.

Pure, unadulterated fucking.

I should have objected, except he felt too good. His cock felt too good. All too soon, my orgasm soared out of control, and I cried out, spasming and coming around him. He gritted his teeth, his hold tightening.

"One more, Red. You're gonna give me one more."

He lifted my leg over his shoulder, changing the angle, still thrusting in long, hard movements. I gasped as he dragged his cock against my clit, the sensation spiraling me into another orgasm. I grasped at his arms, and he threw back his head, shouting and cursing as he came. He was powerful and sexy in his release, his corded neck muscles standing out, his shoulders straining.

Then he collapsed on me, his weight pushing me down into the mattress. For a moment, there was nothing but our heavy breathing.

He moved, getting rid of the condom, then returning to the bed. For a moment, he stared, then tugged on my arms. "Let's get this off of you." He tenderly pulled away the torn material and removed my bra, laying me back on the pillows. He climbed in beside me, tucking me into his arms. His aggression was gone, and the man I had spent the night with on Friday was back. For how long, I didn't know, but I decided to enjoy it while I could.

I lifted my head and he kissed me. Soft, sweet, his lips lingered on mine, his arms a warm, safe spot to be in.

I sighed as he tugged me back to his chest, resting his chin on my head.

The room was silent.

"Tell me a secret," he whispered, surprising me.

"You ripped my favorite blouse."

He chuckled. "I'll buy you a new one."

It was my turn. "Tell me one."

He played with my hair, twirling a piece around between his fingers. "You make the best lemon pie I've ever tasted."

"That's hardly a secret."

He tipped up my chin and brushed a kiss to my mouth.

"Neither was yours."

I chuckled. "Can I ask a question?"

"I think you just did."

"No, um—Maxx. Two x's. That's unusual. Is it a family name?"

It was his turn to chuckle. "No. It was an error. My mom wanted Maxwell, my dad liked Max. He crossed out the 'well' at the end, and the person read it as M-A-X-X, and that was how it was recorded. My mom decided she liked it—it was different, so she left it. My dad never lived it down. I kinda like it too."

I pressed a kiss to his scruff. "It suits you. You're so sexy, you need two x's—like a warning label."

He groaned at my quip. "Now you got a second secret. My turn."

I snuggled back to his chest. "I like it here. It's peaceful and pretty."

He didn't say anything, maybe surprised by my words. His arms tightened a little, then he spoke.

"I hated the feeling I had when I couldn't find you."

I felt a small thrill at his words, but I didn't react.

"I'm sorry. I'll call next time."

"I'll know you're at Mary's gossiping."

"We weren't gossiping. We were playing cards and talking."

"Was I mentioned in the conversation?" he asked dryly.

I remained silent.

"Gossiping," he stated smugly. Then his voice took on a warning tone. "I don't like to be talked about, Red. I value my privacy."

I blew out an indignant sigh. "What an ego you have. Not everything is about you. We had lots of other things to talk about, you know."

He didn't reply.

"Mary knows you, and she knows you're private. You were barely mentioned." I warmed to my annoyance. "And what was that shit about my glasses and wearing contacts? I need them for reading. And I don't own a turtleneck. Besides, it's summer, and I would perish in the heat."

A long deep snore was his response. I tilted back my head, looking at him.

He was asleep. He fucked me like a champion, then passed out.

With a huff, I slipped from the covers, pulled on my jeans, and yanked on his shirt he'd taken off earlier.

As far as I was concerned, he could wear mine.

I held my head high all the way back to my little room.

CHAPTER 12

CHARLY

Maxx didn't come into the office the next morning. He showed up early and went straight to work on an old Toyota Camry that was in the shop. It was in great shape, the original bodywork still in place, no rust that I could see. It was a creamy white and, obviously, well maintained.

I was certain he regretted last night. I had zero regrets, except knowing it would probably make him more distant and grumpier. Plus, I had no doubt he would inform me today it wasn't happening again. Or he would pretend it never happened.

I could do the same thing, except for the slight ache in my lower back and the fact that I was a little tender in spots.

Being ridden hard would do that to a girl. Maybe I would ask him today if I could soak in the tub. I poured him a cup of coffee and carried it out front and leaned against the bumper.

"Morning, boss."

All I got was a low grunt from under the hood.

"I brought you coffee."

"Fine," was the muffled response.

I admired his ass before I spoke. "Nice car."

I saw his back flex as he exhaled in resignation, realizing I was going to keep talking. He lifted his head. "Yes. A nice old Camry."

"Ninety-two?" I guessed. "That was sort of the breakout year."

His gaze was filled with annoyance. "Yes. And it will be ninety-two more years before I get this done if you don't shut up. Don't you have work to do?"

"Yep. Lots of it. I need some reports pulled to do it, though, and you're avoiding me."

He brought himself to his full height, towering over me. "I am not avoiding you." Then his eyes narrowed. "Is that my shirt?"

"Oh." I fingered the collar. "Yes. Mine seems to be missing." I batted my eyelashes, trying to look innocent. "Have you seen it?"

I expected a snarl. A biting comeback. What I didn't expect was the open expression on his face. Or his sudden shout of laughter. Even more surprising was the way he moved, caging me between his arms against the car. "Yes, as a matter of fact, I have. It looks far better on my bedroom floor." He leaned in and nipped my neck. "The password is ThomasR1950. Get your own damn reports. I'm busy."

Then he got back to work. I blinked. Looked around the garage expecting a camera crew and someone yelling "Punked!" to jump out.

"Um," I stammered. "That will give me access to everything."

He turned his head and threw me a wink. "I'm aware. I'm watching you. Remember that."

I stumbled away, heading toward the office. Maxx stood, reaching for his coffee. "Do up a couple of buttons, Charly. Have mercy on my customers." He shook his head. "And me," he mumbled.

I didn't respond. I sat down heavily on the chair in the office and, without thinking, buttoned up. I signed in to the bank and tried the password. I was shocked when it worked, but then quickly pulled the reports I needed, printed off some statements, and signed off.

Maxx was talking to a couple of guys in the garage, listening to what they had to say. I watched him, suspicion creeping in.

What was he up to?

MAXX

I somehow wasn't surprised when I woke up in the morning and found Red gone. She never seemed to be in the same place I left her in. I sat up and ran a hand through my hair, feeling rested and surprisingly calm. I shouldn't be. I had done it again. Slept with Charlynn—Charly—Red—whatever her name was. I swore it wouldn't happen, but it had.

The night before, I had assumed she was in her room as I ate the delicious macaroni and cheese she'd left in the oven. I had another large piece of pie, then feeling guilty that my actions must have made her upset, I took a plate of food to her. But she wasn't there. I checked the house again, then walked the property, but there was no sign of her. After seeing her bag and laptop under the table in the dining room, my panic grew.

Where the hell could she go? It was getting dark, and she didn't know the area that well. I hopped in the truck and drove into town but didn't spot her. I called Mary in case she'd seen her, but there was no answer, and finally, I drove along the road slowly, looking in the vast fields and trees to see if I could spot Charly. Spying a light at Mary's, I pulled in the driveway, the relief at seeing Charly on Mary's porch morphing into anger as I realized she must have been here the whole time. Laughing, eating, talking, while I worried and panicked over her.

Once we were back at the house, my anger morphed into another feeling entirely. The intense heat and passion that sizzled between Red and me exploded, and before I knew it, we were upstairs. I remembered snarling a bunch of things at her, which only seemed to ramp up the heat between us. I was rough with her—far rougher than I should have been, but she was right there with me, orgasming twice, screaming my name. My own orgasm had been powerful, my body locking down as the ecstasy spiked and the aftershocks rippled through me. I had never experienced the sensations Red brought out in me. It was mystifying.

I slid from the bed, spying the torn blouse lying on the floor. I picked it up, holding it to my nose, inhaling the fragrance left behind on the material. My already hard cock lengthened further. I shook my head in frustration. Just her scent made me hard. How the hell was I supposed to get through working with her every day? Seeing her in the kitchen at night? This situation was never going to work unless we somehow stopped the physical draw between us—now.

We struck sparks off each other. Our goading exchanges seemed to ignite the desire between us. Something about her made me growl and snipe at her—as if I was somehow punishing her for the attraction I felt. She never backed down, answering my comments with sassy, smart-mouthed retorts that infuriated and taunted, yet turned me on with her attitude.

Once we started, it was as if someone struck a match and lit the flame. The only thing that calmed the inferno was sex. Until the next conversation.

I stared in the mirror, thinking. Maybe that was the key. Change the conversation. Red seemed to like the grumbly side of me, as she called it. Perhaps if I was just a nice guy, she wouldn't be as interested, which meant she wouldn't argue back. Without an argument, no passion. We could simply be what I wanted. She could be an employee; I would be her boss.

It could work.

The look on her face as I teased her was perfect. She didn't expect it. She looked shocked—so shocked, in fact, she could barely talk.

There was no argument. No argument meant no passion. No passion meant no sex.

My logic was sound. This was going to work. Her expression when I gave her the banking information was disbelief. I didn't bother to tell her I had reread her resume and finally contacted her old boss, Peter Phelps, who informed me that Charlynn was one of the most honest people he knew and would vouch for her anytime. He also informed me she was the hardest working assistant he'd ever had and had been sorry when the company they worked for went under.

"I'd hire her again if I'd hadn't decided to retire. Tell her hello if you hire her," he said. *"You won't regret it."*

I didn't bother to tell him I already had, and I wasn't so sure on the regret part. Yet. I was pretty damn certain I saw a different side of her than he ever had. At least, I hoped I did.

The morning was busy, and Charly was in and out, and despite what I'd told her last night, she dealt with the customers, taking care of their payments. I tamped down my annoyance at the slightly befuddled expressions many of them wore as they left the office. She seemed to charm them all, which put me a little on edge.

At noon, she brought me a sandwich and a cold soda, leaning against the bumper of the Camry.

"Don't you work on any motorcycles?"

"Yes." I chewed and swallowed. "A bunch are coming in this week. Autos are the bread and butter, though."

"Any restorations?"

"I finished one last month. Shipped it back to the States. It was a beauty."

"What kind?"

"Vintage Harley. 1977 XLCR 100."

"Nice."

"I have two others coming—a Ducati and another Harley. One is a partial restoration, the other a complete. I work on those over there." I indicated the third bay. "Spray booth is behind it."

"You do it all?"

"Every last bit. I've got a reputation for being one of the best. I only take on so many a year, and I handle the whole thing."

"Paperwork?" she questioned with a lift of her eyebrow.

"All done and paid. I keep all those files separate in the bottom left-hand drawer."

"Do you keep pictures of the restorations?"

"Actually, yes—not a ton but always before and after. There's a camera in the drawer I use with a memory card. Each file has my concept sketches as well."

"Oh, I could use those for the website."

"So, you really know how to do all that, ah, stuff?"

She waved her hands. "Easy peasy."

Her use of odd sayings amused me.

"Well, knock yourself out."

"What's the most iconic motorcycle you've ever worked on?"

I stiffened, then forced myself to relax. She had no idea what she was asking me. I kept my voice neutral.

"An 1952 Indian Chief."

"Wow. My father loved Indian motorcycles."

I took a long drink of the cold soda. "They're classic."

"Did you ever ride one?"

I almost spat out my answer. "Yes."

She looked around the shop, changing the subject, which cooled my ire. "Are there any photos from when your dad ran the shop?"

"I think there are some in the storage room." I scratched my beard, thinking. "Or in the boxes in the barn."

"Can I look?"

"Like I said—knock yourself out."

"Holy moly, that's awesome. Retro is *in*." She pushed off the bumper and patted the hood. "I don't have a work order listing in the computer for this one."

"There's no charge."

"Maxx, you can't be doing favors for your friends."

"It's not for a friend. It's for you."

She opened her mouth to argue, then realized what I had said. Her eyes widened. "Me?"

"That was my mom's car. My dad bought it new. She didn't drive much, and he kept it in pristine condition. When she had her first stroke, they put it in the barn. I've kept it maintained, even planned on selling it at some point, but never did."

"You're going to let me drive your mom's car?"

I wagged my finger. "I expect you to take care of it. It has a lot of sentimental value." Bending forward, I stroked the still immaculate paint job. "And it's a great little car. It'll do the job."

She blinked at me but didn't say anything.

"The truck is too big for you, Red. This is compact—like you. It makes sense." I growled playfully at her. "And I won't waste my time driving you around."

As soon as the sentence was out of my mouth, I knew I'd made a mistake. I barely had time to brace myself before she flung her arms around my neck and kissed me. And as soon as her mouth touched mine, I gave in. I wrapped my arm around her waist, lifting her, palming her ass as we kissed. I slanted my mouth, kissing her harder, deeper, and not caring about my plan. She obviously didn't care about my tone, and I didn't care how bad an idea this was. Right now, it was pretty damn great.

She plunged one hand into my hair, tugging and stroking. The other, she used to clasp the back of my neck, holding me tight. I wrapped my free hand around her ponytail and yanked at it, pulling her head back and kissing my way across her throat.

"So sexy in my shirt, aren't you, Red? Acting all sweet and demure. You got anything on under those tight little yoga pants?"

She rubbed against me, gasping as I licked my way up to her ear. "No."

"Jesus," I bit out, eyeing the Camry and wondering if there was enough room to fuck her in the back seat.

"Hey, Maxx! Yo, where you at?" a voice yelled.

We broke apart, staring at each other. I set her down, and before I could say anything, she turned and hurried to the office. I heard the door slam just as my one o'clock appointment showed up.

"There you are," my next customer, Tim, said, walking through the garage door.

"Hey," I responded, hoping I sounded fairly normal. I walked around the Camry so the car separated us, praying my erection would diminish and my breathing would slow. All I could think of was if he had been five minutes later, he would have walked into a whole different scenario. One he wouldn't forget.

I glanced past his shoulder and saw Charly headed down the hall, no doubt to go work in the storeroom. It was good planning on her part. If I kept looking at her, I was going to rid of Tim, shut the garage door, and have her.

Out of sight, out of mind—right?

I ignored the chortles in my head.

X

I made it through the afternoon, staying busy with customers. I even followed protocol, typed up the invoices, collected payment, and left the information on the desk for Charly. I didn't want to have to listen to another one of her "I told you" lectures.

I pulled down the overhead door just before four, not wanting to be around in case anyone showed up with an emergency. I was tense, my body still taut from earlier.

I decided to go and work out rather than heading into the house. Rufus followed me to the converted barn, lying down in the wide entranceway after I rolled open the large wooden doors.

One side of the barn was storage. Things from the house my parents had left, some of the boxes I had packed of their possessions and brought back after they had passed. There was some furniture, boxes of papers, and extra things from the garage. There was now a large empty spot where the Camry used to sit, covered and protected. My bike was parked beside the doors.

The other side, I'd turned into a workout area. I didn't need a lot of fancy equipment. I had my weights, a treadmill, and a fitness trainer that did the job of several pieces. There was a shower in the corner for after I finished my workouts, some speakers for music, and a small fridge for cold water. After warming up and doing a full set with the weights, I turned on some music and hit the treadmill, finding my rhythm and forgetting everything else.

Until Charly walked in.

Her hair was a burst of fiery red with the sunlight behind it. It hung well past her shoulders in a mass of curls. She was wearing those damn cute shorts again, her legs looking trim and shapely. I narrowed my eyes at what she had on over top of the shorts but kept my pace.

"What the hell are you wearing?"

She glanced down as if she didn't know, then fingered the

denim sleeve. "I found these in a box in the storeroom! Aren't they great?"

I held back a groan. At one point, my father had denim shirts made for the garage with the logo on them. It had silver snaps instead of buttons and was faded and soft from years of washing. I had forgotten they even existed until now. The old logo was stitched over the pocket, giving it the retro look Charly said was so popular.

But the mechanics never wore them over a tank top with the tails tied up, exposing a sliver of stomach.

My steps faltered a little. "You aren't wearing that getup in the shop," I grumbled, forgetting my earlier rule about keeping my voice neutral.

She pursed her lips. "Yowsers—what a prude. Spoken like the elderly curmudgeon I imagined you to be, Maxx."

"Not a chance, Charly," I warned.

She shrugged, not caring what I had to say on the subject. Then she tugged on the fabric knot. "Will you rip them off if I try?"

I almost face-planted. With a curse, I hopped off the tread-mill and wiped my face with a towel.

She didn't wait for a reply, instead wandering to the other side of the barn. "Wow, there is a lot of stuff here."

I grunted, unable to get the image of peeling that shirt and shorts off her body and having my way with her again.

She stopped, staring at the motorcycle parked by the doors. "Is this yours?"

"Yes."

"You're a Harley guy?"

"One of my faves. I had a Ducati." I paused. "But I don't anymore."

She ran her hand along the gleaming paint. "It's beautiful. You did the restoration work?"

"Yes."

She admired it, touching the chrome, checking out the multi-toned black frosted paint and the custom airbrushing detail. She ran her hand along the hand-stitched leather seat.

"It's a 1983 HDFXRT," I offered.

"It's beautiful," she murmured, then moved on farther into the barn. I watched her with interest, wondering what else would catch her eye. I liked watching her move.

She stopped, staring up, a gasp of delight escaping her lips. "Oh my god!"

I shook my head to clear it, then went over to see what had delighted her so much.

She was looking up, her head bent back so her hair fell almost to her ass. I wanted to touch it. Her hair or her ass—even better, both.

I glanced up at the bicycle hanging from the rafters. It was old, the seat wide, with a basket on the front. I remembered my mother going to Littleburn, returning with groceries she'd picked up in the basket. Sometimes, it would be filled with wild flowers or berries she'd pick.

"The bicycle?" I asked.

Charly grabbed my arm. "Oh, Maxx. Could I borrow it? Please? I would take good care of it!"

Her reaction was surprising. It was just an old bike—she seemed more excited about it than the car.

I rubbed my chin. "I'll have to replace the tires, and you'll need to clean it up, but yeah, if you want it." I looked at her. "You don't want the car?"

"Of course I do. But with this, I can explore and get some exercise at the same time." She flicked her hand in the direction of my exercise area. "I don't like that kind of workout."

I reached up and lifted the bike down, inspecting it. "I'll

check it out, and once I'm sure it's safe, you can use it. The chain is loose, so I need to tighten it."

"Can I paint it? I'll polish it all too."

It needed a good coat of paint and some TLC. "Sure."

She rubbed her hands together. "Oh good, a project."

I had to chuckle over her enthusiasm for the old bike. I set it to the side. "I'll order a couple of tires and check it out."

She beamed at me. Her smile was wide and bright, completely disarming me. It was honest and real, and I found myself smiling back at her. Without thinking, I pushed a curl back over her shoulder, stopping at the feel of the silk of her hair on my hand. I froze, threading my fingers through the curls, rubbing them between my fingers. Our eyes met and locked, the instant heat from earlier returning. I tugged on her neck, bringing her close. She sighed, her eyes drifting shut as I lowered my head and kissed her. Slowly, our lips moved, tasting and giving. I ran my tongue over her bottom lip, and she opened for me, her body quivering as I brought her tighter to my torso.

How she affected me so quickly, so deeply, I would never understand. I wound my free arm around her waist, needing her closer. Wanting to taste her more. Feel her body molded to mine. Despite the height difference, we meshed as if sculpted for each other. Her breath filled my head, fed my lungs, nourished my soul. I bent, lifting her, and she wrapped her legs around me. I stumbled to a covered chair, sitting down, Charly straddling me. Our mouths never separated, our groans mingling, our passion growing, morphing into a living, tangible bubble of heat around us. I ran my hands over her legs, slipping my fingers under her shorts, feeling her readiness. She rolled her hips, making me hiss as she slid against my erection. My tongue explored her mouth, discovering all of her. She whimpered as I undid the ties on the shirt and cupped her breasts. Our fingers grasped and fumbled, and moments later, I was inside her, the heat of her wrapping around me.

"Fuck," I gasped. "Condom."

"On birth control," she assured me, licking at my neck. "Safe. So, so safe."

She moved and I cursed. I grabbed her hips and guided her, lost to everything unique and perfect about this small piece of time.

The sunlight in her hair, the way the dust motes danced in the beams around us. The way she bit her lip as she rode me, tiny gasps of pleasure escaping her mouth. The feel of that glorious hair brushing my knees as I watched her tilt back her head and find her release. The feel of her, all around me. The sights, the sounds, the sensations of this moment, forever locked into a memory. Knowing I would never again see this barn the same way or look at this chair with simply a passing glance. She would be etched into all of it.

She cried out, gripping my shoulders and calling my name. I thrust into her heat, holding her down as I came, a long, low groan rumbling from my chest. Tendrils of pleasure shook me, wrapping around my spine and exploding in bright shards of light behind my eyes.

She fell forward into my chest, her head buried in my neck. I brought her close, resting my chin on her head. Neither of us spoke, lost in our thoughts for a moment.

My plan had backfired big-time. Instead of keeping her at a distance, I had kissed her senseless by lunch and fucked her before dinner. So much for my bright ideas.

She lifted her head, looking up at me, her green eyes soft. I had to smile at her. "Gonna ask me for a secret, Red?"

"I'll give you one," she replied.

I tucked a stray lock of hair behind her ear. "I'm listening."

"I think you're the sexiest man I've ever seen. Especially for an old curmudgeon."

I chuckled.

"Your turn."

"I don't think you're so bad yourself, Red. Aside from this horrid hair color and all the dots all over your face." I winked to let her know I was teasing, then on impulse pulled her in for a hard hug. I grimaced at the feeling of something sharp digging into my skin.

"Ouch," I growled. "What's in your pocket?" I rubbed at my chest. "A knife?"

"Oh!" she said. "I forgot. I found this in the storeroom too." She pulled something from the pocket on the front of the shirt, holding it out on her palm. "I know it's rare. Did you find it for that restoration you did on the Indian bike?"

I stared at the iconic Indian logo emblem. It had been the crowning piece missing from the bike when I last saw it. The final fragment I'd searched long and hard for.

Except I never got the chance to affix it. I thought it had been stolen along with the bike.

Flashes of that day hit me. Coming home early. Finding them together. The fight. Waking up to find them gone, along with the bike.

My entire world crumbling around me as lie after lie was revealed.

My stomach knotted, and a tidal wave of anger hit me. The feelings of rejection, scorn, and humiliation hit me all over again.

I grabbed the piece of metal from Charly's hand, barely controlling my emotions. I lifted her from my lap, almost pushing her off in my haste. I dragged up my boxers, grabbing my sweats and pulling them on.

"Maxx," Charly asked. "What is it? What's wrong?"

I grabbed her by the shoulders, keeping her at arm's length. "Don't touch me," I spat out. "Stay away, Charly. This time, I mean it. No more." I waved my fingers between us. "Whatever *this* is stops now. I brought you here to do a job. Do it and stay clear of me."

I turned and walked away, ignoring the shocked, hurt look on her face.

CHAPTER 13

CHARLY

His words echoed in my head as he stormed away. I watched him enter the house, the screen door slamming against the brick. I tugged on my clothes, feeling remarkably calm considering what had occurred.

I stood in the wide-open expanse of the barn doors for a moment, the sunshine warming my face. I glanced at the beautiful restored motorcycle beside me. Brought back to life with care and passion by Maxx's hands. The same hands that seemed to know exactly where to touch me and how to give me more pleasure than I had ever experienced.

The same hands that pushed me away.

Even when he was shouting, his words intended to frighten and hurt me, all I could see was the pain in his eyes. The fear of getting close—too close—to me was evident, even if he refused to admit it. The woman who had been here before had done a number on him.

Rufus loped over, his golden coat gleaming in the light. Crouching down, I stroked his head, feeling the warmth from the sun on his skin. He was a great dog. Docile, friendly, happy to hang around the garage all day, trotting over to see customers, lying outside, his tail wagging, lifting his head in greeting. He often sat in the office with me, and this afternoon, he'd lain in the doorway while I worked on organizing the storeroom.

My thoughts returned to the metal emblem I had found. There was obviously a story behind the seemingly innocent badge. I knew they were difficult to find, just as the heavy iconic bust of the Indian head some models had affixed to the front tires were rare. They were lost, broken off, or rusted away. My dad had one once, a long time ago in his shop. But where it went, I had no idea. He probably sold it.

I stood and went back into the barn, wheeling the bicycle I had found toward the garage. I loved the old-fashioned look of it, with the wide basket on the front and the big padded seat. I would enjoy exploring the countryside on it on my days off. My steps faltered, and I stopped as a terrible thought hit me.

What if Maxx decided I was too much trouble and ended my employment? My chest constricted. I'd been here less than a week, and I already loved it. Working in the garage, organizing things, and yes, bossing Maxx around, were all part of it, but it was the simplicity of it all that I really loved. The quiet of the small place. The feeling of safety. Seeing the stars at night and not hearing the constant sound of traffic.

I knew I couldn't spend the rest of my life living in a room in the back of a garage, but for now, it was what I needed. I hoped Maxx would keep me on so I could find my feet and save some money, then decide what I wanted to do. I wasn't sure my future included Toronto. Growing up, I longed for the city and the lure of excitement. Living there was a different matter altogether. Maybe small-town living was more my style. But I needed time to figure it out, and I wanted to stay here.

I pushed the bicycle forward, steering it into the empty bay at the side. It needed some work, but I wasn't afraid of getting my hands dirty. As long as Maxx was still okay with me fixing it up and riding it. I ran a hand through my tangled hair, suddenly feeling tired.

If Maxx wanted an employee, that was what he'd get. I was going to do my job so well he would forget about anything else. I would stay busy, out of his way, and avoid being alone with him, and, above all else, arguing with him. That seemed to cause trouble every time.

I would treat him the way I treated my old boss, Peter. With respect and decorum. Peter always said I was invaluable to him, and I wanted to be that for Maxx as well, so I could stay.

I tried not to think about the fact that I never wanted to feel Peter's hands on my body or that I found Maxx utterly irresistible.

I simply had to put aside the overwhelming roar of lust that blasted through my body every time Maxx growled or glared at me. Forget the way it felt as his body moved with mine. The way he tasted and felt. How he made me feel desired, sexy, and safe.

I could do that. From this moment on, he was only my boss. Nothing more.

Easy peasy.

Maxx came into the garage the next morning, going straight to his workbench. I hadn't gone to the house last night, figuring it was best to keep my distance. There were plenty of leftovers for him to eat, and I wasn't hungry. I spent the night organizing my room and chatting with Kelly via text. She hated talking on the phone, so we always texted instead. I didn't tell her much about Maxx except to say he was tough but I was enjoying my job.

Her news was far more interesting.

Kelly: *Terry's been arrested.*
Charly: *What?*
Kelly: *Another tenant complained. She found him in her apartment and screamed down the place, called the cops and the local news. He's up on breaking and entering and harassment charges. He was fired from his job and is in jail. A few other people came forward.*
Charly: *Holy moly. I sent a letter to the cops and the owner of the building before I left Toronto.*
Kelly: *The news piece said they had other complaints from former tenants too. Maybe they meant you.*
Charly: *Wow. He deserves it. I wonder if they will contact me.*
Kelly: *I think they have lots of other people, but they might. They found a lot of little, ah, "souvenirs" he took from people's places.*

I shook my head, staring at the screen.

Charly: *Ugh. I always thought I lost stuff. I hope he rots in prison. At least he is out of the building.*
Kelly: *For sure.*

Then she went on to tell me she was off on another trip with her photographer, this time a longer one, and promised to let me know when she got home. I wondered if she would ever get tired of her nomadic lifestyle and settle down. But Kelly loved her life, and if it made her happy, then that was all that mattered. By the time we stopped texting and I checked out the articles on Terry, my mind was racing over the whole situation and not simply on Maxx's overreaction.

He was not the same this morning, his usual anger-driven stance missing. He moved differently, not stomping or striding quickly. His shoulders were hunched, not the ramrod straight posture I was used to seeing.

Was he ill?

I worried my lip as I wondered what I should do. Take him coffee? Ignore him?

Finally, I decided normalcy was the best route. I poured him a coffee, grabbed my notebook, and went out front. He was sitting at the workbench, staring at a file folder. He didn't notice me approaching, so I cleared my throat.

"Morning, boss."

He looked up, and my breath caught in my throat. Exhaustion was etched into his face, the lines around his eyes deep.

The urge to step forward, cradle his face in my hands, and kiss him was strong. I wanted to take him to his room, pull him down on his bed, and hold him while he slept.

Except I couldn't do that. He didn't want my touch.

I held out his coffee, and he took it, carefully avoiding touching my fingers. "Morning," he rasped.

"I've gotten in touch with everyone who had outstanding invoices. There are only a handful still waiting to pay—they'll be coming in this week with their payments. I'm going to the bank this morning to make the deposits."

He sipped his coffee in silence. He focused his gaze somewhere over my shoulder.

"If you want to leave, Charlynn, I'll give you a month's salary and take you to the bus. There's one that heads to Toronto from Lomand tomorrow."

I stared at him.

"I apologize for my behavior." He scrubbed his face. "I'll give you a reference if that helps."

His words surprised me, but it was the tone he used to say them. Quiet. Worried. Removed.

He fully expected me to accept his offer and walk away. I probably should. The thousand dollars would tide me over until I found something else. Except I didn't want to go.

"Thanks for the offer, Maxx, but I think I'll stay."

He frowned, running a hand through his hair. "Why?"

I shrugged. "I like it here. Organizing this place is a challenge, and I like challenges. I feel safe here, and frankly, I don't want to go back to Toronto."

He studied me for a moment, his shoulders losing a little of the tension. "You didn't feel safe in Toronto? Because of your landlord?"

I recalled Mary's words when she told me Maxx and I had a lot in common. I leaned against the workbench, staying a safe distance from Maxx. I met his curious gaze and told him everything.

"I came home from work one day to find out my roommate was a thief. Aside from a few things she left behind, my apartment was empty, all my money gone, my bank accounts drained, and she had disappeared. Her name, everything, had been fake."

His eyebrows shot up, but he didn't say anything.

"Then, to make matters worse, I lost my job and found out Trish had been trading sexual favors for the rent money I gave her. So, I was behind on my rent, and my ever-helpful landlord offered to let me take her place until I could find the money."

His eyes narrowed, and his hands clenched into fists. "He threatened you."

"Yes. And since I told you the story of how that went for him at the bar the other night, you know I refused." I shivered simply at the thought. "He was vile."

I met his angry gaze. "I tried so hard to be brave, Maxx, but I was terrified about what he would do to me if he caught me. He was so…awful. I was equally nervous about your posting, but I was desperate." I swallowed. "I knew you thought I was a guy, but I decided working for a curmudgeon who was angry was better than staying there. I was sure I could get you to come around and appreciate my work, not my gender."

He didn't say anything, and I told him about my terror and

how I didn't relax until the bus pulled away and my sheer relief at escaping that part of my life. I explained about the wallets and the money, laying it all on the table.

He listened, his expression intense. His brows drew down in anger at parts, his frown constant, but he never interrupted.

I blew out a long breath. "So, basically, I figured you'd be annoyed, but I had to get away. I thought once you saw how good a job I did, you wouldn't be annoyed anymore. I had no idea all I would do *was* annoy you once I got here." I lifted my shoulder. "Or the reaction it would cause between us."

He lifted a brow. "Annoyance isn't the main issue here, Charly."

I was quick to reassure him. "What happens is mutual, Maxx. You don't owe me an apology."

"Yeah, I do."

"Then I accept it."

"I don't want you to feel as if—" He huffed and ran a hand through his hair. "I don't want you to feel unsafe because of me. I am not the kind of man your landlord was. I'm not trying to take advantage of you."

I was touched by his words. "Oh heavens. I know that. You're nothing like him, Maxx. What happens between us is mutual," I assured him. "I understand you wanting to draw the line, but at no time have you ever taken advantage or made me feel unsafe."

"Good." He grunted, sipping his coffee, clearly uncomfortable. "I would hate that," he muttered so low I almost didn't hear him.

I told him the news that Kelly had shared about Terry.

"Will you have to go into Toronto to give a statement?" He scowled.

"I called the cops this morning. They said the chances were unlikely. They have a lot of complaints against him now. If I'm needed, they'll be in touch."

"I'll take you if you have to go."

"Oh. You don't have to do that."

He grunted. "Yes, yes, I do."

I ignored the flutter of pleasure his insistence made me feel. I let his words go and moved back to the gist of our conversation.

"I had no idea who you were that night in the bar," I confessed. "I didn't expect to see you again."

"I know how you feel. I was pretty damned shocked myself."

"Don't send me away, Maxx. I'll do my job and leave you alone. I promise."

"What happened last night—" he began, but I interrupted him.

"Won't happen again. I get it. We're both adults, we can figure it out."

"Let me finish," he growled, and I tried not to giggle. He sounded like Maxx again.

"I was rough and said some things I shouldn't have said. Seeing that emblem hit me and brought up some bad memories. I'm sorry I pushed you away, and I'm sorry I yelled. But the bottom line is, we can't keep doing this. I'm not in the market for a relationship, and you aren't the kind of girl who sleeps with her boss with no chance of a future." He met my eyes, his dark and serious, although I was certain I heard a trace of regret in his undertone. "Because there is zero chance, Charly. Let me be clear on that."

I swallowed my hurt. "I get it. I just want to do my job. Give me a chance."

"Fine. You have the rest of your month trial."

"I haven't finished my two-week one yet," I teased.

"You've proven yourself enough," he muttered and turned back to his workbench. "Don't you have things you can do now?" he asked pointedly.

"Yowsers. Bossy much?" I quipped and stalked away, trying to get him to smile.

"You know it," he called over his shoulder.

I headed back to the office, sitting down heavily in the chair. I felt relief over the fact that I could stay. We had set some ground rules, which we both had to adhere to. I peeked up through the glass. Maxx was leaning on the workbench, holding his coffee but not moving. He looked oddly despondent, and I wondered how much had to do with his decision and how much had to do with the memories seeing that emblem had evoked.

Whatever situation that emblem was attached to was a minefield. He told me he had restored an Indian Chief motorcycle, and I wondered if that had anything to do with it. Add in the Tramp and the ex-friend Mary spoke about, and I had a feeling the story was complex and deep.

I pulled my laptop close and decided to run a few reports then finish in the storeroom. I needed to stay busy and productive. If I didn't, I would give in and try to comfort Maxx. I knew if I did that, I'd be back on a bus, no matter what I wanted.

And I really didn't want to leave.

I stuck to my word the rest of the week. I did my job, stayed clear of Maxx, and finished up the storeroom to stay busy. By the weekend, it was organized, and I had found a treasure trove of pictures and small items that would look great in the garage and the office. I even had plans for the small room in the front that sat unused and vacant. Maxx admitted it used to be a waiting room, but he had done away with it. I planned on showing him why it was needed. In the evenings, I worked on designing a new logo and website. Maxx had told me that picture I had seen was his father, although he wasn't sure how it got on the web. I found the fact that the man who could disassemble any engine, manifold, or carburetor and piece it back together so it worked perfectly yet couldn't grasp the workings of the internet, strangely endearing.

Not that I would ever tell him that.

Saturday morning, I used the car Maxx had fixed and drove to Lomand for groceries. They had a large grocery store with a bigger selection than the small general store in Littleburn. The car drove like a dream—smooth and quiet. Hardly a surprise given what I had seen of Maxx and his work. He was meticulous and cared about the work he did. Even a simple oil change was done carefully. He reminded me of my dad with his old-fashioned attitude toward customer service. No job was too small, no question stupid. I had noticed there were only a few women customers, which surprised me. If I lived here and had a car, I'll be yanking on wires weekly just to come and see him.

In the store, I picked up all the items on my list—and the ones Maxx had added when I told him I was going. He left the list and cash on the office desk last night before he walked out of the garage. I had watched him, feeling sad. It was hard to believe it had only been a week since I had first seen his intense gaze and felt his mouth on mine. So much had happened, it felt like a lifetime. I wanted to ask him to come to the store with me, just to spend more time with him, but I knew that was crossing the line he had set.

As I shopped, I added a few items. I had noticed that while he ate well and took care of himself, Maxx had a bit of a sweet tooth, and his favorite was pie. He had finished the entire pie I had made, and I noticed he casually checked the cupboard I had kept it in every day, looking for more. He never said a word, though. I planned on making a few pies to put in the freezer this weekend. I was so intent on my task I never noticed the people around me until a voice spoke close to my ear.

"Well, who have we here?"

I looked up with a frown, meeting the frosty gaze of a familiar-looking man. He was average height, dirty-blond hair, and a permanent scowl on his face. Not the attractive, broody expression Maxx wore, but a discontented, malicious type of glare. I didn't like the way he stared at me, and my fists tightened on the cart handle.

"I'm sorry, have we met?" I asked.

He sneered at me. "You gonna pretend you don't remember meeting me in the bar last week?" He glanced around. "No bodyguard today?"

It clicked this was the guy who had gotten in my face and Maxx had escorted from the bar. Donner, I think he called him. Wes Donner. I lifted my chin. "I don't need a bodyguard. Nor do I need your attitude. I wasn't interested last week, and I'm still not interested. Go away."

I moved past him, but his hand shot out, grabbing my cart. "You need to learn some manners."

"Unless you want a repeat of what happened in the bar to happen here, I suggest you move to the side, asshole," I stated clearly. "I assume you don't want all these people to be witness to a girl taking you down...again."

His glare became frostier. "Uppity little bitch," he muttered but stepped away.

"Have a lovely day." I moved away fast, refusing to let him see the fact that he made me nervous. I looked over my shoulder, seeing another man join him. They looked similar, so I assumed it was his brother. Maxx had mentioned they were troublemakers in town who liked to throw their weight around.

I turned the corner and pushed them from my mind. I refused to let them intimidate me. I didn't see them again as I left the store. I drove back to Littleburn, enjoying the scenery, planning out meals in my head. It didn't seem to matter what I cooked, Maxx ate it up. He liked simple, good food. He ate a lot of salads, vegetables, and fruit, and I had seen him go into the barn daily to work out, so I knew he took good care of himself.

After talking to Mary last night, I had bought a lot of strawberries and blueberries at the store and planned on spending my time off at her place. We were going to bake pies, using the rhubarb she had in her garden. I would put them in the freezer, so Maxx could have a piece anytime he wanted.

Maybe my pies would be the deciding factor for me staying. I would do anything to make sure that happened.

Back at the house, I unloaded the groceries, then headed to the garage. Maxx was finishing off a job, and I handled the final payment, trying not to be too pleased when I saw he had collected money from everyone who had been there this morning.

He was rolling the overhead door shut as I came from the office. I watched his muscles flex, thinking of his strength. It was evident in the way he handled equipment with ease, how he moved and shifted. He was extremely sexy, and what made it even sexier was he didn't seem to notice—he was just Maxx.

He wiped his hands and indicated the end bay. "I put the new tires on the bike. I got a new seat as well. The other one was in rough shape."

"Thank you." I hurried over, looking at the bike. He followed, and I felt his close proximity without turning.

"You sure you want to take this, ah, wherever you're going?" he asked. "You can take the car."

"No, I want to ride the bike. It's only to Mary's."

"You're going to Mary's?" he queried, surprised.

"Yes, we're going to bake pies, and I'm going to help her weed her garden."

"Huh," he muttered.

"What?"

"I thought you might go into Lomand and have, like, a girls' night or something."

I rolled my eyes. "With what girls, Maxx?" I shook my head. "Not much into the bar scene." I met his gaze. "Last week was unusual for me."

He stroked his chin, not saying anything.

"Besides, I've seen enough of the locals this morning. I don't want to risk running into them again."

"What are you talking about?"

"Wes Donner saw me in the store."

Maxx's gaze turned frosty, his shoulders stiffening. I felt my breathing pick up at the angry look on his face. "What did he do?" he spat.

I repeated our brief conversation, and Maxx's lips quirked. "He wouldn't like that."

"No, he didn't." I lifted my chin. "I'm not letting him bother me."

"Good girl."

"Is he always an ass?"

Maxx lifted a shoulder. "He's rich, spoiled, and likes to get his way. His dad owns a bunch of stuff in town, so he tends to get away with shit. He and his brother, Chase. They aren't dangerous, but annoying. Entitled. Spoiled kids masquerading as adults. They think they can get away with anything." He barked out a laugh. "They did when they were younger but not as much anymore. Still, avoid them if you can."

"I can take care of myself."

His amusement was real this time. "I know you can."

He turned and walked away with a wave. "Enjoy your time off, Charly."

I felt a strange sadness as he disappeared. I was looking forward to spending time with Mary, but a small part of me had hoped Maxx would ask me to stay and spend my time with him.

Silly, but true.

CHAPTER 14

CHARLY

I loaded the wide basket on the bike with the fruit and my knapsack and rode to Mary's, enjoying the scenic route. I was grateful when I got there, my legs unused to the workout. She had lemonade waiting, and we sat on the porch, relaxing.

"How are things with you and Maxx?"

I pursed my lips. "Tense most of the time." I met her gaze. "And strictly employee and employer."

She nodded in understanding.

"May I ask a question?"

"You can ask it. Can't guarantee I'll answer."

That was fair. I knew she protected Maxx.

"Does an Indian motorcycle figure into the equation of the Tramp and the bad friend?" I asked.

Her expression became dark. "Very much so, but—"

I interrupted her. "I know, it's Maxx's story to tell."

"Why would you ask?"

I told her about the emblem. Maxx's reaction to it. The way he'd shouted. I did leave off the part that we were naked when it happened, but I was honest and said Maxx informed me we would never be anything but coworkers.

She took a sip of her lemonade, her voice pained when she spoke. "They really did a number on him, Charly. Have patience."

I smiled sadly even as I shook my head. "I'm not pushing anything, Mary. I want this job—I need this job too much to risk it."

"But you have feelings for him."

I stared at the open fields across from her house, the breeze kicking up dust over the pasture. "I am drawn to him. I was the night we met, and it hasn't changed. I like him." I chuckled. "Even when he's all growly and gruff."

"Or maybe especially when he's all growly and gruff?" she teased.

"Maybe."

"He's always been that way. He was a broody teenager, and he became a taciturn young man. Serious and stern. But he was always kind and helpful. And to the people who knew him best, he was loving and caring. Funny." She shook her head. "The anger and dismissiveness started after...well, after everything happened last year."

I understood. Whatever happened hurt him deeply. Add in the fact that he was still reeling from losing his parents not long before that, and it wasn't a shock he had changed. I had seen glimpses of the funny, caring man she described. I only hoped he would slowly rediscover that side of himself.

Mary stood. "Enough about the boy who is no doubt brooding at his house or tinkering in the garage to pass the time. At least I know he isn't writing any more ads."

I grunted as I stood as well. "I hope not."

She linked her arm with mine. "Let's attack that garden."

We spent the rest of the weekend in the garden, sitting on the porch sipping wine after dinner, and playing cards. Baking an endless number of pies.

I took the bike apart, spray-painted it a bright yellow, and scrubbed and polished the chrome. I let it dry overnight, and then I put it back together. Mary had laughed over my color choice, but agreed it was better than the faded white—and much preferable to the shocking pink I had almost chosen.

Later Sunday afternoon, I loaded my basket with pies to go into the freezer at Maxx's. Mary had a larger chest freezer where we put the other dozen we had made, so I could come by and take them as needed. Using small pie plates, I had made her a bunch of individual ones to enjoy whenever she wanted one. She was thrilled, having admitted pies were something she couldn't really make. She had held up her hands. "Too strong. My pastry is like cement every time."

I waved goodbye and cycled myself back to the garage. The breeze was cooler today, blowing in my face, which made the ride back a little harder. By the time I arrived, I was winded and thinking I needed to avail myself of Maxx's treadmill to strengthen my legs.

Maxx was out front with Rufus, throwing the ball as I came up the driveway. His motorcycle was parked next to his truck, both of them gleaming in the sun, obviously freshly washed and waxed. The Camry was parked off to the side, also having benefited from some detailing work. The creamy white glowed in the sun. I stopped beside the truck, noticing something looked different. I had to bite back my smile when I realized there were now running boards on the truck. He would never admit it, but Maxx added those so I could get in the truck easier.

He came around the truck, eyeing the bike. "What the hell did you do to it?" he asked. "Yellow?"

I shrugged. "It was this or pink."

"I would have painted it in the shop. And a better color."

"I didn't need you to paint it, Maxx. I like the color—it's pretty. I'm perfectly capable of handling a can of spray paint," I stated dryly. "I polished the chrome too."

He grunted, and I couldn't help but tease him.

"Besides, it looks as if you were plenty busy. Nice running boards."

"I've had them for a while. First chance I got to install them is all. Don't read anything into it."

I ignored the growly tone. "Wouldn't dream of it."

He got down on his haunches, inspecting my handiwork. I had taken my time and been careful. I used a rust-inhibiting paint, even smoothing down the rough spots before I covered them. He stood. "Nice job."

"Thanks." I lifted two containers from the basket, handing one to him. "These are frozen, so I need them to go in the freezer right away."

"What are they?"

"Pies."

His eyes lit up. "Yeah?" Then he frowned. "Why are they frozen?"

"So I could pile them in the basket and bring them home." I held up the other container. "This one is still warm. You can have it after dinner."

His face broke into a wide smile, transforming his features. Stern and unflappable was attractive on him. Excited and happy was incredible. His eyes crinkled, his teeth flashed, and his face became intoxicatingly handsome. Dimples appeared by his mouth. His countenance changed entirely. He was devastatingly sexy.

He shoved the first container back at me, taking the still warm pie plate from my hands. "Nope. I am having a piece right now."

He turned and began walking toward the house, calling over his shoulder, "I hope you bought ice cream yesterday, Charly."

Still enthralled over his sudden openness, I followed slowly, trying to recover my senses. I thought growly was hot on him. If pie did that to him, I'd be baking every day. Holy moly.

"It was on your list, Maxx, so yes, there is ice cream. I can read, you know."

He must have heard me because his laughter floated through the air. I shook my head. This was not good. If he was going to be sexy all the time, I didn't have a hope in hell of resisting him.

I walked to the utility room, putting the pies in the freezer. I wanted to add some premade meals for nights I didn't feel like cooking or on the days I was off, but it was a pretty small freezer and I had already filled it with frozen vegetables and fruit. I wandered into the kitchen, stopping at the sight of Maxx leaning against the counter, shoving pie and ice cream into his mouth.

"You know," he mused. "If the internet had a smell factor and you'd flashed one of these pies, I would have hired you just for that, regardless of the fact that—" he grinned widely, his eyes crinkling in that sexy way again "—you chap my ass constantly."

It was all I could do not to launch myself at him. He was so appealing right now. Tall, rugged, teasing, and at ease. Eating pie. Throwing my favorite expression at me.

I rolled my eyes. "Jeez, were you raised in a barn? You wanna chew that pie, Maxx? I spent a lot of effort making it—at least slow down and taste it."

He shoveled another mouthful in. "I am tasting it. It's the best thing I ever ate." Then he held out his fork. "Taste it."

My feet carried me closer, hardly able to believe what he was offering. As I got near, he slipped his fork into my mouth, the tartness of the warm rhubarb and strawberries exploding, highlighted by the cold sweetness of the ice cream.

I closed my eyes and licked my lips. "Damn, that is good," I admitted. I opened my eyes to see Maxx staring at me. His dark gaze was intense, focused on my mouth. Our eyes locked as he lifted the fork and drew it between his lips, his tongue sliding over the tines in a long, sensual lick.

"Yeah," he uttered. "It really is."

My breath came out in a long shudder. I waited for the explosion. Either him yelling at me, or lunging, maybe taking me right there on the counter. Despite his angry words the other day, I knew he wanted me. The evidence of it was in his stare. The bulge in his jeans. The dark, frank look in his eyes.

But nothing happened. He dropped his gaze and finished the pie in two fast mouthfuls. Then he cut another slice, added more ice cream, and walked away. "Help yourself, Charly. You get one piece. The rest is mine for later."

"It's all yours, Maxx," I mumbled, my knees feeling weak.

I heard his chuckle as he walked outside. I also heard what sounded like him saying, "I wish, Red. I wish."

But I was certain I was mistaken.

I made a concerted effort to stay away from Maxx again. I spent the week acting like the perfect employee. I did my job, made sure he had his meals, and spent the evenings in my room, often taking a bike ride and enjoying the scenery. I found it incredibly difficult to try to remain aloof. Watching Maxx without him noticing became an art form for me. I could peer at him as he talked to customers. Paced while on the phone. Ogle his fine ass as he bent over the hood of a car. Groan with barely suppressed lust as he slid underneath the hood on a creeper, his torso disappearing. I wondered how he would react if he felt my hands on his thighs, stroking him, unzipping those jeans and taking him in my mouth, all the while not being able to see me.

I almost fell off my chair imagining the snarls and cursing that would happen under the car. And what he would do to me when he rolled out. More than once, I had to squeeze my thighs together to ease the ache between them.

My little room was the only place I could totally relax. I longed for a bath but hadn't yet asked Maxx if I could use the tub in the house, worried that would be overstepping. I felt lonely at times, yet fairly content.

Saturday, I did the shopping again, happy not to have run into Wes. Mary and I went for supper later at Zeke's, enjoying a good burger and some fine cocktails. She always had interesting stories to tell me, some including Maxx and his parents. When we were walking out of the restaurant, Wes Donner and his brother were getting out of their truck. He leered at me, saying something to his brother that amused him and made him eye me up. I ignored them. Mary shot them a look that shut them up.

"I wish I had that talent." I smirked.

"Years of practice," she replied with a wink. "Those boys are trouble. I never know who is worse—Wes or Chase. They're both overgrown children who need a good spanking."

I snickered at the image. If anyone could do that, it would be Mary.

"You be on your guard for them. Especially Wes since you embarrassed him. He doesn't like that."

Maxx had said the same thing.

"I am," I assured her.

"Good."

Then she changed the subject.

Sunday, I helped her plant some vegetables, and I baked Maxx another lemon pie. Mary got one too.

That night, I fell into bed and slept soundly, exhausted from the long week of avoiding Maxx, while fighting the desperate longing for not avoiding him. I wasn't sure how long I could keep up this charade. He seemed to be handling it just fine. He was polite and courteous but went out of his way to avoid me. He thanked me for his meals, always complimented them, and I knew he'd already taken another pie from the freezer. He was a great boss, but the bottom line was, I liked him better as growly, unpredictable Maxx.

On Monday, I carried a sandwich into the garage, setting it on the workbench. It had been a hectic morning, and I'd barely had time to talk to Maxx at all. At one point he'd received a call that he'd walked outside to take, and when he came back, his glower was deeper than usual. I knew better than to ask him about it, though. Instead, I stayed busy.

Maxx was talking to a customer as I went by. He was busy with his hands as he worked on a nice-looking Yamaha. But he glanced up, and I offered him a smile. "Your lunch, boss man, whenever you're hungry."

He nodded, his attention on the man he was talking to. The man chuckled. "Wow—she's good. You get lunch?"

Maxx made a low noise, and the customer stepped forward, his hand outstretched. "Cam."

I shook his hand. "Charly."

"Pleasure." He indicated Maxx. "You're far cuter than this lug. You smile too."

I had to laugh. "It's part of the service now."

"What else is included?" Cam teased.

"I want those numbers this afternoon, Charly," Maxx snapped. "Stop flirting and get to work."

Cam threw back his head in amusement. "I hope you get paid well for putting up with the attitude."

"I think Maxx considers that one of the perks."

Cam chuckled and looked at Maxx. "I like this one."

Maxx snorted. Like a real blow the air through your nose and huff at the same time sort of snort. He glared at Cam. "Hands off my staff. I have a firm no mixing business with pleasure policy. Charly can't date my customers."

I managed to hide my surprise at his words. He had never mentioned anything of the sort. And I highly doubted Cam was looking for a date. His tone was teasing and friendly but not personal. He didn't look remotely interested in me. His next words confirmed that.

Cam frowned. "My wife will be happy to hear that, Maxx. Relax. I was just being nice." He eyed him. "You might want to try it."

"I'm plenty nice."

I had to turn and walk away to stop my laughter. Cam spoke again. "Back to the event. You have to go, Maxx."

"I can't. I'm booked solid."

"Can't you put it off?"

"No. I can't just close the garage, Cam."

"It's an amazing opportunity."

My steps faltered. *What opportunity?*

"I guess it's one I will simply have to say no to."

Cam huffed and called my name. "Charly!"

"Um, yes?"

"Can you reschedule your boss here so he can be gone for a while?"

I met Maxx's expression. It was filled with warning, intense and dark. Telling me not to speak.

I decided to push back a little. I was tired of being quiet. "I can check."

Cam smirked and crossed his arms. "Great."

Maxx stepped forward, gripping my arm. "The office," he snapped.

I tried not to feel the thrill of his touch or the way his voice made me shiver. In the office, he spun me around. "Stay out of this, Charly."

"Stay out of what? Looking at your schedule so you can go somewhere?"

He crossed his arms, narrowing his gaze. I could feel the anger rolling off him, and I found great delight in it. He had been far too polite and lackluster the past few days. That wasn't Maxx. Growly, snappy, and terse—that was him.

I mimicked his stance. "It might do you some good to get away for a while."

"I'm not interested in your opinion."

I shrugged and sat down. "Fine. Act like a martyr."

"I'm not acting like a martyr. I'm acting like a sensible business owner."

"Uh-huh."

"I can't just leave the garage. I have commitments."

I crossed my arms and glared at him. "Are you trying to convince me or yourself, Maxx?"

Dark eyes glared back at me, lethal and threatening. His glower was furious, the knuckles on his hands white as they fisted at his sides.

"Where exactly would you be going?"

He dropped his head, shaking it in resignation. "I was offered a chance to be part of a convention in the States. Los Angeles. They had a last-minute cancellation, and my name came up. I would be talking about motorcycle restoration." He paused. "All expenses paid. I would give a series of talks and demonstrations. They supply everything."

"Maxx, that's amazing!"

"I was pleased to be asked," he said, the words all the more telling from the undercurrent in his voice. He wanted to go.

"Think of the networking, the chance to get your name out there. The business this could bring you," I urged. "You have to go."

"And what, just close the garage and leave you to run amok? I don't think so," he sniped.

I almost laughed at his attempt to piss me off.

"I was at the general store a couple of times last week. Mr. Conner's son was there."

Maxx frowned. "Brett?"

"Yes. He told me the shop he worked at in Toronto had a fire. He's out of a job until it's rebuilt, so he's back home. He's a mechanic."

"I know he's a mechanic." He stopped as my words sank in. "You want me to have Brett cover here?"

I detected a note of worry in Maxx's voice, and I knew this was thin ice I was walking on.

"You've known him all your life. He told me you went to school together."

A strange looked passed over his face. "Sometimes, that means nothing."

I held back the retort I wanted to say. Instead, I shrugged. "Sometimes, it does."

"I'd be gone a whole week. They want me to fly out tomorrow, and I would be gone until next Tuesday. That's a lot of arranging to be done," he muttered.

"You could at least talk to him. If you're worried, you can change the bank password and only let Brett have access to the front. I'll work in the office on other things and take the payments. Get Mary to come babysit us if that makes you feel better. Put a spy cam in the garage—whatever you have to do. But don't simply walk away from an opportunity like this, Maxx."

He stared at me, silent and brooding. I waited for his eventual dismissal of my ideas. I was shocked when he nodded and spun on his heel. "I'll think about it."

Refusing to give him the chance to overthink it, I opened my laptop, brought up flights to LA, and checked the schedules. I made a quick phone call, printed out a few options, then went out front, laying the paper beside him. Cam watched us, looking amused.

"Just in case, these are some flight options. And, ah, Brett is going to drop by shortly. Just to talk. Either way—your decision." I scurried back to the office before he could yell. It was an incredible opportunity for him, and the break might do him some good. Maybe he would relax and enjoy himself. Make some good connections.

Maybe when he came back, I wouldn't annoy him so much.

I shut down my laptop and walked through the garage, hoping to escape unnoticed. I felt Maxx's glare follow me, and his voice boomed out as I reached the door. "Meeting at three, Charly. I expect those numbers to be ready."

"Yep," I squeaked. Then, like the coward I was, ran.

Maxx stormed through the door of the house around two thirty. I was upstairs, changing his sheets. I heard his heavy footsteps on the stairs and swallowed. He walked into the room, which seemed to shrink and close in around us. But when he spoke, his voice was deceptively mild.

"What part of 'stay out of it' did you not understand?"

"Um, the whole part?" I replied, keeping my voice light. "I just made a phone call. Easy peasy. If you don't want to go, you don't have to."

"Well, since it seems there is nothing stopping me, I have no choice."

"Why don't you want to go?"

He rubbed his face. "It's complicated."

"Most things are with you."

He narrowed his eyes. "I trusted my best friend with this

shop, and he screwed me over. I find it difficult to allow anyone to get close now."

I was surprised he had told me that much.

"You can control what Brett has access to. Me as well," I offered. His next words shocked and pleased me.

"I'm fine with you, Charly."

"Yeah?" I asked.

He ignored my question. "I spoke to Brett. He's happy to come in and work while I'm gone. Keep things running out front. You handle the back."

"So, you're going?"

He held up his hand. "On two conditions. I need you to look after Rufus, and I'm not happy about the thought of you being here alone all the time. It's pretty secluded."

"Oh." I had to admit, I hadn't thought about being here alone.

"Brett is going to move in to your room. You can have one of the rooms down the hall from mine. Whichever one you want."

"You want me to live in the house?"

He sighed and shut his eyes. "You should have been in here all along. I only put you out there to test you, Charly. After... Well, frankly, it was safer for you to be out there."

"Safer?"

He opened his eyes, meeting my gaze. "For both our sakes."

Heat pulsated, filling the room so quickly, it was intense. I knew what he meant. If we were down the hall from each other all night, one of us would crack. It was inevitable.

He swallowed and spoke, breaking the tension building between us.

"You can stay here while I'm gone. Rufus will protect you and be happy. Brett will be comfortable in the garage, and I'll feel better knowing he is here."

"And when you come back?"

There was a beat of silence. "We'll address that when I get home."

"Okay. So, you're going to do this?"

"I guess I am."

"Maxx, it's so exciting. Think of the networking. The business. You might get more restoration work."

"I can't take on much more. The garage is busy."

I shook my head. "Holy moly. Always short-sighted."

"What are you talking about?"

"If Brett works out, you can bring him on. Ease your workload so you can take on more restorations. You'll be there to supervise and watch, but you can do more of what you love."

"You have this all planned out, don't you, Red?"

He stopped talking, realizing what he had called me.

"Easy peasy, Maxx. Leave it to me." Attempting to lighten the situation, I tried teasing him. "You go and have a great time. I'll hold down the fort while you're carousing and drinking, being a celebrity."

He rolled his eyes, exasperated. "It's a bunch of bikers and distributors. I'm not a celebrity."

I shook my head. "With those sexy smolders, the women will fall all over you—" I stopped speaking abruptly, an image coming to mind. The women would go crazy over him. I mean, who could resist? I didn't want him to meet anyone, and I certainly didn't want him to sleep with anyone else. But I couldn't say anything. I had no ties on him, and if I did say something, it would be crossing that line.

I suddenly hated the thought of this trip. Him being gone. Surrounded by sexy biker chicks who would most certainly want to ride *him*. I gripped the pillowcase I was holding so tight, my knuckles turned white as jealousy raged through me. One word echoed in my head—one word I dared not speak out loud.

Mine.

As if sensing my inner turmoil, Maxx's eyes bored into mine, the silence around us building. The air pulsed with the passion that lurked beneath the surface every time we got close. I swallowed my suddenly dry throat, clutching the pillow tighter. Maxx's gaze drifted to the bed, then back to me. His gaze darkened further, and I felt my breathing pick up. It was as if I could feel his touch from across the room. Sense his deep need. A need that matched my own. We were like a moth and a flame—getting too close would cause devastation, yet we seemed powerless to resist. I almost whimpered as his hands fisted tightly against his sides as if forcing himself not to reach out.

"I don't think so," he murmured. Then he turned and walked away, not stopping until he was at the bottom of the stairs.

"Clear my schedule, Charly. I'm out of here."

CHAPTER 15

MAXX

The next morning, I carried my bag downstairs to find Charly waiting in the kitchen. She handed me an iPad and patiently showed me how to use the feature she'd added. All my latest restorations were there, the pictures in order from start to finish. My concept sketches were in the files as well. I shook my head in disbelief. "How?" I asked.

Charly shrugged. "Magic."

"No, Charly, how did you do this?" I studied her face, noticing the shadows under her eyes. "Were you up all night working on this?" I had been busy packing and getting organized. Charly had carried her things to her room down the hall and her door was shut when I looked before retiring, so I'd assumed she was in bed. She must have been working on this in the office.

"Yeah. Honest, Maxx. It was easy peasy. I know it's not a PowerPoint or anything, but maybe they can hook it up to a larger screen, and you can just scroll through the photos if you want."

I didn't know what to say. It was an incredible, thoughtful thing for her to do. I had planned on grabbing the memory card from my camera and trying to figure something out once I got there, and now I didn't have to.

"Thank you, Charly," I said simply. "You're the best."

"Well, will you look at that? The man has manners."

I chuckled.

She handed me some coffee. "You're welcome."

"Go back to bed."

"Nope. I have a busy week ahead of me."

"What do you have planned?"

"I don't want to tell you, but I think you'll like it."

Not being told her plans should have made me nervous, but it didn't. Charly was a different breed of woman, and I trusted her. It surprised me since I never thought I would trust another woman again, but with her, I knew my faith wasn't misplaced.

"Maxx, can I, ah, have like a hundred dollars for, ah, stuff?"

"Stuff?" I teased. "Business stuff or personal stuff?" Then I smacked my head in realization. "I need to pay you. You must need cash."

"I'm okay until you get back, but I need some money to make a few little changes."

"Doesn't sound like much to keep you busy for a week."

"I can make a buck go far," she retorted.

"There is two hundred in petty cash in the bottom of the file cabinet. I need receipts."

She rolled her eyes. "Duh."

I dug in my pocket and handed her another two hundred. "Here's an advance."

She hesitated.

"Charly, I told you if you did your job, you would get paid. You've outdone yourself. Take it."

She took the money, slipping it into her pocket.

I glanced at my watch. "I have to go."

She jumped up, suddenly looking upset. She wrung her hands

in an oddly nervous gesture for her. "Okay. Travel safe. You have your passport?"

"Yes."

She prattled on, waving her hands in the air, looking like a little redheaded bird flapping its wings. "Don't take rides from strangers, okay? Avoid the sun and the desert. Did you pack sunscreen? Do you have your credit card? Flight information? Did you pack clean underwear?"

I gaped at her strange behavior. "Yes to all but the last one."

"You didn't pack underwear?"

I shook my head slowly, enjoying the flush of color that rushed to her cheeks. "Nope, going commando all week." I bent and brushed a kiss on her warm skin. "Think of that while you're dipping into the petty cash and causing havoc."

She stilled, and I winked at her as I bent and grabbed my duffle bag. "See you in a week, Charly."

"Maxx…"

I paused at the door. "Yeah?"

"I'll be right here, waiting."

I cocked my head, her words sinking in. She looked tired, worried, and altogether too sexy standing in my kitchen, saying goodbye. Reassuring me. Exhausted because she had been awake most of the night doing something to help me. I had to fight the impulse to walk back to her and kiss her senseless.

"Good to know."

LA was hot. So fucking hot, I hated leaving the air-conditioned coolness of the hotel. It was loud and crowded, the roads clogged with congestion, and the sidewalks overrun with people.

The convention was massive. People came from all over for it. I got to meet other presenters, talk about motorcycles and restorations. It was great to converse with bike enthusiasts, exchange ideas with fellow restoration specialists, some of whom I had long admired. I wandered around the vast convention center, looking at bikes, parts, and new machines I itched to purchase for the shop. My lectures went well, and I was surprised how much I enjoyed giving them.

Surprisingly, the only fly in the ointment was the women. Charly had been right when she'd said there would be a lot of them around. Normally that wouldn't be an issue, but for some reason, the advances I received made me uncomfortable. Some were friendly and wanted to talk motorcycles, discuss ideas they had for their rides—others, not so much. There was just one thing on their mind, and they weren't getting it from me. For a couple of them, that seemed only to spur them on, and nothing I did, short of telling them where to go, seemed to dissuade them. In fact, it only seemed to encourage them, as if getting me in bed was a challenge.

Luckily, it was one I was up for. I had zero interest in a hookup. I tried hard not to delve too deeply into the reasons behind it.

I woke on Saturday, hearing the bustle already outside the hotel, even though it was still early. LA never seemed to quiet down, even overnight.

I missed the peace of Littleburn. Waking up in the stillness of dawn, Rufus at my feet. Working on cars and motorcycles. Talking to people I knew.

And dammit, I missed Red. How she had wormed her way under my skin and past my defenses, I had no idea. I knew I liked her, but how much became apparent once I was away from her. She was always in the recesses of my mind, peeking out at the strangest times. I found myself thinking about her several times a day, storing away bits of information I knew she would like.

Taking pictures I thought she would enjoy seeing since she wasn't there with me.

Wishing, at times, that she were.

She made a point of calling me every day. She'd tell me what was happening with the garage, assuring me she was keeping an eye on Brett.

"He's doing a great job, Maxx."

I'd grunt my response.

"Want me to send you the work orders and deposits?"

I rubbed my eyes. "No."

I still had alerts come in, and I saw Brett was staying busy. I didn't care about the deposits; I cared about talking to her.

"Rufus misses you. I'll send you pictures."

And she did—every day. A new one of him lying on the grass in the sun. Sleeping on the floor of the office. One arrived last night of him on the foot of her bed, making himself comfortable. I tried not to be jealous of my dog, sharing her bed. I recalled how it felt to be beside her at night. The way she tucked herself into my chest, nestling tight. She liked to be held, and I had enjoyed having her close.

It was easier to admit that when she was twenty-five hundred miles away.

She never told me what she was busy doing, although I imagined it was a lot. She wasn't afraid of hard work, and she was damn good at the organizing part.

Best non-male Girl Friday I had ever hired.

I looked forward to her daily calls. The pictures. The way she made sure I was still connected to my life back home. I found myself teasing her, purposely asking her questions I knew would make her respond with one of her odd expressions.

"How'd you do that, Charly?"

"Oh, easy peasy!"

"That sounds like a lot of work."

"Holy moly, mister. You have no idea."

"I appreciate all you're doing."

"Oh my. Would ya listen to that. The man has manners again."

"That must have made you mad."

"Totally chapped my ass."

Each exchange made me smile and, somehow, miss her more.

I flung back the blanket and got up.

I was connected to her—in ways I never expected.

I cursed as I headed for the shower.

This was more complicated than I had thought it was. And I had no idea how to stop it.

Or, if I even wanted to.

Later that afternoon, I headed across the lobby, needing a couple of Tylenol and a break. The event was packed, the auditorium overflowing, the noise level high. I had done three lectures and had three more to go later. For now, I needed a little quiet—and some room service.

"Maxx!" a voice behind me called. "Wait!"

I stifled a groan. Monique was one of the women who refused to take no for an answer. She was at every presentation, her leer frank and steady. She appeared no matter where I went, always a look of calculated surprise crossing her face when we would "bump" into each other. I turned down all offers of drinks, dinner, or her not-so-subtle offers of a quickie in the stairwell. Some men would be flattered by her attention, but I was finding it aggravating. She was one of the sponsors of the event, so I was careful and polite, but she refused to take the hint.

She stopped in front of me, smiling widely. "I saw you leave. I thought maybe we could get a bite together." She pulled on a long, carefully sculpted blond curl, lifting her shoulder so her prominent breasts pushed forward from the leather vest she was wearing.

"Thanks, Monique, but not now. I have a headache, and I'm heading to my room."

Wrong thing to say.

"Oh, I give great neck rubs," she cooed. "I could come with you and, ah, *ease* that ache. Any of them you might have." Her gaze dropped to my crotch, and I wanted to roll my eyes and tell her not to bother. There would be no response from my dick for her.

I was saved from telling her exactly what she could do with her neck rub by the sound of my phone ringing. I had never been as grateful to see the garage number flash across my screen as I was at that moment.

"Sorry, I need to take this. It's my fiancée," I lied.

Turning my back, I answered the phone, praying Charly would forgive me for what I was about to do.

"Hey, baby," I crooned. "I was just thinking about you. Christ, I miss you."

There was silence on the end of the line.

"I was heading to my room. Maybe you could finish what you started this morning when you called, you little minx." I chuckled low and deep in my chest, knowing Red liked that. "I think my cock was about to slide between those pretty lips of yours?"

I heard Monique's huff of exasperation and watched as she stormed away, her high heels clicking on the marble floor. I had a feeling she wouldn't be bothering me anymore.

I went back to the call. "Charly?"

A throat cleared, and a voice I didn't expect replied.

"It's Brett. I assume you would like to talk to Charly and not me. I doubt I can help you with what, ah, you are looking for."

I shut my eyes, cursing and muttering. I headed toward the elevator.

"What can I do for you, Brett?" I asked through tight lips.

"I need a part for a Lincoln. It's backordered, but there is a dealership in Toronto that has one. I was going to drive in and get it. It would save us the courier charges, but I'd be gone the rest of the day. I'll catch up tomorrow. I wanted to okay it with you. Charly said you needed to approve it."

"Sure. That's fine."

"Okay. Hang on."

I let my head fall back in the elevator, part of me hoping it plunged to the basement and ended my embarrassment.

I heard murmurs and Charly's loud screech.

"He said what?"

Her voice came on the line. "Holy moly, Maxx Reynolds, are you drunk?"

I started to laugh. Loud guffaws that echoed in the empty elevator. The doors opened, and I walked down the hall to my room, still chuckling. "No, but I think I'd like to be."

I explained about Monique, relieved when Charly huffed, then giggled. "I don't remember getting a ring," she sniffed.

"An oversight."

"I told you to watch out for the women."

"Yes, as usual, you were right."

"I'm sorry, can you repeat that?"

"Nope. You're breaking up, Charly. I didn't hear you."

"Gosh dang it. I aid you in your time of need, and I don't even get the satisfaction of you groveling." Then she began to giggle. "And I'm not sure Brett will ever recover."

"I'll explain when I get home. He'll understand."

"Right now, he thinks I call you for phone sex. Thanks for that, Bucko."

Bucko? That was a new one.

"You can tell him."

"Nah, let him think what he wants. He already surmised we were sleeping together."

"Why would he think that?" I toed off my shitkickers and relaxed back on the bed.

"I think you went a little overboard on the protectiveness thing when you spoke to him. He's been very, ah, respectful."

"Good. He should be." I frowned. "Any trouble with Wes?"

"I saw his brother in Lomand while I was in town yesterday with Mary. Aside from his staring, nothing else."

"Okay. Keep your eyes open."

"As I told you, I can take care of myself."

"And as I said, I know that. Just saying, be careful."

She muttered something about chapping her ass, which made me grin. "I have to go. I really need some food and some Tylenol."

"Okay. Put a cold cloth on your head. Or even better, ask for an ice bag and put it on your neck."

"I will. Thanks. And, Charly?"

"Yeah?"

"Sorry about earlier. I didn't mean to embarrass you."

She sighed, the sound breathy and low over the line. "It's fine. I expect a huge bonus for that, though."

"What would you like?" I asked, playing along, wondering what she would ask for. Her reply slid into my heart, warming the unused organ.

"For you to come home. I miss you."

She hung up before I could reply.

CHAPTER 16

CHARLY

I dropped my head into my hands. Why did I say that to him? It was far too personal—yet the words had come out before I could stop them. I did miss him. Staying in his house, working at making it better for him, made his absence seem bigger. The silence in the house louder.

I looked down at the file I had discovered earlier. It was stuck in the back of a drawer, caught on the railings. I had to work it out carefully, and I had been shocked to discover the contents.

I glanced up, making sure the doors were shut. Brett had left while I was on the phone with Maxx, Rufus was napping at my feet, and Mary wouldn't arrive for a couple of hours. We were going to finish the wall I had been working on in the garage.

I opened the file, once again perusing the documents, the story they told unfolding before my eyes. I had sorted the thick folder once I had realized what it contained, and now I read through it.

The mystery of the 1952 Indian motorcycle was revealed in front of me. Maxx's dad had bought the first parts, slowly finding pieces to begin restoring it when Maxx was about twenty. Years went by as they searched and discovered more original parts. There were a few grainy photos, some handwritten notes—everything to do with the bike kept and stored in this tattered file. He and his dad invested years of time, and hundreds of man-hours, finding, restoring, and rebuilding the bike. There was a gap in the file, which I assumed was when his mom became ill the first time, and after that, it was all Maxx's handwriting in the file. Pictures of the bike, complete. Set up in the large bay window at the end of the shop. I glanced toward the window, now vacant, understanding why. There was a police report for the stolen bike. Another one for theft of cash and valuables. The suspects' names listed: Shannon West and Billy Rines. From the little I had gleaned from Mary—Maxx's girlfriend and best friend.

They had stolen from him, taken off together, and left him broken.

I picked up the picture of the bike. It was spectacular, the fluid lines clean and sharp, the color an intense red with lots of brilliant, gleaming chrome. Beautiful airbrushing along the unusual fenders. The only things missing, the front figurehead and the emblem.

Maxx must not have attached the emblem before it was stolen. He hadn't yet located the figurehead. Otherwise, the bike was perfect.

It was worth a lot of money, but I had a feeling it was the sentimental value of the bike that made losing it so hard for Maxx. Add in the betrayal he felt, no wonder he had trust issues.

I recalled Mary telling me that Maxx and I had a lot in common. She was right, although Maxx had suffered far more loss than I had. He was left with deeper scars.

I tapped the file, finding a thicker, safer accordion case to keep it in, and put it back in the file cabinet. Maxx must have forgotten it was there when he told me about the petty cash hidden at the back of the cabinet.

I had to tell him I knew and let the chips fall where they may. He hated lies, so better I tell him than for him to find out and think I was hiding it from him.

"Child, what is making you look so pensive?"

I glanced up, startled. I hadn't heard Mary come in. Her arms were full, and I hurried over to take some of the piles of pictures from her arms.

We stacked them on the table in the garage, then headed back to the office. I handed her the file. "I found this."

She flipped through it. "Ah."

"So, that's the story," I surmised. "Why Maxx is so distrustful."

She exhaled hard. "That's the gist of it. He needs to tell you the rest."

"If he's willing. I'm not sure he wants to share."

She tapped my nose. "You have no idea, do you?"

"About?"

"Maxx has called me several times. Hypothetically to check on the garage, but his questions were mostly about you. He cares more than he's willing to admit." She shook her head. "He's been away before—I don't remember getting more than a quick call once or twice while he was away."

"Do you think he can trust again? I mean, trust me—enough to tell me and let me in?"

"I hope so. You're good for him." She looked around the garage. "You're good to him. He will not be expecting this when he gets home."

"I hope he isn't mad." I indicated the wall. "I worry he'll think I took this too far."

"Give him some time. If he truly hates it after a few days, we can paint over it and take the pictures down, but I think you'll be surprised."

"I am not sure he'll be happy with the money I've spent." I

grimaced with worry. I had used all the petty cash and my own two hundred, but the difference was incredible. Mary had given me her credit card so I could purchase the domain name and rebuild the website, so Maxx owed her for that. His reaction to that information worried me more than his reaction to the changes. I liked Maxx growly and annoyed. Not angry.

"Nonsense. It's business. Maxx understands that." Mary tilted her head. "Has he given you the impression he is in the poorhouse?"

"No. I see the balance in the business accounts. I get the feeling he is a bit of a, um…" I trailed off.

"A tight ass?" Mary finished. "He is, but he knows a good investment, and I believe what you have done is exactly that. Now, let's finish it. He comes home in a couple of days."

Those words made me smile. I was looking forward to having him back—I hoped the time away helped clear his head some.

I glanced at the garage.

I hope what waited for him pleased him.

Maxx had an early morning flight, and with the time difference, his plane should land about two. With customs and driving home, I expected him around dinner. I made him his favorite chicken and rice casserole, planning on slipping it into the oven around five. Brett was booked solid all day, and I was busy between the last-minute additions to the waiting room and the final piece for the wall. Once it was hung up, I stood back and looked at it, wondering on a scale of one to ten, how much Maxx would hate it. I only had it dry-mounted, so it wasn't expensive. If he was furious, I could get rid of it easily. But I hoped he would like it.

Brett looked at it, threw back his head in laughter, and patted me on the shoulder.

"That is brilliant."

"Will he hate it?"

"Probably. But it's eye-catching and I like it. He'll get used to it. You know Maxx, it takes him a while to warm up to things."

Even with the garage busy, I couldn't settle. I flitted from job to job, finding it hard to concentrate. Finally, I left the garage and went to make Maxx a pie. I told myself I was simply anxious about Maxx's reaction. The truth was, I had missed him terribly. All sides of him. His growls and glowers. The glares he threw my way when I annoyed him. Our verbal sparring.

His honest, quiet thanks for the meals I made him. The caring way he was with Rufus. The respect with which he treated his customers.

The odd moment when he would look at me with tenderness. His gentle teasing. The rare treat of being close enough to smell him. The subtle fragrance of his cologne and just him. The heat that bubbled in the air between us at times. Hot and aching—the way he left me feeling a great deal of the time. Even if he had no intention of doing so.

I liked all sides of Maxx.

With a sigh, I finished beating the meringue and piled it on the lemon, still steaming from the pot. I fluffed the egg mixture with the fork for peaks, then slid it back into the oven to brown. I washed up the dishes and took the pie from the oven, sliding it onto the counter to cool. It looked beautiful.

His favorite meal and dessert. That alone should tell him I missed him.

I only hoped it was enough to soothe any anger he had over the changes.

Brett finished about five and left to head home. He assured me he would be back in the morning to talk to Maxx. He was hoping Maxx would take him on for a while in the garage, and maybe allow him to stay in the room out back. He was a quiet guy and enjoyed the privacy. He usually ate his meals on his own at night, the way I did, and went for a long run every evening. He had confessed to not wanting to go back to his father's place simply because his dad expected him to work in the small store, and he really didn't like it.

I wasn't sure how that would work since I assumed Maxx would be sending me back to the room in the garage, but I wished him much luck with his talk. Brett would be a good addition to the garage and help free up some of Maxx's time. His email had exploded since the weekend with inquiries about hiring him to restore motorcycles. He was so talented, I hoped he would focus on that endeavor.

I paced around the garage, finally heading over to the house about six. I had thought Maxx would be home by now but decided his plane must have been late. I slipped the casserole into the oven, fussed in the living room, then began to regret everything I had done.

He was going to hate it. I just knew it. I had crossed the line, but once I'd started opening boxes in the garage, I couldn't stop myself. Maxx's house was so sterile and plain. What I discovered in the boxes was all him. His past. His life. He should have it around him.

I fidgeted with the edge of a small throw blanket, worrying the fringe when a throat clearing from behind startled me. I jumped, spinning on my heel.

Maxx stood in the door, Rufus pressed against his leg, happy to have his master back. I had been so deep in my thoughts, I hadn't heard him arrive. Maxx's expression was inscrutable as he stared at the room, taking in the changes.

Finally, he spoke.

"What have you done?"

MAXX

The garage overhead door was shut as I pulled into the driveway, so I assumed Brett must have been done for the day. I knew he had worked extra to keep up while I was gone. Rufus nosed open the screen door of the mudroom and rushed out to greet me, his tail wagging as he weaved around my legs, happy and excited. I patted his haunches and stroked along his back, as pleased to see him as he was to see me.

I straightened, eyeing the house. There was somebody else I was anxious to see. I had expected Charly to greet me as soon as I arrived, waiting and apprehensive. My gaze skittered toward the garage. Had she moved her things back into her room, so she hadn't heard me approach? I hoped not. I planned on talking to her about that situation.

I planned on discussing a lot of things with her.

I headed for the house, opening the door and stopping in the kitchen, inhaling. She had dinner for me, and it smelled incredible. Sitting on the counter was a lemon pie, the top browned and glistening. My mouth watered just thinking about tasting it. I moved farther into the house, noting how spotless everything was.

I caught sight of Charly in the living room, and I strode toward her, stopping in shock before I walked into the room.

For a moment, it felt as if I had gone back in time, the room looked so familiar.

Except better.

I made a strange noise low in my throat, and Charly looked

up, startled. Our eyes locked across the room, her nervous green meeting my confused brown.

"What have you done?" I managed to rasp.

Her movements were a blur. She rushed toward me, her hands flapping, talking the entire time. "Holy moly, Maxx. I didn't hear you. Way to give a girl a heart attack. Don't be mad. Well, be mad if you want, but don't stay mad. I can change it all back. Easy peasy."

She reached me, her hands still fluttering. She touched my shoulder, arm, tapped my chest, then clasped her hands across her breasts. "You're mad. Oh god, you're so mad, you can't even speak." She cupped her cheeks, staring at me in horror. "Are you gonna throw me out?"

I blinked, feeling disoriented. How could anyone talk so fast and flitter around like a mad magpie? And how did her touching me make me feel so completely relaxed?

I reached out and pulled her hands from her face. "I am not throwing you out."

"Oh, thank god."

Then she launched herself at me. I stumbled back a step or two, then steadied myself and gripped her hard.

"Don't be mad," she repeated. "Please don't be mad."

I looked around the room, still in shock. Gone were the bare, white walls. The room had been painted in a deep charcoal—the same color it had been before Shannon moved in. The only white now was on the chair rail and the trim. The pictures I'd had on the walls were back, my favorite chair in the corner. There were new pieces, small items that belonged to my parents scattered in places. Some bright cushions on the sofa. A warm rug I recalled being in one of the bedrooms upstairs covered the hardwood floors. Curtains hung at the windows. The room was warm and homey.

Still holding Charly, I walked forward to the center of the

room, turning my head to her ear. "Tell me how," I demanded. "How did you do this?"

I set her on her feet. She looked up at me, her hands on her hips.

"You told me I could look in the barn for things. I found the paint and boxes marked living room. I looked inside, and Mary told me it was stuff you used to have in here. She recalled helping you pick the paint color." Charly waved her hands. "This room wasn't you, Maxx. Everything in the boxes I found was—plus a few items Mary told me belonged to your parents. I thought you'd like them out where you could see them."

She lifted her chin higher, as if bracing for a fight. "You hired me to make your house comfortable. So, that's what I did."

I looked around again. She was right. The room was comfortable, and it was me. Shannon had hated everything about it, preferring modern and minimalistic. She'd packed everything up one weekend while I was away and painted the walls a sterile white. I hadn't liked it much, but it seemed to make her happy, so I decided not to argue. It was better than listening to her talk about how much she hated the old house. She wanted a sleek, modern place, and I had no desire to live in one. Nor did I want to spend the kind of money she wanted on having a new house built.

It should have been an early warning sign, but as with everything else wrong between us, I had chosen to ignore it.

And now it had happened again. The room had been changed—except this time, it had been done to please me. To make me happy.

It was an odd feeling.

I looked down at Charly, her expression tugging at something inside me. Her chin was jutted out, proud and strong, her stance rigid, but her eyes were filled with worry and trepidation, giving away her inner turmoil.

"You did good," I murmured. "It's exactly right."

Her shoulders sagged in relief. "Yeah?"

"Yeah." I hesitated, then tapped her nose playfully. "Thank you."

She sighed, appraising me nervously. "Okay. One down."

I frowned. "One? What the hell else have you done?"

"Don't start with the growling, Maxx Reynolds."

"Then answer me, woman. What else have you changed in the house?"

"Nothing," she replied, her gaze skittering over my shoulder then back to my face.

I turned and peered out the window in the direction she had focused on.

"What have you done to the garage?" I snapped, thinking of the last surprise that had awaited me in the garage. It hadn't been the least bit pleasant. Without waiting for an answer, I spun on my heel and stalked outside, heading for the building. Charly followed, grabbing at my arm. I shook her off, glaring at her when she rushed in front of me, blocking the door.

"You have to keep an open mind, Maxx. Promise."

I was particular with the garage. I had it set up exactly the way I liked it, and the thought of her messing with that made me angry.

"Out of the way, Charly." I scowled.

"Please," she begged. "We all worked on it so hard."

"We?" I asked, confused.

"Me, Brett, Mary, and a couple of your customers."

My customers?

I huffed out a long breath, knowing if Mary was involved, she would never allow anyone to do something to the garage I would hate.

At least, I didn't think she would.

"Just open the damn door, Charly."

She twisted the handle and stepped in, never turning her back to me. She flicked on the light and stood back, letting me follow her.

At first glance, everything seemed to be normal. The bays in order, the tools in the right spots. Then I saw it. The walls had all been painted a fresh coat of beige. The long wall by the office was a deep, rich red. It was covered with pictures. I walked closer, narrowing my eyes as I took them in. The entire history of the garage was on that wall. Pictures of my dad working in the shop, repairing lawnmowers, bikes, and cars. Me beside him, growing up over time. All three of us standing by the sign at the end of the driveway, my dad's arm thrown over my mom's shoulder. Images of my mom in the office. There were photos of the various bikes I had restored, ones I'd worked on with my dad.

It was a wall of memories.

The next thing that caught my eye was the old sign that used to hang at the end of the driveway. It had been cleaned up and hung in one corner, a tribute to the old days. In the opposite corner was a later sign, still outdated, but part of the history of the place.

It was the center sign that made me frown. I moved forward, studying it.

The old signage had been a tire and the name. Reynolds Restorations. Simple.

This one was bold. Black. The image of a muscled arm gripping a wrench in the middle.

Reynolds Restorations and Repairs
Hard as Steel.
Performance Guaranteed.

Hard as steel?
I turned my head. "What the hell?"

"A new look."

Before I could reply, she held up her hands. "Open mind, Maxx. We can discuss it later once you hear all my ideas."

I exhaled hard. "Fine."

Charly flicked on the light in the unused waiting room, and I went inside. The old metal and vinyl seats had been recovered and polished. The walls painted. There were more pictures. Old tools that were no longer usable, but my dad had never tossed out, had been shined and hung intermittently. Some of the old license plates my dad collected were hung between them. There was a water cooler in the corner.

I shook my head, unable to take it all in. I returned to the garage, looking closer at everything. The pictures. Discarded items that Charly had made important again and hung as a tribute to the past all around the garage, but in places where they were out of the way so as not to interfere with the purpose of the building. One of the old garage shirts, a set of coveralls. More tools and a few spare parts. It made the garage eclectic and…fun. It gave it a look and feel that was somehow what I had been looking for and unable to find.

And it had been done by a slip of a girl. A sassy, mouthy redhead I loved to give a hard time. Who somehow reached into my mind and figured out what I would like and made sure it happened.

I prowled around, exploring, seeing it all with new eyes. Finally, I stopped in front of Charly. She was anxious, paler than I had ever seen her, the freckles on her skin standing out in sharp contrast to the white of her skin. Her hands were clenched in fists by her sides. I had never known her to be so silent for so long. I could tell how much this meant to her, how desperately she wanted my approval.

I searched her eyes, the anxiety evident. The need to erase

the worry tore through me, rendering me silent for a moment. It wasn't a feeling I was used to.

Our gazes were locked, a battle of wills happening between us. She expected me to argue, yell, or tell her I disliked it. Demand she take it down. If I did that, she would yell back and call me ungrateful and a grump, then storm away, mad and hurt.

Except, that wasn't what was going to happen.

"We're talking about that new logo."

"Okay."

I drew in a long breath. "Good job, Red."

Her eyes widened, and before she could react, I hauled her against my chest, and I kissed her.

CHAPTER 17

MAXX

E verything I had pushed out of my mind when it came to kissing Red came roaring back to life once my mouth was on hers again. She was life. Air. Passion. I lifted her, amazed at how well we fit together. She wrapped her arms around my neck, twisting the ends of my hair between her fingers, whimpering as my tongue stroked along hers. She was so right in my arms.

And completely wrong.

With a low groan, I released her, setting her on her feet. Slowly her arms slipped from my neck, and she opened her eyes, meeting mine.

"You *kissed* me."

"I did."

"I don't recall asking you—"

I cut her off with my mouth again. I loved it when she was spitting fire at me, all indignant and pissed off.

She bit my bottom lip, yelping as I smacked her ass then lifted her back into my arms. She wrapped her legs around me, and I palmed her ass. She had a great ass, fitting into my hands perfectly.

I stumbled in the direction of the waiting room, sitting down heavily on one of the newly refurbished benches. Red straddled my lap, sliding her hands into my hair, grinding down on my aching cock. I slipped my hand under the loose shirt she was wearing, tracing along her spine, my thumbs stroking the edges of her full breasts. She gasped into my mouth when I dipped under the lace and my fingers found and stroked her nipples. She pulled back, her breathing erratic.

"What are you doing?"

"Do I really need to explain this to you, Red?"

She narrowed her eyes. "You keep calling me Red. You only call me that when you're about to, you know…"

I lifted one eyebrow. "You know?" I repeated.

Her voice dropped. "When you're about to fuck me."

Charly rarely ever swore. Hearing her say the word *fuck* did something to me. I grinned at her.

"Keep grinding on me like that, and there's no doubt one of us is going to be fucked."

She jumped up, slamming her hands on her hips. "If you think you're going to defile me in this clean waiting room, Maxx Reynolds, you have another think coming, mister. Gosh dang it, I worked hard to get this room ready, and you wanna lube up your dipstick and mess it all up?"

I gaped at her tirade, trying to quell the quirking of my lips at her vehemence.

Defile her? Had we returned to historical times?

"I mean, it's a great dipstick and all, but have a little respect." She turned and flounced out of the room, strutting across the garage. I swear to god she was sashaying those hips of hers far more than necessary.

It didn't help my erect…dipstick.

Then the humor of the entire situation hit me, and I began to laugh. Huge guffaws of mirth burst from my mouth. I dropped my head back against the vinyl seat and let it out. The stress of the last few days, the amazement at what she had done while I was away. The instant passion I felt whenever she was close.

How it felt to see her standing in my house, looking as if she should be there. Greeting me every day when I walked in the door. The shift in my chest when I saw what she had accomplished in the garage. Her quiet desperation she couldn't hide from me, hoping I would like it.

And how fucking right she felt in my arms. Under my mouth.

I had been right. Red hadn't straightened my world. She had blown it to smithereens.

The question was—did I want to try to fix it?

When I finally stopped laughing, I walked around the garage again, noticing more details. The wipe-off boards, the price list on the wall. I tried not to smirk when I noticed that although the services were neatly written out, the prices had not yet been added. Red was waiting for me to tell her what I wanted those to be. I ran a hand through my hair, trying to take it all in.

How the hell had she done all this in less than a week? Plus the changes to the house? Another thought occurred to me. How the hell had she paid for all this? Even if she used all two hundred bucks in the petty cash, that wouldn't even cover paint.

I grunted in frustration. I hated owing money. I hated not knowing how much money I owed. I locked up the garage and headed toward the house. I needed to find out.

Red was in the kitchen, leaning against the counter, eating her dinner. When I walked in, she met my eyes, then dropped her gaze.

"I'll eat and get out of your way," she mumbled. "You must be tired."

I stepped in front of her, halting her movements, her fork hanging midair. I braced my arms on the counter, boxing her in. "You aren't going anywhere until we've talked. Go sit at the table and I'll bring my dinner and join you."

"You-you want to eat with me?"

With a wink, I grabbed her fork and guided it to my lips, the chicken and rice casserole flavor exploding in my mouth. I chewed and swallowed. "Damn, I like this one."

"You can have your own, Maxx. You don't have to eat my dinner."

"I wonder if it will taste as good," I mused, smiling when I saw how flustered she was becoming. She blinked and looked around as if she were making sure I was talking to her and not someone else in the room.

I pushed off the counter. "Sit. I'll get some of my own, and we can eat. Then we're going to talk. You better have the right answers, Red."

"I always have the right answers. Depends if your grumpy ass listens to them."

I swatted her butt as she went by, amused at her yelp. "Show some respect," I repeated her words from earlier. "My grumpy ass always listens."

"Whatever," she muttered. "You listen with one ear blocked, and the other is already deaf."

I chuckled as I scooped a massive amount of the casserole onto my plate and grabbed some cutlery. I sat beside her, and we ate in silence for a few moments. She got up and came back with glasses of ice water, setting one down in front of me, then taking her seat again and continuing to eat.

She was a slow eater, small mouthfuls, chewing thoroughly between bites. She patted her lips often with her napkin and took long drinks of her water. Compared to the way I dove into my meal, devouring it and refilling my plate, she was refined. Delicate.

That word almost made me snort. Delicate wasn't a word I would associate with Red. Ballbuster, maybe.

I must have made a noise, because she looked up from her plate. "What?"

I shook my head around a mouthful, chewing and swallowing. "Nothing."

She frowned.

"You're a slow eater." I pointed out.

"I was always so busy making the meals and doing the dishes after, eating was my chance to relax a little," she admitted. "I savored my dinner, even if it was simple."

"Nothing wrong with simple. This is delicious."

"Thanks." She pushed her plate away. "Did you want pie?"

"Later." I finished my dinner and took both the plates to the kitchen, returning to the table. I rested my elbows on the table and studied her. She looked tired.

"Aside from changing the garage and my house, anything else happen while I was gone?"

She pursed her lips. "Oh—Terry pled guilty. He's in jail and will be there a long time. I won't need to go give a formal statement or anything."

"Good. That's good."

She shrugged. "That's about it, really."

Silence hung in the air, and I smirked.

"How did you do it all, Charly?"

She crossed her arms, leaning them on the table. "Now I'm Charly again."

I shrugged. "You're both. But right now, yes, you're Charly. I want to know how you did all you did in less than a week and with two hundred bucks."

"Well, the living room cost nothing but a paint tray and a

gallon of white trim paint. That was fifty bucks. Mary had the material, and we made the curtains."

"And the garage?"

She fidgeted a little in her seat, then snagged a file off the chair beside her. "I paid cash for the paint. I traded Brett some extra food to help me paint after hours."

"Extra food?"

"He likes breakfast and cookies."

I liked cookies too, but I refrained from mentioning that.

"Brett knew a guy who did dry mounting," she continued. "I traded him a tune-up and some oil changes on his motorcycle and his wife's car for all the pictures. He helped me hang them for free because he thought it was a cool idea." She slid some papers my way, and I scanned them. It was a basic agreement of what she had stated.

"Mary had a friend who knew how to reupholster stuff. I paid for the supplies and traded some more oil changes and a tune-up on her car for the work." She slid another paper my way. "The water cooler I got at a garage sale for less than ten bucks, and I cleaned it up. I bought the jug and the cups, which cost another twenty. I bought a couple of containers of CLR to clean up the tools. Brett's dad gave me a discount."

More receipts slid my way.

"Most of what was done was labor, and that was free. Brett and Mary helped. Cam dropped by to see how things were going, and he helped move things in from the barn. He called another friend of yours—Jack—and he came and helped too."

I was silent for a moment, amazed at what she had done and how she had accomplished it. Mentally, I added up the money spent and scrutinized her. "This is more than two hundred, Charly."

"I used the money you gave me too, and Mary loaned me the

rest. I owe her $147.53." She twisted her hands. "I went over budget—sorry."

I stared at her. Over budget. She had spent less than six hundred bucks, and my garage was epic. My house felt like me again. Charly had no idea.

"*I* owe her. And you." I drummed my fingers on the table. "That money I gave you was for you—to buy things *you* need."

"There was nothing I needed. This was far more important."

Her words reverberated in my head. *Nothing she needed. More important.*

Once again, Shannon came to mind. She constantly needed. Wanted. Always asking for money, complaining about her lack of…everything, it seemed.

"You'll have your money in the morning. And your paycheck."

"I'm not worried. I trust you."

The words were out before I could think. "I trust you as well."

Her eyes grew round. "What was that? I didn't hear you."

"I am not repeating that. You heard me." I scowled.

"Oh, there he goes, all grumpy bear-man again."

"You seem to bring it out in me more than other people."

"It's okay, I like it—most of the time."

"Most of the time?"

"I like your growls and when you're kinda grouchy." She tilted her head. "It's rather hot. I don't like it when you're angry."

"So growly Maxx, not angry Maxx. I'll try to remember that."

She slid one last piece of paper my way. "I had to register the domain name and pay for the website I'm building. That required a credit card, which I don't have. Mary let me use hers, so you owe her for that."

I scanned the document. "I'll pay her this right away."

Silence fell as I looked over everything, then slid it all back into the file Charly had on the table. She was very organized and detailed. I appreciated it more than she could understand. Then I gazed at her.

I couldn't take my eyes off her. Sitting at my table, her legs pulled up to her chest, she looked as if she belonged there. She watched me watch her, the air around us beginning to heat the way it always did when we were close.

"You should hire Brett," she blurted, instantly breaking the mood that was descending between us.

"Why?"

"The customers like him, he does great work, and he likes it here. He even likes his little room. He says it gives him a break from people. I think he means his dad." She rubbed the end of her nose, scrunching it. "I think his dad treats him like he's still sixteen when he's there."

"Yeah, I remember Brett saying that before."

"Your email box is filled with inquiries about taking on motorcycle restorations," she said.

"I know. I saw a bunch before I left the hotel." I smiled at her. "That iPad of yours came in very handy for the presentations and keeping up with email. Thanks."

"We should get you one. I could find a used one for you. Great to take pictures I can access easily."

I nodded in agreement. "Sure—do that."

Her eyes lit up. "Okay, I will."

I sat back, regarding her. "I'll talk to Brett. With the interest about hiring me for bike restorations from the conference, plus the fact that they asked if I would do another event with them, you're right. I'm going to need help. If he's willing to stay on for a while, with me supervising when needed, I can concentrate on that aspect of the business."

Her eyes grew round. "They did? Maxx, that is amazing!"

"I was surprised," I admitted. "But pleased."

"So, the conference was great?"

"Many aspects, yes. I enjoyed giving my talks, I met some great connections, and I bought some things for the shop that are being shipped."

"What aspects weren't so great?"

I hesitated. "It was hot and crowded. Made me miss home. There were a few people I didn't enjoy meeting as much as others. I'm going to leave it at that."

"Told you the biker chicks would be after you."

"Charly," I growled in warning. "Leave it."

As usual, she ignored my warnings. "You don't like being chased. You're too alpha."

"Alpha? What the hell does that mean?"

"You like to be in control."

I had no response. She wasn't wrong about that.

"Were they pushy?" she asked.

"Like you, you mean?"

She huffed. "I'm not pushy, I'm interested. I worry about your poor morals being compromised."

I burst out laughing. "Compromised?"

"Whatever. I bet you beat them off with a stick."

"My dipstick, you mean?"

She stood with her own growl, stomping to the counter. I watched her, kind of enjoying her reaction. She was acting almost—jealous?

She opened the cupboard, grabbing a plate. "I'll give you your pie and go get my things."

Like an invisible thread drawing me to her, I followed, once again trapping her against the counter. "No."

She looked over her shoulder, peering up at me. "No?"

I spun her, caging her in. "You stay in your room—in the house—from now on."

She looked uncertain.

"I'm going to ask Brett to stay on. You said he liked the room. He can stay there. You stay upstairs."

"Is that a good idea?"

I sighed and tucked a strand of hair behind her ear. "You're safer there." I really couldn't believe I had made her stay in that room behind the garage. I should have given her a room in the house right away, regardless of the pull I felt toward her.

"We're adults." I pointed out.

"Sort of my point, Professor. We get to do whatever we want to do. Sort of like your time in LA."

I touched her chin, running my finger back and forth along the soft skin. "I had nothing to do with any woman while I was there, Red. Nothing."

"You didn't?"

I wanted to tell her I had no interest as long as she was around. She was the only woman I could see. But I held back those words, knowing how she would interpret them.

"No. I did my job, I talked to a lot of people, and I came home." Two more words slipped from my mouth without thinking. "To you."

"Maxx," she whispered.

I hung my head, then met her gaze. "I know there's...*something* between us, Charly. But I think it's different for each of us."

"How so?"

"You're looking for your life. Your place. I'm not it. This is just a stop on your road. This place is my life. I'm happy here. Alone," I added before she could say anything. "You want a relationship."

"What do you want?"

I shrugged. "Not what you deserve."

"So, sex without attachments? No feelings?"

I couldn't lie to her. Not anymore. "I do feel things. I think you're amazing. Sexy. Funny. But I am not looking for that to be a permanent thing."

"What if I'm not either?"

I cocked my head. "Are you sure of that?"

She jutted out her chin. "Yes. Maybe I just want you for sex too."

I tapped her stubborn little chin. "Little fibber."

She glared. "How do you know that?"

"You have a major tell when you attempt to lie. And I mean attempt because you're horrible at it. It's easy to tell when you try."

"How?" she demanded.

I ran my finger over her cheek. "When you get upset, you go pale. Really pale. These little dots are like a Morse code on your skin, screaming your feelings."

"What does that have to do with lying?"

"It upsets you to lie. I've watched you try—even to a customer. You simply can't do it. You went as white as a ghost when you said you just want sex."

"Well, fudge."

"I'll sleep with you anytime you want, Red. Say the word. Arch that sexy eyebrow my way, and I'm yours. But it's only for now. I can't make that any plainer."

She chewed her lip, her silence saying it all.

"Go to bed, Charly. You must be exhausted with everything you've done. In fact, take tomorrow off. Sleep in, go into town shopping, see Mary. Take the day and enjoy it."

"But I wanted to show you the website and the logo and everything."

"Tomorrow night after supper. And no more eating on your own. If Brett's around, he can eat with us too. If not, you and me."

"Really?"

"Yeah, it's nice to have someone to talk to while I eat."

"Okay, we'll see how it goes."

"How it goes?" I repeated.

"You'll probably get tired of me prattling on and decide you want to eat alone again."

"I doubt it, but we'll see what happens. Now, go. I'll leave your paycheck on the desk. Grab it before you go."

"All right. Um, I've been using the claw-foot tub at night."

"Not a problem."

She ducked under my arm, making me realize I had been touching her face throughout our whole conversation. She paused at the foot of the steps. "Night, Maxx."

"Night…Charly."

I wasn't surprised she'd backed away after my honesty. No matter what she said, she wasn't a love them and leave them girl. She felt deeply. Cared too much.

And I had already accepted far too much from her to let her think a physical relationship would change anything. We'd both wind up hurt.

Still, watching her disappear up the stairs was one of the hardest things I had ever done.

CHAPTER 18

MAXX

It felt awesome to be in my own bed, but I didn't sleep as well as I thought I would. I tossed and turned a great deal in the night, finally giving up and heading to the garage around five. I wrote out some checks, including one to top up the petty cash. I would ask Charly to stop by the bank while she was in town. I also wrote out one for groceries because Charly mentioned she was planning on shopping today since she'd been too busy while I was gone. She could just give me the receipts—she had proven herself more than trustworthy on so many levels.

I glanced around the small office. Somehow, she had managed to spruce it up as well. I hadn't even looked in here yesterday. She'd painted the room, shifted the desk and file cabinets, and added a few items on the walls. I tried not to grin when I realized the pictures in here were taken more recently and were mostly of me with a motorcycle. She was surrounding herself with me.

And I liked it more than I should.

I was going through the emails, listing the assorted requests, and wondering if Charly could somehow figure out a way of sorting and detailing the various offers, when Brett walked in. It was just after seven, but I somehow wasn't shocked he would arrive early.

He poured a cup of coffee, took a sip, and grimaced. "Obviously, Charly didn't make this."

"I gave her the day off, so you're stuck with my tar."

He sat down. "She deserves the day."

I looked around. "I have no idea how she did all this in such a short time."

"She worked nonstop," Brett stated. "Sweet-talked everyone she could into helping. Handed out oil changes and tune-ups like candy. Bartered like a pro." He chuckled. "Watching her delve into boxes and come up with the most obscure items and get so excited about using them—" he shook his head in amusement "—she was a little force unto herself. You're lucky to have her."

"She's a great asset to the garage," I admitted. "An amazing assistant."

He snorted and drained his mug. "I think she's more than that, judging from the phone conversation I had to endure."

Laughing, I explained the call. He joined in my amusement, but after the laughter died, he studied me. "She's astonishing, Maxx. Don't write her off so lightly."

"I'm not in the market for what she needs."

"That's a shame." He stood and poured another cup of coffee. "I think you're what *she* needs."

Before I could question his statement, he changed the subject.

"So, about me staying on."

"Right." I laid out my thoughts, and we discussed the future. I was surprised when he informed me he didn't know if he wanted to return to the garage he'd been working at in Toronto.

"I will only ever be a mechanic there. There are no rewards, no place to go, nothing to aim for, except maybe manager. I do my job and go home." He scrubbed his face. "There's no pride in my work, if that makes any sense."

"Totally does to me," I agreed. "Where do you see yourself in a few years, Brett? Surely not sleeping in the back of a garage working for me?"

"No, I'd like a place of my own, eventually." He rubbed the back of his neck. "I'll be honest, Maxx. My apartment in Toronto wasn't much bigger than the room back there, and not as comfortable either. Plus, it didn't include Charly's meals. Right now, that suits me. As for working, I need to prove myself and earn your trust. Maybe one day I can be more than a hired hand. But I have to start somewhere, and I like it here." Amusement filled his eyes. "With everything Charly has planned, plus what I hear about the offers you have, you're going to need help."

I had no idea what Charly's plans entailed, but I knew I needed help. And I liked Brett—he had always been a decent guy.

We talked salary and hours, then shook hands. He stood and stretched. "Another guy I worked with in Toronto is looking. Name is Stefano. Amazing with carburetors. A touch like I've never seen. And his passion is airbrushing. Might come in handy with your expanded area."

I mulled over his words.

"He's coming to see me next week. Wouldn't hurt to at least meet him?"

"I suppose not."

"Great. I'm gonna get my stuff, throw it in my room, and get started." He winked. "I have a couple of tune-ups coming in today, courtesy of the whirlwind named Charly."

I had to agree. Whirlwind described her well.

She appeared around nine, dressed in a pair of jeans that clung to her ass in the most appealing way possible and a frilly blouse. I noticed when not in the garage, she liked girly clothes. Frilly things, with lace. Never much for such things, I did think they suited her.

I followed her into the office, staring openly at her ass until she turned and faced me. I kept my facial expression neutral.

"Quit ogling my ass, Maxx."

"I'm not."

She rolled her eyes and fluttered her fingers in the air. "Duh, windows all around. I watched you."

Busted.

I bent low, meeting her eyes. "It's a rather spectacular ass, Charly. It needs to be ogled."

She huffed out an exaggerated puff of air, and I grinned at her little display of annoyance. I picked up the checks and handed them to her.

"Your paycheck, what I owe Mary, money for groceries, and if you're at the bank, the petty cash replacement."

"Okay." Then she paused. "Maxx, my check is too much."

"Nope. Consider it a bonus for all you've done. Go shopping, buy yourself something." I flicked the lace on the sleeve of her blouse. "Maybe another frilly one of these." I leaned closer. "To replace the one I ripped."

Her cheeks flushed, and she slapped my hands away. "Stop it. I don't need a bonus."

I leaned against the desk. "Too bad. You're getting one."

"I didn't do this to get extra money," she protested.

"I know," I snarled. "I gave you the bonus because I wanted you to have it. Jesus, woman, why are you always so difficult?"

"Why are you always so grouchy?"

There was no thought. One second, she was talking; the next, my mouth was on hers, hard, heavy, and powerful. I kissed her until she softened under me, until my head was so full of her, I could barely break away.

I pressed my forehead to hers. "Because you make me grouchy, Red. You make me feel a lot of things I don't want to feel, and it pisses me off."

"Oh," she replied, her breathing fast.

"Now, take the check, put it in your account, and go shopping for god's sake before I throw you down right here and Brett gets one hell of a show."

She blinked at me, her eyes still unfocused. She reached for the checks and stuffed them in her purse.

"Okay, boss. Good talk. Thanks. The bank. Yeah, okay. Easy peasy."

"Oh and, Charly?"

"What?"

"Order the computer and the software, as well as the iPad. Whatever one you want."

"Really?" she breathed.

"Yep. I can hardly wait to see what you do with it."

She was almost vibrating with excitement, which amused me. Then she turned and walked into the wall. She yelped, and I reached out to steady her. "Careful."

She shook off my hold. "No more touching, gosh dang it. Kissing, computers… You mess with my head, Maxx."

"You do the same," I murmured.

She rolled her eyes. "Whatever." She walked out, my gaze following her long after she disappeared.

She had no idea how much she messed with my head. Or what she did to my heart.

I wasn't sure which one was more dangerous.

CHARLY

I had coffee with Mary, enjoying the unexpected day off and the time to sit and do nothing for a change. I gave her the check, and she wasn't surprised when I handed it to her. "Maxx is just like his father. He hates to owe anyone. Thomas Reynolds hated credit," she explained. "Yet he never hesitated to extend it to someone who couldn't afford to pay their bill all at once."

"Maxx said something about hating to owe money."

"The apple doesn't fall far from the tree." She leaned forward. "What did he say?"

"I think he was so shocked, I haven't seen his entire reaction yet. But what he took in, he liked."

"The new logo?"

"We're going to discuss that tonight. He hired Brett today, so that is a good step."

"It is. For Maxx, it's huge."

I finished my coffee and carried the cup to the sink. "I'm going to Lomand to the bank and the store. Anything you need?"

"I'd appreciate some milk."

"Sure. I'll drop it off on my way back. Easy peasy."

I drove to town, listening to some music. I stopped at the bank, opened an account, then got the petty cash and grocery checks cashed and put the money back into the envelope the checks came from. I held the envelope in my hand, heading to my car, thinking over what I needed at the store when I ran into something, or as it happened, someone.

My purse fell to the ground, the envelope slipping from my hand and landing on the gravel. I fell on my ass, then scrambled quickly to my knees, looking up to see what, or whom, I had hit. I met the smarmy smirk of Wes Donner, and I had to resist rolling my eyes. The idiot simply didn't get it.

"Excuse me," I stated, gathering up the items that fell from my purse. He didn't move, watching me from above with a shit-eating grin on his face. I tugged at the envelope he had placed his foot on, holding it against the ground. Reining in my anger, I looked up. "Move your foot."

His grin got wider, making it all the uglier somehow.

"You look good on your knees in front of me."

I tugged on the envelope, trying not to show my revulsion. He slid his foot forward, trapping more of the packet under his sneaker.

"I bet you're good on your knees, aren't you?" he muttered. He peered down, focusing on the logo on the corner of the envelope. "Reynolds Restorations. Is that where you're hiding?"

I tugged on the paper, even though I knew it wasn't going to budge until he lifted his foot. And that wouldn't be until he decided he'd intimidated me enough. I glanced around the parking lot. It was empty except for my car and the few that belonged to employees. The lot was tucked at the back of the bank, so there was no one else around.

"I'm not hiding. I work there. And I'm expected back any minute, so unless you want Mr. Reynolds to rearrange your face, I suggest you lift your foot."

"Mr. Reynolds," he drawled. "Is that what you call him as he fucks you? How often does he have you on your knees? I bet he likes it like that."

His tone and his questions were so filled with hate that a long shiver went down my spine. He wasn't going to stop, and I knew I had to take matters into my own hands. Good thing I had practice.

I lifted my free hand and ran it up his leg, feeling his jolt of surprise as I touched him. "Is that what *you* like?" I asked. "Being called *mister*?" I moved my hand higher, fighting the revulsion I felt.

His face went lax as I slowly stood, letting my fingers drift higher. I inched closer, keeping my voice low. "You like girls on their knees in front of you, Wes?"

"Yes," he grunted.

"You know what I like?" I whispered.

His eyes drifted shut as I ran my fingers up his thighs. I was pretty sure he was getting hard, but I was also certain I understood part of his aggression now. He wasn't packing much heat. I only hoped my aim was good.

"What?"

I slowly rose to my feet. "I like bringing assholes down a peg or two."

His eyes flew open just as my knee met his groin. The exploding pain showed on his face, the shock in his gaze. He stumbled, falling to the ground, clutching his groin. I reached down and grabbed the envelope, hissing as his foot kicked out, catching me in the arm. I ignored the flash of pain and headed to my car as fast as I could.

"Have a good day," I called, gunning the engine and getting out of the parking lot in a hurry. He was still lying on the gravel as I checked my rearview mirror.

It was a job well done.

I did the shopping, feeling oddly jumpy, even though it was broad daylight and the store wasn't busy. After I was done, I drove to a little clothing store Mary had said had some nice things, and I bought a couple of blouses and a new skirt. The woman who ran it, Sarah, was very chatty and helpful. She was pleased to know Mary had sent me. There were lots of articles of clothing that caught my eye, but I didn't want to linger, and I told her I would come back with Mary another time. I used the groceries in the car as an excuse, but the truth was, I was feeling jittery after my run-in with Wes.

I stopped at Mary's, grateful she was out, and left the milk in her fridge, then drove to Maxx's. I felt better simply pulling up in front of the building, knowing Maxx was inside and close. I headed to the garage, walking through the wide doors, feeling relief. Brett was working on a car, and he waved as I walked through. Maxx was at the desk, writing something. He looked up as I strolled in, trying desperately to appear casual.

I slid the envelope on the desk. "Petty cash, the grocery receipt, and the change. You bought Mary some milk."

He grunted. "Holy shit, it's been crazy."

"Well, holy moly, why didn't you call? I would have come back."

He pushed off from the desk. "Because I gave you the day off. We managed." He picked up the envelope and brushed it off, looking at me quizzically.

"I dropped it. Sorry."

"Are you all right?" he asked.

"I'm fine."

He studied me, then let it go. "Brett filled up the propane tank. We're going to barbecue dinner, so you don't have to worry about it. I found some steaks in the freezer."

"Oh. That's a nice surprise. I'll make a salad, and I got some new potatoes we can have. Easy peasy."

"Great. Then you can tell me about this website thing."

"All right." I paused. "I need some help carrying the groceries in."

"Sure." He followed me to the car, lifting out the bags. "Peaches?" he asked as I grabbed the small basket.

"I was going to make cobbler."

"I love cobbler."

"Well then, it's your lucky day."

He followed me into the house, setting down the bags.

"Did you fall or something while you were out?"

My hand stilled as I opened one of the bags. "Sorry?"

"You have dust on your ass and down your leg."

"Oh, um, yeah, I tripped in the parking lot of the bank."

"Are you hurt?"

"Nope."

He eyed me speculatively. "All right. You get stuff prepped. Brett and I will handle the cooking."

I sniffed. "Will it be edible?"

I wanted to rile him up a little. Make him come closer. My comment did it. He stalked over to me, crowding me against the counter.

"I grill well, I'll have you know."

"You certainly grill me," I retorted.

"You have no idea how much I want to grill you." He scowled, trying not to laugh.

That was what I needed. His gruff words, his closeness, even for a moment. Without thinking, I looped my arms around his waist and hugged him. For a moment, he was stiff with shock, then he wrapped one arm around me, holding me close. His voice was quiet when he spoke, filled with a gentleness I wasn't used to hearing.

"Charly, what's wrong?"

I pulled back and ducked under his arm. "Nothing. I just needed a hug. Now get out so I can put away the groceries and enjoy the rest of my day off, gosh dang it." I wagged my finger at him. "Dinner better be good."

He was quiet, then nodded. "It will be. Your reasons for that new website better be good as well."

"Don't worry, Maxx. I won't disappoint."

He turned and left, muttering. I thought he said, "You never do," but I could have been mistaken. After all, that would be a compliment, and Maxx had reached his limit on those yesterday.

Surely, I couldn't expect them two days in a row.

I headed upstairs to change out of my dirty jeans, wash my face, and get ready to face him and his attitude after dinner.

MAXX

Something was up with Charly, but what, I didn't know. She seemed anxious. Maybe it was having to talk about the website and the new logo she had come up with. Except her unexpected hug made me think it was something else.

It was as if she was seeking shelter for a moment. It made me feel odd and somewhat angry. What had occurred that she needed to feel safe?

I watched her during dinner. She seemed fine, and I relaxed. Women were a strange lot, and I never thought I understood them. Perhaps she had been having a bad day and needed a hug. My dad used to hug my mom close if she was upset or having a difficult day. *"Come along, sweetheart. I got you,"* he would croon as he rocked her. *"Let the day go. Just let it go."*

My question was—what made Charly have a bad day? That question lingered in my head, making me restless and a little edgy. The fact that it bothered me at all made me even edgier.

Brett and I cleared the table, then Brett left to go pick up more of his stuff from his dad's place, leaving Charly and me alone. He clapped my shoulder before he left.

"She has some great ideas. Listen to her."

She set her laptop on the table and opened it. "Dinner was great. And not doing the dishes was a treat. Is that going to happen all the time?" she teased.

"Nope. Don't get used to it."

She sighed dramatically. "Fine."

She tapped some keys and showed me the new website. It was bright, bold, and clear. The new logo she had designed was featured on each page. She even had a history of the garage, and there were pages about the restoration side as well as the services offered.

"You have very few women clients," she informed me.

"We have a couple," I argued.

"You should have more. There is a huge untapped potential for business. I looked around in Lomand and Littleburn. Hundreds of women drive cars and trucks, even motorcycles, but where do they have them serviced?"

I scratched my beard. "No idea."

"We want them coming here." She pulled in a long inhale of air. "For most women, going to a garage is overwhelming. It's a language many of us don't understand. Our vehicle doesn't work right, but often a mechanic doesn't really listen since we don't speak 'car.'" She paused. "Even if we do, often we aren't listened to because of our gender."

"I don't treat my woman customers that way."

"Exactly. So, we need to get the word out that Reynolds Restorations and Repairs is different."

"How do you want to do that?" I crossed my arms over my chest. "And why did you add repairs?"

"I added 'repairs' so people know you do more than restorations. I will mention you're a full-service garage in all the ads and marketing. As for getting the word out—some basic classes. Teach women how to speak car. What the parts are. How they work." She held up her hand before I could speak. "If I get how something works, then I understand it better. I feel more comfortable asking questions. I'm not talking in-depth, do-your-own repairs, Maxx. Simple one-hour classes offered every month—free of charge. Brett says he's happy to do some."

"I don't want to have to corral a bunch of women in the garage. They'd all be talking and comparing lipsticks instead of listening," I groused, imagining the scene.

"You just love to chap my ass, don't you? I thought this through. We'll keep it limited—more exclusive. Before you know it, we'll have a waiting list."

I was silent, mulling over her words. It made sense. I had always wondered why I had so few women customers. Maybe Charly was onto something. She'd obviously given the idea a great deal of thought, but I wasn't ready to give in just yet. She would never expect me to capitulate so easily. I hadn't growled near enough yet to please her. And for some reason, I wanted to please her. On lots of levels.

She clicked to another page, and I studied it. "I thought we agreed I would set the prices," I said, my voice low and challenging.

"Holy moly, I just filled them in—they're suggestions." She sounded frustrated. "Maxx, I checked every garage within a ten-mile radius of you. I got Brett to get me the price lists in Toronto. Even if you raised your prices to what I have listed here, you're still one of the lowest around. And with my projections, your profits go up substantially—even with paying Brett." She slid a paper my way. "You can even afford to hire another body and concentrate on the restorations. Those profit projections are on the back."

I studied the page, then turned it over and whistled. "Are you sure these are accurate?"

"If we bring in more customers and produce a higher output, yes."

I scrubbed my face. "You're asking for a lot here, Charly."

"What do you have to lose, Maxx? If I'm wrong, you let

Brett and his friend go. You fire me, and you go back to business as usual. Easy peasy. If I'm right, you get to free up your time and do what you love and have the garage too. We're already seeing an increase in business with Brett here. He let some of his customers who lived this side of Toronto know where he was working, and they came here. Others will too. The same with his friend. Add in the new advertising I'm planning, the outreach to the women of the community, and I see a real upswing."

I grunted, letting her know I was thinking. Part of me was so damn proud of her, I wanted to kiss her. She was brilliant, and she had no idea. When I placed that ad, I had no clue. I had hoped for someone to upgrade the website a little. Tidy the office. Cook a few meals. Maybe help sort out that part of my life so I could sort out the mess in my head.

She had stepped in and, with her mouthy, quirky attitude, became more than I dared to wish for. She had become some-thing vitally important to me. She was more than I hoped for—and way better than I deserved.

She was simply Charly. And that, I realized, was something incredibly special.

Even if she drove me mental most of the time.

I was quiet too long, and she started rambling in that nervous way of hers.

"We can adjust the pricing. It was only a suggestion."

I grunted.

"Brett could handle the women's classes. They'd love him. Easy on the eyes, funny, and sweet. He'd bring them in in droves. Tall, good-looking, and that curly blond hair and his blue eyes? They'll love it."

I glared at her. *She thought he was easy on the eyes? And when did she decide she liked blond hair and blue eyes?*

A small rumble emitted from my mouth.

"With any luck, his friend will look good in the coveralls I plan on them wearing. We women love a man in a uniform."

"Coveralls are not uniforms." I scowled.

"Oh, but they are." She warmed to the subject. "A hot, sexy, somewhat greasy mechanic in a pair of coveralls talking about tightening your fan belt? Or your overheating chassis? Total turn-on. We'll pack them in."

"What if I taught the courses, Charly?" I asked through gritted teeth. "How would they do then?"

She fanned herself. "All growly and rough? Telling them to make sure to change their oil regularly and rotate their tires for optimal performance? We'd be booked solid, and they'd all request the grouchy bear-man."

I cursed under my breath, shifting in my chair, feeling my erection kick up. I was going to show her an optimal performance, all right.

"So," she began. "Next. The new logo is fun. Eye-catching. Maybe a little sexy," she stated. "You know—to attract new customers."

"Performance Guaranteed?" I snarled.

She licked her lips. "It's true. You are, ah, good, with your, um, tools."

Instantly, the conversation took on a totally different meaning.

"Even when I'm *hard as steel*, Red?" I questioned, my voice gruff.

The way I am right now? I wanted to add, feeling my cock pressing against the material of my sweats.

"Oh." She looked confused. "Well, you're a little…ah, it depends on, you know… the kind of mood you're in. Sometimes, you're faster than others. Your tools are, um, good. I mean, great. Well-handled. And you always satisfy. I mean, the job is always well done." She stuttered and stammered.

Her usually pale cheeks were flooded with color. Her hands were waving in the air the way they did when she was flustered. Her gaze bounced around everywhere, never meeting my eyes and never settling. She shifted in her chair, unable to sit still.

I knew those tells. She wasn't thinking about the logo or the website any more than I was right then.

The only tool she was thinking about was the one currently hard as steel—for her.

In one movement, I slammed the laptop shut and dragged her onto my lap. She gasped, grasping my neck as I held her close.

"You did this deliberately, didn't you, Red? Thought all this up, knowing how I would react." I ground myself up into her heat, groaning at the feel of her pressing back against me.

"Only after," she whimpered. "I realized how you would take it."

"Oh, I'm going to take it all right. Just as soon as you ask me nicely."

She pulled my mouth to hers, and we kissed. I plunged my tongue into her mouth, tasting the peaches from dessert, the sweetness highlighting her flavor, which I found addictive. I gripped her hips, fisting the silky material of the skirt she'd changed into. I liked the way it swirled around her knees as she moved, showing off her sexy legs. She moaned deep in her throat as I licked my way up her neck, cursing into her ear as she undulated over me.

"Up," I commanded, pulling up the material that separated us in my hands and bunching it around her. She made fast work of the sweats I was wearing, yanking them down, then crying out as I sat back down and pulled her back to my lap, the only thing separating us the thin silk of her thong.

"Maxx," she gasped. "Oh god, you're so big. Massive."

I scowled. "You drive me fucking crazy. But I meant it. Ask me, Red. You have to ask me."

"It's just sex," she replied, the statement sounding more like a question.

"Yes," I snarled, thrusting up, desperate to be inside her.

"But I want you," she murmured, her lips at my ear. "You want me?"

"You can feel how much I want you," I groaned. "My cock is aching." I fisted the tiny lace straps on her hips. "Put me out of my misery, Red."

"*Holy moly.* Fuck me, Maxx. Use that big tool and tune me up," she breathed, the word fuck never sounding so sexy before now.

The straps broke under my hands. In seconds I was deep inside her, the heat and wet of her surrounding me. She buried her face in my neck as I drove myself upward, gripping her hips and guiding her. She cried out as I hit that spot inside her that drove her to new heights. I wrapped one arm around her, imprisoning her against me as I moved. She gripped me tight, her embrace locked around my neck. She whimpered and moaned, her lips against my ear. She pleaded and begged. Cried out my name. She strangled my cock, her muscles clamping down and holding me prisoner. My balls tightened as she began to orgasm, her body stiffening as she bent back, crying out her release.

I kissed my way down her throat, sucking on her nipples through the thin material of her T-shirt, the lace showing through the wet spot on the fabric as I moved between them. I kept moving, grunting and roaring out in my need. Her eyes flew open wide, her breathing becoming harder.

"I'm going to...oh god...I'm going to come...*again*. Maxx, please, I can't... *I can't.*"

"Yes, you can, Red. Come all over me again. Soak me. I want to feel it. Feel you." I reached between us and found her bundle of nerves, stroking over her lightly. Just enough to send her over the edge again.

She cried out, her climax hitting her again, pulling mine from me like I was in a vortex, spinning my world on its axis. I roared her name, dragging her up my chest and kissing her as if my life depended on the feel of her mouth underneath mine. I needed her oxygen to breathe. I had to have the taste of her in my mouth as I came. I needed her as close as possible to survive.

Reality returned slowly. She was clutched in my arms, her head on my shoulder, her body limp in my embrace. I was a mass of loose limbs and sweat-soaked skin, gripping her to me. The laptop was halfway across the table. The chair had left marks on the wooden floor where the feet dug into the wood. The light over the table swung slightly in the aftermath.

And Red was crying.

I sat up straight, running my hands over her. "Where? Where are you hurt?" I asked, frantic.

"I'm not," she hiccuped.

"You're crying." I had never seen Red cry before. She was always brave and feisty.

"It's just a release," she sniffed and wiped her eyes. "I'm good. I'm really good."

I sighed heavily, pulling her head back to my shoulder.

"That was pretty intense," I agreed.

"I needed it after today."

I frowned against her hair.

"Tell me."

She was quiet, and I held her tighter.

"Tell. Me."

"I ran into Wes."

"Fuck. What did he do?"

I listened as she told me what had occurred. I was furious at his words, then felt my lips quirk when she described taking him down with a knee in the groin. She was small, and he wouldn't expect that, even after what happened in the bar. I got mad again when she mentioned the way he had kicked at her.

I sat straight. "Which arm?"

"I'm fine. I'm not even sure he meant to. I think he was just kicking in reaction to the pain in his nuts."

I noticed she was pulling down the sleeve on her right arm to keep it in place. I grasped her wrist carefully and tugged up the sleeve, cursing at the bruise forming, turning the milky skin a mottled mass of blacks and blues.

"Bastard," I hissed. "I'm going to kill him."

"No, you're not. You're going to stay away from him."

I shook my head. "This wasn't words or taunting, Red. This was him touching you. Way different."

"As I said, I don't think he meant to. I kneed him pretty hard. He was in a lot of pain. I'm certain he was just moving too much. I got too close trying to get the envelope."

"You should have left it."

"I doubt that. It was five hundred bucks, Maxx."

She had a point. "He needs to be taken to task for what he said."

She studied me, a small grin playing on her lips. "Is he wrong, though, Maxx?"

"What?" I demanded.

She ran her lips up my neck. "I bet you'd love it if I called you Mr. Reynolds while I was on my knees in front of you, wouldn't you? Taking your cock in my mouth—"

I cut her off with my lips, a new, frantic hunger taking hold. I stood, taking her with me, my cock already growing, wanting back inside her.

I headed for the stairs, all rational thought gone. She was going to call my name, all right. Mine, God's, and I didn't care if there was a mister in front of it or not.

As long as it was her voice saying it.

I'd save rearranging Wes's face for another time.

Right now, I had other needs.

Hard, pressing needs only Red could soothe.

And soothe, she did.

Brilliantly.

CHAPTER 19

MAXX

I woke in the morning with Red beside me—or I should say, all over me. Her head was buried in my neck, her breathing small puffs of air on my skin. She was half on top of me, her leg thrown over my hips, snuggled tight to my body.

In return, my cock was hard and snuggled tight into her. All it would take was a shift of my body and a subtle movement of my hips, and I'd be inside her. I could feel her heat surrounding me.

Her mouth pursed and moved, ghosting my skin with kisses as she slumbered. Her fingers moved on my skin restlessly, and she whimpered low in her throat. I listened carefully, grinning at the words she whispered.

Maxx.

Please.

Want.

Please.

I couldn't refuse. I was done denying both of us. I turned and gripped her hip, groaning as I sank into her. I tipped up her head, kissing her soft skin.

"Red, baby, open your eyes."

She blinked as I moved, slowly easing in and out of her, her body moving with mine without any thought. Her breath caught in her throat as she woke fully.

"Holy moly, what are you…" She trailed off with a groan. "*Maxx.*"

"You asked me," I growled. "You begged. I'm giving you exactly what you wanted."

"Yes," she whimpered. "Give it to me." She hitched her leg higher. "All of it."

With a snarl, I rolled over her, bracing on my elbows. I sank deeper as she wrapped her legs around me, and I moved faster. Powerful thrusts of my hips as I took her. Claimed her.

She was beautiful under me in the early light of dawn. Her red hair was wild and spread out over the pillows like a river of molten fire. Her sleepy eyes were half closed, her lips parted as she moaned and sighed my name. She gripped my shoulders, ran her hands over my chest, pulled me in deeper as she arched her back and tightened her legs.

I kissed and lapped at her skin. Her full, sexy breasts. I sucked at her nipples until they were red and wet from my mouth. I did the same to her lips.

Then, with a long roar, I came. I sat up, pulling her hips with me, driving into her as my orgasm raged through me. Pleasure spiraled down to the point our bodies connected, sending out long spasms of ecstasy so great, I was certain I would explode from the sensations. Red keened my name, gripping the sheets and twisting them in her fists as she climaxed, milking my cock, her muscles holding me within her in the most intimate of embraces.

Then, at long last, we stilled. I dropped my head to my chest, breathing hard. Red made a strange noise, her body still quaking.

I slid from her, then dropped beside her and gathered her in my arms.

For a moment, there was nothing but the sound of our breathing. Then she spoke.

"Good morning."

I chuckled and tucked her to my chest, kissing her forehead. "That it is."

"I expected to wake up alone or in my own bed," she murmured.

"Hard to do since you were all over me when I woke up." I nipped her neck. "And already ready for me, begging me to take you."

"Oh."

"A man can only take so much, Red."

"I see." She slid from the bed. "I need a shower."

I followed her, enjoying sharing the water and steam. My hands lingered on her skin and more than once my lips followed their path. Red nuzzled at my chest as I held her under the flow. She felt oddly right in my embrace.

We stepped out, and I wrapped a towel around my waist, smiling as she patted at her skin, thinking how soft it was under my tongue. A small smile played on her lips.

"So, your early morning attack was justified?" she questioned, her lips quirking.

I laughed low in my throat, making my chest rumble. "That was hardly an attack."

She peeked up at me, her gaze mischievous. "No?"

I lifted one eyebrow slowly, looking at her. Gripping a towel, her body on full display for my eyes and my eyes only, she was a vision. Sexy, curvy, and enticing. So very enticing.

"No," I replied. "I can show you an attack if you insist."

She tilted her head questioningly. Her gaze widened as she took in my growing erection. I already wanted her again. I was insatiable when it came to her. Add in a challenge?

It was so on.

She hurried into the bedroom, holding a pillow in front of her. I leaned on the doorframe with a smirk.

"You think a pillow is gonna stop me, Red?"

Her eyes grew rounder as I stepped toward her. "Come quietly. If I chase you, you're gonna pay for it," I warned, staring at her.

"Pay for it, how?" she asked, her lips curling into a teasing invitation.

"Wherever I catch you is where I take you. Might not be as comfortable as the bed," I growled, ready to spring.

With a squeal, she tossed the pillow at me and ran, her giggles floating behind her. I laughed low, liking this game.

No matter what, we were both going to win.

I caught her in the living room and lifted her to the top of the sofa, grabbing her knees and pulling her legs apart. She whimpered, looking almost frightened. "No one has ever… I mean…" She trailed off.

I didn't think I could be harder, but I was wrong. "Then I'm claiming you, Red. All of you."

Then I dropped to my knees, and slid my thumbs between her legs, opening her up to me. I groaned at the soft, wet pink warmth waiting for me. For my touch. I covered her with my mouth, dragging my tongue firmly along her slit. She gasped and grabbed at my hair. I touched and teased her, flicking at her clit with my tongue as I stroked her folds with my thumbs. I swirled my tongue around, gathering her wetness and moaning at her taste. Rainwater, honey, and musk—and all Red. I slid a finger inside and lapped at her as she cried out, the grip on my hair just short of painful. I opened my mouth and drew in her clit, smiling at the little cries and the pleas falling from her mouth. I suckled the stiff little nub, alternating teasing sucks and hard pulls. I added another finger, pumping hard. She screamed my name, lifting her hips, pushing forward, wanting closer to the pleasure. And I gave it to her. Licking, nibbling, sucking, biting—drowning in her sounds and her. The gasps, cries, pleas, and garbled words. Then she stiffened, her legs shaking as she came, flooding my mouth and orgasming hard. Her walls gripped my fingers, her pleasure rippling through her body.

Before she could recover, I was inside her, thrusting hard, clutching her hips and pounding into her. One orgasm morphed into another for her, and she wailed. Actually wailed my name. I lifted her from the back of the sofa she encircled my waist with her legs as I grasped her ass, using it to move her over me as I orgasmed. She was hotter, tighter, and perfect this way with her head buried in my chest, her little cries of pleasure huffed out on my skin.

Until, finally, we were both sated. Quiet. Exhausted. Too exhausted for even Red to talk.

I carried her upstairs, smiling and snuggled in my arms, and placed her back under the blankets. She was out right away, and I looked down at her for a long time, wondering what I was going to do. I wasn't in the market for a relationship, but she was slowly worming her way into my heart. I couldn't deny it. But I wasn't sure I could ever be the man she deserved. That I could ever return her feelings fully—and she deserved that above all else. Someone who could love her completely.

I got ready and was in the shop early. Red—Charly—was still asleep in my bed, exhausted after round three this morning. Brett walked in from the back about thirty minutes later, and we discussed the day and the appointments. We talked about Charly's new website and ideas.

"She is pretty damn clever," he said.

"That she is. But let's not tell her. Otherwise, I'm not sure we can live with her," I stated dryly.

"Live with who?" Charly asked, walking into the office.

It was all I could do not to react. She was wearing one of the old garage shirts, the sleeves rolled up, the tails tied in front, with a pair of tight yoga pants and glittery pink sneakers. Her hair was tied up high on her head with a bandanna holding it back. She looked like a fucking pinup girl.

My cock lengthened at the sight of her. I had to turn away and pretend she didn't affect me.

"Nice of you to finally show up," I snarked. "The shop opened fifteen minutes ago, and there isn't even any coffee made."

Brett chuckled and headed to the garage.

She rolled her eyes. "Sorry, *boss*. My alarm clock didn't go off, so I guess I slept in. It won't happen again."

"See it doesn't."

She draped over me, her breasts rubbing against my arm. She traced her finger over the blotter, tapping it. "The first appointment isn't for another half hour. It's all good." She pressed closer. "My alarm clock needs to be reset." Her breath drifted across my ear. "It behaved very badly this morning."

I held back my groan. Her scent surrounded me, and I felt the hardness of her nipples on my skin. Little minx was playing with me.

I refused to rise to the bait.

I stood so fast she almost toppled over. "Get coffee going, and I want to see some more numbers from your ideas later today."

She bit back her smile, playing with the ends of the shirt. "On it."

She puttered around, making coffee. I had no idea why I stayed to watch her, but I couldn't seem to make my feet move.

She reached up to grab a filter, the shirt lifting, showing a sliver of skin between the waistband and the ties of the shirt.

I leaned close. "Change your shirt. You shouldn't wear it like that."

She looked down. "Like what?"

"Tied up and showing skin."

"I'm not showing any skin!"

"You did," I insisted. "When you reached up. I saw it."

"That would happen whether I wore a T-shirt or this shirt," she protested. "It's called gravity."

"For god's sake, stop arguing and change."

She put her hand on her hip, staring at me. "For god's sake or yours, Maxx?"

"Take it off," I warned.

She grinned, tugging at the tails. "You plan on giving Brett that show, do you?"

"I meant change it." I scowled.

She undid the ties so the shirt fell past her hips. "Better?" she asked sarcastically. "Will that satisfy your puritan eyes?"

Fuck.

She was even sexier with the shirt billowing around her. It was huge—swallowing her up, making my imagination run wild with what it was hiding. My cock knew what it was concealing, and it wanted under that shirt.

What the hell was going on with me?

"Hardly," I snarled at her and turned and walked away.

Her low laughter followed me.

She was a beacon all day. It was as if something had shifted inside me and everything revolved around her. I could pinpoint her location in the garage every moment. I heard her voice even over the sound of the machinery and the music we had playing. I knew when she was close. I wanted to bark at every customer who went into the office to pay their bill and made her laugh. I stomped in with some lame excuse whenever I thought the customer was hanging around too long. I glowered at many. Found reasons to need Charly on another task and took care of the payments myself.

Everyone commented on the garage and the changes. They admired the pictures, and a few of them shared stories of my dad. I had to grudgingly admit it was all Charly's doing, which only brought their attention to her even more.

I sighed in relief when she disappeared midafternoon to take care of her "other duties," as she called them. At least hidden in the house, she was out of sight.

Until I realized the reason many of the customers weren't hanging out in the new waiting area was because she was working outside on a blanket with Rufus, and the customers were out there, talking to her.

My shitkickers dug into the grass as I marched over, glaring and angry. Three customers sat on lawn chairs, staring at her as she spoke, her hands waving in the air as she made a point.

With the bright light glinting off her hair, her pale skin touched by the sun, and wearing the old shirt, she was vibrant, sexy, and clueless as to her draw.

"Waiting room is inside, gents," I snapped. "All new and shiny for you."

One of the customers smirked as he replied, "Charly was telling us about the women's clinic you're going to run. My sister would be very interested. She hates going to a mechanic—says she feels stupid."

Another customer nodded. "My wife would love it. Like Charly says, if she understood it, she'd be more comfortable. I have to take her car in all the time."

Carl, the oldest man, observed my stance behind Charly with a wink. "You got yourself a treasure here, Maxx. Full to the brim with ideas."

"Full to the brim with something," I muttered, my anger deflated but still tense. I didn't like Charly surrounded by men.

They all laughed and said goodbye to Charly. She bowed her head and typed on her laptop. "What are you doing?" I hissed, hunching down behind her. "You're supposed to be inside the house."

She rolled her eyes. "I'm done getting dinner ready, and the house is clean. I decided to work outside. They just came over to chat, so I took the opportunity to tell them about the women's classes we are going to offer."

"I never agreed to them. I said I would think about it."

"I think you've thought about it enough. You heard their reaction. It's a good idea, Maxx. Gosh dang it, stop being so stubborn."

I moved closer. "You are going to pay for your little stunts today, Red. Big-time."

Her fingers faltered, then resumed their typing. "Whatever, Maxx."

I slid my hand under her chin, lifting her face and kissing her hard and fast. "You won't be saying *whatever* later. You'll be screaming my name."

I stood and stomped toward the garage.

"I look forward to it!" she called out.

The next day, she appeared in another shirt, worn over a tank top and another pair of yoga pants. These ones were bright blue and hugged her ass like a second skin. Her hair was hanging down her back in a long, bright swath of color. I was hard the instant I walked in and saw her across the garage. I had to turn around and pace behind the building before I could go back in. I refused to look in her direction.

Apparently, the wild sex on the stairs and in the claw-footed tub she loved so much, or the orders I issued about what she should or shouldn't wear in the garage hadn't sunk in. I had been certain I was clear on the yoga pants thing, but she found a loophole.

As she was sliding a sandwich beside me while I sat at the workbench, I grabbed her hand. "What did I say about yoga pants?" I snarled.

"You said no black yoga pants. These are blue."

"I told you to stop wearing those old shirts."

"You said I couldn't tie them. You never said I couldn't wear them as a cover."

"Consider yourself warned on both counts."

"Hmmph."

After work, I was surprised to see her filling her basket on the bike. "Where are you going?"

"To Mary's. Remember the lady I told you I met on the bus? Turns out, she knows Mary, so I'm going there to have dinner with them."

I crossed my arms. "And what about me?"

She tilted her head, a smile pulling at her lips. "You want to come with and have girl talk, Maxx? You might be a little bored."

"I meant my dinner."

"It's in the fridge. It's warm today, so I made a big salad with grilled chicken. Easy peasy for you to help yourself."

The words were out before I could stop them. "I like eating with you."

"I'll be home in the morning and here tomorrow night."

I covered her hand with mine, frowning. "You're not coming back tonight?"

She patted my hand. "Nope. You get the house to yourself all night."

Somehow, I didn't like the idea, which was odd. I usually enjoyed some solitary time. I felt a slight frisson of annoyance ripple through me. She hadn't even mentioned not being here.

"There had better not be yoga pants making an appearance tomorrow, Charly." I swore to god she was trying to kill me with those things and the shirts. She was already far too distracting without adding in my sudden obsession with her wardrobe choices.

She shook her head. "No yoga pants. Jeans. Simple jeans and a T-shirt."

I narrowed my eyes. She was caving too quickly. "What are you up to?" I groused.

She rolled her eyes. "I only have so many clothes, Maxx. I still don't get your beef with my pants—they cover me from waist to ankle. And it's not as if I wander around in a bikini top—those shirts are huge."

She was right on both counts, except the pants fit her like a second skin and the shirts looked sexy on her. She didn't see it that way.

"You're blind," I snarled. "I see the customers looking at you."

She climbed on the bike, shaking her head. "Holy moly, what an imagination." She gave me a little wave. "See you tomorrow!"

I watched her disappear down the driveway, the urge to follow her and make sure she was okay, strong.

She didn't see herself the way I did. How she looked in the outfits she wore. How alluring she was no matter what she wore. Even on the weekends in sweats and a loose shirt, she was sexy.

But at least I wouldn't have to suffer the yoga pants again.

Nothing could be as torturous as that.

The house seemed too empty without her. I ate dinner on the porch outside, the salad and chicken delicious as always. Charly was right—her cooking was simple, but it suited me. Everything was tasty and fresh—way better than the shit I had eaten before she came along.

Brett was gone, having agreed that Wednesdays were the quietest in the shop, so he would take them off. He headed into Toronto for a night with friends and wouldn't return until tomorrow evening, so I had the place to myself. His friend was coming with him tomorrow for me to meet him. That should be interesting.

I sipped a beer and polished off the dinner, then ate the last piece of pie, hoping another one would appear tomorrow. Or maybe more cobbler. I wondered if I could convince Brett to mention those cookies Charly owed him. I had a feeling they'd be damn awesome as well—as long as he shared them.

I wandered the house, drinking another beer, listening to the silence. Had it ever been this loud before? Charly had only been around for a few weeks, and in the house for an even shorter time, yet the place felt empty without her.

I had no idea what to do about her. She insisted she had no desire for anything but sex, but I still had my doubts. Sex with her was incredible. Hands down the most intense passion I had ever shared with a woman. She could light me up with a single look. The way she taunted me, goaded and teased me. Found ways to irk me so I growled and snapped at her, which for some reason, turned her on. I found that a little disconcerting, yet typical of Charly. She didn't do anything halfway.

But it was what happened after sex with her that confounded me the most. It was I who took her to my bed every night. She loved—needed—to be held. And I liked holding her—far more than I should. The feel of her molded to my chest, her hair spilling down her back over my hands was becoming addictive. I found the tighter I held her, the more she melted into me. It was hard to figure out where I stopped and she started at times.

And then there were her little conversations in the dark that always started the same way. *"Tell me a secret."*

I knew about how lonely she was since her dad died. How devastated she had been when her brother passed. How she struggled when she realized her father would never recover from that loss and she would be alone soon.

She whispered how terrified she was I would send her away that first week. *"I had nowhere else to go, Maxx. And I already loved it here."*

All her confessions told in the safety of the darkness, where I couldn't see her face but could hear the pain in her voice.

They all made me hold her tighter as if I could stitch the pieces of her broken heart back together with my embrace.

I wasn't as open as she was, but I talked about losing my parents, my worry about the shop and doing them proud. She listened, always finding the right words to assure me of her confidence in my choices. I did confess to planning on sending her away at first but was honest and promised she had a place here for as long as she wanted it.

And that, right there, was the thing. She would want to move on. Sooner or later, living in a room in my house, having sex with me, and facing the reality that I was twelve years her senior, set in my ways, and not interested in marriage or much else aside from my garage, would wear her down. She would want more. And she deserved more.

I sighed in the stillness of the house, sitting in the darkness of my living room. Rufus was at my feet, somehow sensing my mood and staying close.

I dreaded that day, yet I knew it would come.

At least, this time, I set the rules. I was prepared, and when she left, I would wish her well and be grateful for the time we had together.

I was a here and now.

Not a forever.

I ignored the thought that if there were a forever, Charly would be the one I chose to spend it with.

I couldn't deal with thoughts like that.

CHAPTER 20

CHARLY

I climbed off the bicycle, parking it inside the barn. I ran my hand over my head and smiled. Mary had French braided my hair last night, and the thick band hung down my back. It felt different, the air on my neck, but I liked it. I had no idea how to French braid, but Mary had been patient, showing me as she went along. I hoped I could do it half as well as she did next time.

It had been a fun evening and so great to see Monica again. She and Mary had been friends for years, and it was nice to spend some time with both of them. Monica cupped my cheeks before she left.

"You look so much happier, child."

"I am," I assured her.

"Good. Come see me soon, yes?"

"I will."

"Bring this Maxx of yours. I want to meet him."

I felt my smile falter a little. We were closer, but I doubted he would ever be truly mine. He was adamant about the future—that we had none. Still, I nodded. "You should come to the garage and meet him. Have your car serviced. They do great work."

"I will do that."

I wiped my hands off on my jeans and tugged down the new T-shirt I wore. My yoga pants were far more comfortable, but I decided to give Maxx a break today. They seemed to drive him to distraction. Hopefully, an evening away from me would have done him some good. He probably enjoyed the peace and quiet.

I headed directly to the garage, smiling as I walked through the large space. It looked so different. Many of the customers this week had commented positively, engaging Maxx in conversation about the pictures, some sharing memories with him about his parents. The chats seem to lift his spirits, and I was so glad I decided to go with my gut on the pictures I chose. The garage's past was so tied up with his parents and his life, and the history should be celebrated.

I set my bag beside my desk and went to the back of the office to make coffee. I filled the pot with water, then looked around for the coffee filters, spying them on the second shelf. I rolled my eyes, knowing either Brett or Maxx had put them up there, forgetting it was I who would use them next. I stretched up as high as I could go, reaching for them, muttering under my breath about tall men and their thoughtlessness. I startled when a strong arm wrapped around my waist, and a hand reached past me to snag the pile of filters.

"No need for all the mutterings, Red. I got them."

I relaxed back into Maxx's firm chest. "You need to leave them on the bottom shelf."

"You shouldn't leave the coffee to me or Brett—for many reasons," he replied, his voice a low hum in my ear.

"Then stop being so impatient in the morning and wait five minutes until I come in. If you weren't so intent on sexing me up all night, I could get in here a little earlier."

He chuckled darkly. "I like sexing you up."

His arm tightened, and I moaned. "Is that a dipstick in your pocket, Maxx, or are you just happy to see me?"

He ran his lips down my neck, licking and nipping at my skin. "I'm very happy to see you, Red." He sucked at my earlobe. "I like the hair."

"Mary did it for me. It's going to be hot today, and she thought it would keep my neck cool."

He flattened his hand on my stomach, rubbing his finger under my waistband in long, slow passes.

"I'm feeling pretty hot already," he growled.

I gasped as he tugged my braid, tipping up my head. His mouth covered mine possessively. He stroked along my tongue in slow, intense passes. His lips worked mine hard, holding me prisoner against his body. He ran his hand over my breasts, plucking the nipples through my shirt, making me squirm. He made fast work of my button and zipper, then his fingers, his talented, wicked fingers, slipped under the material and strummed at my clit. I arched against his touch, suddenly desperate for the feel of his hands on me.

He pulled away from my mouth, dragging his lips across my cheek to my ear. His voice was low, demanding, and intense. "You're always ready for me, aren't you, Red? You knew I'd come for you."

I could only whimper. I was wet five seconds after he kissed me. Only he could do that to me.

"You left me alone last night. I didn't like it." He pressed one finger inside me, then added a second, keeping his thumb on my clit. My legs began to shake, and I moaned at the sensations he was creating. "Don't do it again."

I reached between us, running my hand over his erection. "Maxx, please."

"No," he hissed, his hand moving faster, pressing harder. "Just this. Give it to me, Red. I want to hear you."

The bell rang, signaling a car was out front. I shuddered, and Maxx sped up his movements.

"Come for me, Red."

"The bell—"

His snarl cut me off. "They can fucking wait. I can't." He pressed harder and crooked his fingers inside me, making me see stars. "You come now." He bit my earlobe. "Right. Fucking. Now."

I cried his name as colors exploded behind my eyes. Like a cat in heat, I arched my back, pushing myself closer to his touch, riding out the waves of ecstasy. I bucked and moaned, my legs shaking, gripping his neck and almost sobbing as my orgasm crashed around me, peaked, then ebbed, leaving me a boneless, shuddering mess in his arms.

Maxx kissed my neck, slowly withdrawing his touch. He tugged my braid, kissing my mouth, gentle and light. He stepped back, one hand still on my back, making sure I was steady. I turned to him, glassy-eyed.

"You—" I began.

He kissed me again, tugging up my zipper. "You owe me, Red. Later, on your knees, I'll collect. You got me?"

I nodded, then felt my cheeks flush as he slipped the fingers he'd had inside me into his mouth.

"This will hold me until then." He winked. "That and coffee." He spun me back, facing the shelves. "Get to it."

I peeked over my shoulder as he sauntered away. I grinned as I watched him adjust himself before he opened the door, waving at the customer, then heading to the sink to wash his hands.

I gripped the shelf, resting my head on my hand.

That was one way to say good morning.

His words drifted through my head. *"I didn't like it. Don't do it again."*

I wondered as I went through the motions of making coffee if, perhaps, he was a little more mine than I realized.

Maybe he was a little more mine than *he* planned.

Without Brett there, Maxx was busy all day. The phone was steady, and next week was already filling up. I stayed in the garage, only heading to the house to pull out some burgers to grill later and make sure I still had lots of salad stuff. It was hot, so I put on the air conditioner and shut the windows before heading back with a sandwich for Maxx. I munched on mine as I walked across the grass, thinking of this morning.

Every time I was close to Maxx, I felt his eyes on me. The heat of his stare made the back of my neck prickle. His voice seemed to reach my ears no matter what I was doing. His laughter as he talked to customers seemed darker—richer. I felt him all over my body, the ache between my legs growing all day. I had dated prior to Maxx. Had sex before he entered my life, but what happened between us was so much more than just sex. The passion and need he inspired when he was close at times over-whelmed me. His growls and snarls turned me on. His possessive nature and the way he controlled me were both a surprise and a shock. I had always liked sex, but with Maxx, it was becoming an addiction.

I sighed, entering the fresher interior of the garage. On hotter days, Maxx kept the doors shut and the air as cool as possible, using the huge exhaust fan to keep the flow moving. It was warmer than usual, but better than the heat of outside. The thick cement walls helped, but there was still a change in temperature.

Maxx was crouched beside a motorcycle, working away as I went by.

"I brought lunch."

He stood, wiping his hands. "Great. I just finished, and I'm starving."

He followed me to the workbench and sat down, reaching for the sandwich and taking a large bite. I watched him for a moment. His T-shirt was soaked, his arms glistening in the tight sleeves. He wiped his forehead, taking another bite. "What?"

"You're drenched."

"It's hot. I'm putting out a lot of manual effort." He shrugged. "It happens."

"Are you drinking lots of water?"

"Yes."

"You should change your shirt. Wear something lighter."

He glanced down. "I guess."

"You should have a shower and cool off."

He chuckled. "You worry too much."

"No, I'm being sensible. I'll go get you a fresh shirt." I frowned. "We should get you some lighter pants or long shorts for days like today."

"I like my jeans."

"Some cotton ones that breathe would help keep you cool."

He wiped his forehead again, and I went to the washroom and soaked a towel, coming back and draping it on his neck. He jumped as the towel touched his skin, then relaxed.

"That feels good."

There was a small restroom off the office—a sink, toilet, and a shower stall. "Shower, and I'll get you some fresh clothes."

"I'm quite capable of doing that myself," he griped.

"I'm aware you can dress yourself. I'll just get you the clothes."

He huffed, and I shook my head. "Stop being stubborn, Maxx. Let me help."

"I'm not used to anyone looking after me," he admitted in a low voice.

"Well, you have me now. So, stop arguing."

He met my eyes, his gaze intense and searching. He reached out and stroked my cheek, his fingertips rough, yet so gentle on my skin. "I guess I do. For now," he added quietly. "Okay, Red. Get me some clothes. A shower would feel good."

Fifteen minutes later he emerged, his hair damp, and a frown on his face as he plucked at the gray T-shirt I had left him.

"What, exactly, is this?"

"I ordered those last week. They arrived while you were in the shower. You get to wear the first one!"

He stared at me, then looked down. It was a simple cotton T-shirt with the new logo on it, large and vivid.

"I hadn't approved the logo last week. I still haven't," he rumbled.

"I only ordered a few. Besides, I knew you'd like it. It looks good on you."

He filled out the extra-large perfectly. It clung to his chest and arms, the gray looking nice against his tanned skin. The rounded neckline wasn't too high, so it was comfortable.

He grunted, obviously not too pleased.

"I'm wearing one too—look!"

I stood, and Maxx's face went lax. "What the hell are you wearing?"

I looked down, confused, then realized what he was staring at. "Oh. My, ah, jeans were hot. I changed."

His face was like thunder.

"You said no yoga pants. This is all I've got left."

"A miniskirt?" he asked through tight lips. "You're wearing a miniskirt?"

"No," I explained slowly, noticing how his eyes were darkening more than usual and his voice becoming deeper. Richer. "It's a skort."

"A what?"

I twirled around, showing him. "A skort. Shorts, with a skirt over top. Perfectly acceptable."

"To whom?" he snarled.

"To everyone?" I offered, although my reply sounded more like a question.

He shook his head. "Not to me, Red. Not to me."

MAXX

She stood in front of me, sex incarnate, wearing a T-shirt emblazoned with my new logo, a miniskirt/skort thing, with a ponytail. French braid. What the hell ever. And sparkly sneakers.

A wet dream, looking confused and still so sexy, my cock, which had been semi-hard all morning, roared to life.

"You have no idea what you look like, do you, Red?"

"Ridiculous?" she questioned.

"No." I shook my head slowly. "Like you need to be down on your knees in front of me right now. Sucking me off while I pull that braid and ride your sexy fucking mouth."

Her cheeks flushed, and she licked her lips.

Licked her plump, full lips because I told her I wanted her mouth on me. I glanced at the clock. "We have fifteen minutes, Red. You up for the challenge?"

She tilted her head, her gaze sweeping down my torso,

landing on my groin. My erection was obvious, straining at the zipper.

"Lose the shirt," she rumbled. "I want to see your muscles as I suck you." Then she grabbed the cushion off her chair and dropped it onto the floor in front of me. "And Maxx," she purred. "I only need seven."

I lasted six.

She had my jeans around my knees before I could ask. She took my cock in her hand, stroking it as she ran her other hand over my abdomen.

"You are so sexy," she murmured, then licked along my shaft and cupped my balls. She teased the crown, lapping and swirling her tongue along the head as she twisted her hand, pumping me. I dropped my head back with a long hiss of enjoyment as she sucked me deep in her mouth, doing things with her tongue that should be illegal. She lifted my hand to her head, staring up at me, her eyes bright and mischievous under the lights. She wanted this as much as I did. I had never been this free with a woman, asking, demanding my desires. Never had a woman be on the same wavelength or be as giving as Red. She was amazing.

I gripped her head, guiding her gently. She growled low in her throat, the sensation running down my cock right to the base. I tightened my grip, stroking harder. She hummed, sliding her hands up my thighs, gliding over my pelvis and abdomen. I groaned as she took me deeper, swallowing around my length. The feel of her mouth, of her tongue, was intense, and I grunted.

"You look so good with my cock in your mouth, Red. So fucking sexy," I praised her, touching her cheek. She cupped my balls, then gripped my ass, beginning to move faster. Stroke harder. Take me deeper. All the while looking up at me, her eyes wide and filled with lust. I leaned back, my legs beginning to shake. I grabbed the counter and held her head, muttering and cursing, our eyes locked on each other.

"Yes, Red. Just like that. So good. *So fucking good*. I'm going… Fuck…baby, I'm going to come. You need to—"

My orgasm hit me, and I dropped my head back in a long, low roar of pleasure. Red never let up, licking and sucking until I was spent, swallowing around me and taking all I had.

I collapsed against the counter, my hand still resting on her head as she pulled back, glanced at the clock, and smirked. "Told you."

I sniggered weakly, looking at the time. "Bragger."

She stood, pulling up my jeans, smiling. "Whatever."

I caught her face in my hands and kissed her. She tasted of me, of her, of us. Moments passed of our mouths moving together, unspoken words passing between us as my body settled, my mind cleared, and all I could feel, all I could think of was her.

Red. Charly.

Another word exploded in my head.

Mine.

For the first time ever, the last one didn't upset me.

I wiped my hands as Charly came out of the office. Since our little interaction, she had been funny. Sweet. Almost shy. It was rather endearing and very different from her usual in-my-face actions.

She looked excited, and I lifted my eyebrows. "What's up, Red?"

She waved a flyer. "Look. There's a motorcycle event about two hours away on the weekend."

I took the flyer and looked it over. "Yeah, I've been to this one before. It was a good one. Do you want to go?"

Her eyes widened. "Really? Could we?"

"Sure, we'll close at noon and drive up. There's usually a concert at night. Old rock bands."

"I'd like that."

"Good. Me too. Pencil it in, Red."

She bent and kissed my cheek then hurried away. I watched her go, her little ass looking fine in that skort. Maybe I would tell her to get a few of those. If she was going to drive me crazy, I might as well enjoy it.

She disappeared around five, and once I finished up, I closed the shop and headed toward the house. The skies overhead had turned darker, the sudden heat of the day bringing a storm. From the look of the heavy clouds, it was going to be a bad one.

As I opened the door, I heard voices. Brett's car was parked by the garage as well as an unfamiliar vehicle, which I assumed belonged to Stefano. I was still unsure about hiring another mechanic, although I had to admit it would have some advantages. Charly had shown me the ads she wanted to run, the posters she planned on putting up, the Facebook page and redesigned website she had ready to go. She was correct when she stated there was no point in doing any of it if the garage couldn't keep up with the demand for work. She was working on a complete file of all the restoration work I was getting requests for, doing it, as usual, in her meticulous method. If I was busy with restorations, and garage business increased, a third body would be needed.

Inside, the air was cooler and felt good on my skin. Brett was sitting at the table, his friend beside him. They were a study in contrasts. Both tall, well-built guys in their early thirties, but Stefano was the dark to Brett's light. Deep brown hair and olive skin set off his wide smile and white teeth. A smile he was currently directing at Charly, who was sitting at my table, grinning back.

A roar of unusual jealousy tore through me. I tamped down

the anger and the urge to tell him to keep his smiles to himself, instead walking over to the table and forcing a neutral expression to my face. I stood behind Red and casually laid my hand on her shoulder, then extended my other hand toward him.

"Stefano, I presume."

He stood and shook my hand. "Maxx. Good to meet you. Brett and Charly have been singing your praises."

Charly peeked up at me, her glance quickly straying to my hand still on her shoulder. "Everything okay in the shop?"

"Yep." I squeezed her shoulder a little, enough so Stefano saw the movement of my hand. Our eyes met, and a look of understanding passed between us.

Hands off. She's taken.

He chuckled low in his throat and brushed a hand over his scruff, meeting Brett's eyes quickly. "I look forward to the chance of working with you. Brett tells me you're a master at restorations."

I relaxed and sat down. Charly stood and headed to the kitchen, bustling around. It felt right listening to her as she moved around, asking Brett to light the barbecue, telling me the burgers were ready to grill. She seemed a little tense, and I wondered if she was worried about my decision in regard to Stefano.

We kept conversation light during dinner, enjoying the food and getting to know one another a little. I did ask Stefano where he planned on staying if he worked here.

"I'll find a small place. Brett and I were discussing getting a place together if things worked out."

"It's pretty quiet around here. You won't miss the big city?"

He laughed. "I'd like a little peace and quiet. I lived over the garage until the fire, and I've been bunking in my parents' basement while I looked around." He ran a hand through his hair. "I've had quite enough of family togetherness for a while."

"You don't get along with your family?"

His grin was wide and white in his face. "I love them all, but they are far too close. Mama loves to cook for everyone, so one of my sisters or brothers is always around. Often many of them, plus their spouses and kids. The house is busy all the time, and there is zero privacy."

"How many siblings?" I asked, curious.

"Six of us." He paused. "I'm the only single one. Eight nieces and nephews." He rolled his eyes. "And Nonna's house is where they all like to hang out, it seems. And Zio Stefano is their favorite jungle gym."

I chuckled at his description.

Charly had been unusually quiet until now, but she spoke up. "Mary is thinking of renting a room out for the summer since she isn't hiring anyone this year. You could go talk to her. It's close, and that way, you can see if you like it here."

Stefano chewed and swallowed a large bite of burger. "That is a good idea. Then we can take our time looking for a place." He met my gaze. "If things work out, I mean."

I had to admit, I liked him. He seemed straightforward and honest. He and Brett got along well, which would make working in the garage easier. I could recall the bustling atmosphere in the past when my dad and his crew worked together. I had been on my own so long, it would take some getting used to, but it might be a good change.

Charly stood, taking her plate to the kitchen. She hadn't eaten much, which was odd. She had a healthy appetite, which I liked. There was no pretense with her.

But something was off tonight.

A small niggle of doubt began in my head.

Had I been too rough with her today? Stepped over the line? Was she regretting what had happened between us?

She appeared to grow more ill at ease as dinner progressed. Almost folding in on herself. I tried to pinpoint when it happened but couldn't. I had noticed her tension earlier, but it had grown beyond that.

A plate of cookies appeared on the table, and Charly put a pot of coffee beside them.

"I'll leave you guys to your talk."

Now I knew something was really wrong. Charly always wanted in on the discussions about the garage—especially when it was her idea.

"Feel free to join us," I said, trying to catch her eye.

"No, I'm tired." She pushed a file my way. "Here's all the numbers you need." Her gaze flitted around the table, not really looking at anyone. "Goodnight."

She climbed the steps, not looking back. I watched her leave, Rufus following her. She looked fine, except I knew her. Her face was pale, the dots of cinnamon vivid on her skin, which meant she was upset.

Something was up. I eyed Brett and Stefano, but they didn't seem to notice anything. She had been fine earlier—hadn't she? I couldn't think of anything either of them had said or done to upset her. Stefano had been polite and respectful toward both of us. Brett knew there was something between us, and he was fine and acted no different.

So, what was I missing?

Brett cleared his throat, and I turned my attention to what we were together to discuss. I asked Stefano some questions, and he was open and honest with me. He showed me some of his work, and I was amazed. I was good at airbrushing and detail work, but my designs were simple, and I stuck to clean lines and patterns.

Stefano was an artist. His work was impeccable and eye-catching.

"Why are you not with one of the big shops in Toronto?" I asked.

He shrugged. "I was for a while. But I hate being told what to do. Having my work pigeonholed. So many of these places have set designs or insist on it being done their way. I like working with customers and finding out what they like and creating something special for them. Most of my work, I do on the side, but then I have to rent out space. I have my own machine, which I'd like to bring with me, if that's okay."

I nodded in understanding. We all had preferences for the types of equipment we liked to use. It was personal and what you became used to using. Like tools. I had certain manufacturers I trusted and some I disliked.

We began a discussion in earnest between the three of us. Where I saw the garage going. What I wanted to see happen. The business end compared to the love of the art of restorations. What they were looking for—now and long-term. I was honest about my worries of taking them on, only to have them leave to open their own shop, or worse, work for a competitor. They, in turn, were frank with their goals.

Brett rested his elbows on the table. "In the short time I've been working here, Maxx, I can tell you this place is going to explode. With your little firecracker on the team, she is going to launch you into the next century. I want to be part of that. Part of being a team and working toward a goal." He waved his hand toward the garage. "You have a great spot, with room to expand if you wanted. Another whole building to do nothing but restorations if that was what you decided to do. I want to know I have a place, a future."

I eyed him. "Partner type future?"

"We can discuss that at another time. Take me on, let me be part of it, and reward me. You'll get my loyalty. I'll sign an employment contract that will make you more comfortable if you want."

I glanced at Stefano, who was nodding in agreement. "Brett showed me the garage. I saw your work. I'm tired of Toronto and the rat race. Of being a hired nobody with no say in the jobs I do or don't do. I want to be part of something." He rubbed the back of his neck. "As weird as it sounds, I want to be part of *this* something. There's a feeling I can't explain. Talking to Charly earlier, I caught her excitement."

A sudden gust of wind hit the windows, rattling the glass. We all glanced toward the noise.

"I think that storm they're calling for is about to hit," Brett mused. "You need to head to the hotel, Stef."

Storm. Wind.

It hit me why Charly was acting so strangely. The first secret she shared with me.

"I hate the wind," she'd whispered in the dark.

She wasn't upset. She was anxious.

I stood. "Come back in the morning, Stefano. Look around, see how we work. Ask some questions. I'm sure I'll have some for you. We can talk again over lunch."

He stood and shook my hand, not questioning my sudden ending to the meeting. I assumed he thought I agreed he should head to the hotel before the storm broke, but the truth was, I wanted to get upstairs. I had a feeling my presence up there was desperately required.

They left, and I eyed the sky overhead. Heavy, dark, and threatening, I knew the storm wouldn't bother Red as much as the wind that was bearing down on us. The branches of the trees were bent low with the force, and I feared it was only going to get worse. I made sure the barbecue was in the barn and the doors locked firmly, then headed for the house. I locked up, then took the stairs, my shitkickers making a heavy thump on the treads as I went up.

My bedroom was empty, and I headed down the hall, not knocking as I pushed open the door to the room I had given Charly. I was surprised to see her bed unoccupied until I saw why. She was curled up in the chair that she'd pushed into the farthest corner, her legs drawn up to her chest, with her hands wrapped around her knees. Her eyes, those soft green orbs, were round with anxiety, and I didn't think it was possible for her to make herself smaller. Up here, the wind was even louder, the glass rattling in its frame, old and needing to be fixed. I knew she was terrified sitting here alone, unable or unwilling to ask for help.

Rufus sat beside her, his great head resting against the chair, a silent but unhelpful guard.

I knew what she needed.

Me.

Without a word, I went to her, scooping her into my arms and carrying her to my room. Rufus followed and curled into his bed in the corner as I placed her on the mattress. The wind was more muted in here, not hitting this side of the house directly, but it was still violent. A long shudder ran down her body, her arms gripping me tighter as I tried to move back.

A wave of unusual tenderness hit me, and I held her close for a moment. "I just need to get undressed, Red. I'm not leaving."

She dropped her arms, and I held eye contact with her as I yanked my shirt over my head and toed off my boots, then slid my jeans off, leaving only my boxers on. I gathered her back up and sat down, resting my back against the headboard, the pillows providing a nice softness to lean against. I held her close, a small ball of terror, stiff and scared, not talking or moving. I ran my hand over her head, stroking her hair and talking in a quiet voice. I told her what happened downstairs, and that Stefano would be back tomorrow.

"You wound your magic around him, too, Red. He thinks you're awesome and wants to work here." I huffed out a chuckle. "All I wanted was some order to my life. I had no idea what was going to happen when I let you get in the truck."

Finally, she spoke, her voice quieter than I had ever known it to be. "What happened?"

I pressed a kiss to her head. "You brought the sun back into my life, Red."

She let out a long, shuddering breath. "Oh."

I tilted up her chin and kissed her. It was a different kiss than any other we'd shared. One of comfort and caring. Appreciation and honesty. I was tired of fighting her. Fighting her draw. I hated that she was scared. I loved that maybe I could help her not be.

I kissed her, knowing somehow tonight, things would change between us.

Our kiss deepened as I slanted my mouth over hers, holding her closer. Burrowing my hands under the blanket that protected her and surrounding her with my touch. Slowly she relaxed, forgetting the noise and the storm, losing herself in us. We touched and kissed, discarding the barriers between us and feeling only our bodies sliding together. The silk of her hair on my hands. The satin of her skin against mine. I rolled her under me, using my body as a shield from what frightened her. I pressed her deep into the mattress, murmuring nonsensical words, kissing and tasting her. Allowing, for the first time, the adoration I felt for her to soak into my words, drift through her mind, and sink into her skin. Everything I found appealing, I whispered to her. Praised her.

I lifted on my elbows as I settled between the cradle of her open legs. Our eyes held in the dim light as I slid into her body, groaning at the sensation of coming home. I moved in long, unhurried glides, our fingers intertwined in the pillow over her head as I loved her. Kissed her mouth, her neck, and nuzzled her breasts. She whimpered and moaned, no longer fearful, but passionate and lost with my touch. I covered her mouth, sharing her breath as she peaked, shuddering and clutching me tightly within her, until I followed, spent and complete.

With her.

I gathered her into my arms and held her, keeping her close, needing to feel her as much as she needed to feel me. She drifted her fingertips, light and gentle, along my forearms and hands.

Moments passed of silence, then I spoke. "Tell me a secret, Red."

She stilled her movements and inhaled a slow, deep breath. "It might make you angry."

I frowned against her head. After what we had just shared, I doubted she could anger me.

"Tell me."

"I found the file on your motorcycle. I know what happened. What they did to you," she whispered.

I stiffened for a moment, then relaxed. It was bound to happen. "When?"

"While you were away. It was stuck in the back of the file cabinet behind the petty cash box."

"Hmm."

"I shouldn't have looked."

I felt a smirk form on my lips, and I kissed her head. "But it's you, Red. You couldn't help yourself."

She made a little noise in her throat. "I'm sorry. What they did was so awful. No wonder you don't trust me."

"That's the rub, Red. I tried not to. I tried not to like you. I failed at both."

"You-you like me?"

I laughed, pressing a kiss behind her ear, which made her shiver. "After what we just shared—after the last few days—you doubt that?"

"I was too afraid to hope."

I tightened my arms. "I more than like you, Red. And I trust you. More than I thought I could ever trust someone again."

"Oh."

I sighed, knowing I owed her an explanation.

"I met Shannon at a real low point in my life."

"You don't have to tell me."

"Hush," I growled. "Yes, I do. I need you to understand. I'm going to tell you, and then it's done. I don't want to talk about it, understand?"

"Like, ever?"

"Ever." I nipped her ear. "Are you going to listen or keep talking?"

"Yeesh. I'll be quiet."

I gathered my thoughts, surprisingly calm about talking about such a painful time in my life. Somehow holding Red and telling her wasn't as difficult as I expected.

"I lost my parents pretty close together, and it hit me hard. I was lonely and Shannon seemed to be the right fit for me. I met her at one of those motorcycle events, and I thought she was great. She came to see me here a few days later, and well, she just stayed."

"I see," came her soft reply.

"She helped in the shop, doing deposits and the like. She sort of moved in and took over. She changed the house, changed the way I did things. My best friend Billy worked with me at the shop, and they got along well. Shannon—she had a way about her."

"Like me?" she whispered.

"No, not in a good way. Demanding, controlling in ways you didn't realize you were being controlled, if that makes any sense. Until she was gone, I didn't realize how tired she made me. After the first little while, nothing was good enough. She was always wanting more. More money, more things, more—just everything." I sighed, knowing I wasn't explaining things very well.

"She was a taker," Red murmured.

I barked out a laugh. "That's what Mary called her. She disliked her right away, and Shannon made it plain she hated Mary. I had to choose between them, and I chose wrong. Luckily, Mary forgave me—she even made it possible for me to see her on occasion without Shannon around so we could keep in touch. And when it all blew up in my face, Mary never once said 'I told you so.'"

Red chuckled. "I bet that took a lot of restraint on her part."

I smirked. "I bet it did."

"So, what happened?"

"We were fighting—a lot. Shannon and I. I was arguing with Billy too. Nothing I did was right with Shannon. I started noticing the business was being neglected. Monies weren't being deposited. She always had an excuse, and at first, I believed her, then I started not to. That led to more fights. Then she started in on my parents. She thought I was weak to have been so close to them." I snorted. "Mama's boy, Daddy's brat—she had lots of names for me. Finally, things got so bad, I knew it was over. We'd said too many hateful things, yelled too often. This place felt like a war zone, and I couldn't escape it. It followed me to the garage, so I never got a break. I'd had enough, and after another disturbing visit to the bank, I came home early, ready to have it out with her. I wanted her gone. I knew she was stealing. I also realized she had no feelings for me. And never had. I was simply a pawn to her."

"Oh, Maxx. How awful."

"I walked into the shop and found Billy fucking her. Right in the middle of my shop, bent over some customer's car."

"Oh no."

"We had a huge three-way fight. I fired him. Told her to

get out. Things got really ugly, and I turned to walk away and call the cops, and the world went black." I rubbed my hand over the back of my head, recalling the pain I felt when I woke up.

"When I came to, they were gone. So was anything of value, including my Indian motorcycle. She knew it was valuable, so did Billy. She had tried on more than one occasion to talk me into selling it, but I refused. But they both knew the sentimental value was worth more than any monetary value because…" I trailed off.

"Because you did it with your dad."

"Yes. It was a part of me. And she took it. Along with some expensive tools, a bunch of cash, and my Ducati."

"Maxx, what a betrayal."

"It was more Billy than her, if I'm being honest. Things were so bad between us, I was almost grateful for her to be gone. Billy had been my friend for over ten years."

She lifted her head and pressed a kiss to my jaw. "I'm sorry."

Her soft words eased something in me.

"It would be hard to move past all that," she mused.

"I went for some counseling. I needed some help to clear my head."

"Do you think it helped?"

"I was able to sift through some thoughts and ideas—clear out the cobwebs, so to speak. The guy I went to was no-nonsense. Gruff. Spoke his mind. Called me an idiot more than once."

"Oh. Um, the two of you must have gotten along well."

I chuckled. "We were fine. He told me I was a grumpier sod than he was, even more so after we finished our sessions. I guess that's just my true nature."

She looked amused. "Not really a surprise."

"Watch it," I growled playfully. "He helped straighten me out some, and I see him on occasion if I need to." I paused. "Frankly, having you here and all the changes you have made has done more in moving me forward than he managed to do."

"It was too hard for you."

I smiled at her fast defense of me. "I cleared out this room. Took all the furniture I hated to the flea market and put a sign up for free and walked away. Then I built this bed and the furniture."

"You made all this?"

"Yeah. It was a good way to occupy my hands and mind. I hated the stuff she had bought. Minimalistic, I think she called it. Cheap, ugly shit, I called it."

"I like this furniture."

"I like how this bed looks with you in it."

She giggled and burrowed closer. I noticed while we were talking, she was able to ignore the wind. It was beginning to die down, and I hoped she'd be able to sleep once we were done talking.

"Did you try to find it? The motorcycle I mean?"

"Yeah, I put out feelers, got the word out I was looking for it. Heard nothing. I assume they are long gone and the VIN number on the bike replaced and sold, or they pulled it apart for pieces. I had to give up dwelling on it and move forward."

"Did this happen last year?"

"Yes. Why would you ask?"

"I noticed your files went from meticulous to barely done about a year ago."

I scrubbed my face. "Yes. Thanks to Mary, taxes and every-thing are up to date. I need to fix the files—sort them and do a bunch of matchups. It's all there in the storeroom, just jumbled."

"I already started," she confessed.

"Red..." I breathed out, surprised yet not shocked she would have simply taken on such a project without saying anything.

She asked me a few more questions, then fell silent. I was

touched by her reticence in bombarding me with queries or opinions. It felt good to clear the air between us. A relief, almost.

"Do you regret placing that ad?" she whispered.

"The ad that brought you here?"

"Yes."

I tilted up her chin and pressed a kiss to her lips. "Best ad I ever placed. I got you."

"Yeah?"

"Wanna hear another secret?"

"Okay."

"You drive me crazy in the very best of ways, Red. All your little habits and sayings. The way you put me in my place. Flutter around the garage with zero idea how sexy you are to me in your little outfits. The food you cook. Your goddamn delicious pies. All of it rolled into one smart-mouthed, sassy little redheaded snippet." I kissed her again. "My little redheaded snippet."

She stilled.

"Yours?"

"I'm done fighting this, Red. I'm attracted to you. More than I should be. I don't know if I can be—if we can be—any more than what we are right now, but I'm not going to make myself miserable anymore. So, if you want that, you got me."

For a moment, she was silent. "I want that," she replied.

"Okay. We go from here, then."

The room was quiet, and I thought she had fallen asleep. Until she lifted her head.

"You aren't going to go all soft on me, are you, Maxx? Be all sweet and nice suddenly?"

I chuckled. "You don't want sweet and nice?"

"No, I want Maxx. In all your growly, snarly magnificence, glowering at me in the garage and telling me off. I like that."

"You are a strange girl, Red."

"Holy moly, buddy, you're one to talk," she snorted. "Only

you could come out of counseling even grumpier than when you started."

I rolled her under me, hovering over her. "I'm going to show you grumpy in about three seconds, Red," I promised. "And I don't plan on treating you any differently than I have been. I'll chap your ass daily. So, get used to it."

She pulled me down to her mouth.

"Yowsers. Perfect."

CHAPTER 21

MAXX

I was busy with Brett and Stefano when Red sashayed her way into the garage the next morning. I had left her sleeping in my bed, thoroughly exhausted from a night of being woken up by my wandering hands and growly demands. She was curled in a ball, her bright hair a mass of messy curls around her face as she slumbered.

We all lifted our heads at the sound of the side door opening. She walked in, carrying a tray of muffins, Rufus following her closely. But it wasn't the muffins that had me slack-jawed. It was the outfit she was wearing today. Worn, I knew, to drive me mental.

It worked.

She had taken a pair of the old mechanic coveralls, cut off the sleeves, and tied the shoulders up with a pink ribbon. She left the top billowing open, giving me a glimpse of a tight tank top, also pink, underneath the worn beige material. She'd rolled up the legs of the pants so they ended at her knees, showing off her shapely calves. The waist was cinched in with more pink material, and her hair was in pigtails, with a bandanna holding it in place. And those damn sparkly sneakers again. It got worse as she drew closer. My name, MAXX, was embroidered on the lapel of the front pocket. Of all the coveralls she could have chosen, she was wearing my old ones.

She was feminine, sexy, and yet still appropriate for the garage.

But not for me.

"Jesus," I muttered.

Stefano and Brett exchanged a look and chuckled. "She's a handful," Brett muttered.

"Yep," I replied.

She stopped in front of us, a falsely innocent look on her face as she smiled. She knew what she did to me in those outfits. "Muffins?"

They each took two, then decided they needed to go to the office and get coffee, leaving us alone. Red pushed the tray my way. "I made these."

I took one, glaring at her. "I don't recall giving you permission to cut up any coveralls."

She tossed her head, the damn pigtails bouncing around her shoulders. "The sleeves were torn. I figured you wouldn't mind."

"You think that outfit is suitable for a garage?" I snarled.

She rolled her eyes, enjoying this too much. "Duh. They're coveralls, Maxx."

I stepped in front of her, tracing my name over her breast with my finger. "Any reason *these* coveralls, Red?"

She met my eyes, hers dancing in delight at my reaction. "So I was covered in you all day."

Her words went directly to my cock.

"Find an excuse to be in the storeroom at lunch. You and I need some privacy to discuss your choices in outfits," I hissed.

She tilted her head. "If you say so, *boss man*."

It was all I could do not to throw her over my shoulder and carry her into the storeroom right then. I wanted to fuck her against the shelves, holding those pigtails and making her cry out my name.

"I say so," I growled.

"All right." She pressed closer so I could feel her nipples straining against the material. "Just so you know, I'm commando underneath. I figured it would save you some time."

She placed another muffin on the table in front of me. "See you later." She winked and moved toward the office. I watched her go, a smile tugging on my lips. Things would never be dull while she was around.

And I wanted her around for a long time.

Saturday afternoon, I sat astride my motorcycle, waiting for Red. I watched with narrowed eyes as she hurried across the lawn, stopping in front of me.

"Go change," I ordered

She looked down at the tank top and shorts she was wearing. "But it's going to be hot!"

"Fine." I yanked my Henley over my head, exposing my bare chest.

"You can't go like that," she protested.

"Neither can you."

With a huff, she dug in her bag and pulled out one of the old garage shirts, putting it over her tank. "There."

I reached into my leather saddlebag and tugged a black muscle shirt over my head, sliding it under the waistband of my jeans.

Her eyes widened. "No way. That's worse."

I lifted my eyebrow.

She dropped her bag and dug inside it again, muttering the whole time.

"Holy moly. He calls me stubborn... They'll be all over him wearing a muscle shirt. Walking sex on legs. Seriously."

I enjoyed her frustration. Now, she knew how I felt. Hopping on one foot, she pulled on a pair of pants, right over her shorts. "Better?"

"Did they shrink?" I griped.

She slammed her hands on her hips. "They're capris, Maxx! Stop chapping my ass and put your gosh dang shirt on!"

I chuckled and pulled my Henley back over my head. Silently, I handed her a jacket, and she took it, holding it up.

"It's warm standing in the sun, Red. Not on the back of the bike. You need the cover." I shrugged mine on and waited.

She slipped it on, running her fingers along the old leather. "Is this..." She let her voice trail off.

"It was my mom's. I know it's a little big, but it will block the wind."

In a nanosecond, she was on me, her arms locked around my neck, kissing me. I grabbed a handful of her ass, holding on tight, taking control of the kiss and letting her know who was in charge. At least at the moment.

I stood and deposited her back on her feet. I slid a helmet over her head, tugging on the braids, then locking it in place. I bent down and kissed her again, then swung on my bike.

"Get on, Red."

She scrambled behind me, wrapping her arms around my waist. I patted her hand and gunned the engine.

"Hold tight."

She snuggled against my back. "I plan to."

I wrapped my arms around Red's waist, swaying in time to the music, listening to the covers of the old rock band, and enjoying myself. I couldn't remember the last time I felt so relaxed. I had a great day with her. She was excited and dragged me around, looking at the various bikes, the arts and crafts, and talking to everyone. I saw some familiar faces, caught up with a few people, and watched with amusement as Red handed out business cards like candy, talking about the shop, my talent, and the restoration work I did. Little minx even had pictures on her phone. I hadn't been to the event in two years—too sad when my dad died since we usually went together, and still too raw after the shit Shannon and Billy had pulled. I had gone to one event with Shannon, but her attitude had ruined the entire day for me. Red was easy, just as happy to stand beside me and listen to me talk as she was to explore items in the craft area. She held my hand the entire day, often wrapping her arm around me for a kiss or to share one of the treats she picked up along the way. I tried to growl at her, but today, it was impossible. She was too adorable, and I was too caught up in her spell.

She rested back against me, lifting her head and meeting my eyes. I bent over her and captured her mouth with mine, groaning low when she turned in my arms and returned my kiss with passion. No one paid us any attention in the crowd, everyone enjoying the music, some high from the drugs being passed around, some caught up in the simple pleasure of being outside under the stars and enjoying life.

I lifted her off her feet, my lips telling her silently what my mouth couldn't yet say. She dragged her mouth over to my ear.

"Ever had hard, fast sex on your bike, Maxx?"

"No," I growled.

"You want to?"

I didn't respond. Instead, I flipped her over my shoulder and stalked toward the field where people were parked. My bike was in the far corner, close to the trees, and would now be deep in the shadows. People laughed and cheered as I pushed through them, Red hanging on to my ass for dear life and grumbling in protest. I smacked her rounded ass, grinning as she yelped.

She'd be hanging on harder soon. And yelping in another way entirely.

I'd make sure of that.

The next couple of weeks, I found a new rhythm. The garage buzzed every day. We took a day and rearranged the work areas so we each had a bay. Charly kept the schedules for everyone, handling all the paperwork, parts ordering, and behind-the-scenes items like a pro. Every day, she made lunch for all of us, and Stefano occasionally stayed for our nightly meals—usually barbecue and salad. Mary joined us a couple of nights, and I enjoyed the time we spent around the table, talking and laughing. It reminded me of the early days of the garage when my mom cooked and the crew stayed for dinner. There was a shared feeling of camaraderie. I liked it.

Charly didn't bother to pretend to even use her room. She was in my bed every night, and I had no desire to change that. When we were alone, she was Red. My Red. I tried to call her Charly during business hours, although at times I slipped. Especially when she'd walk in wearing some outfit I deemed inappropriate, which was often. She always found my reactions amusing, and I was certain she based her decisions on how often she could get me to growl and snap at her. It was a game between us. One I usually won since I ended up with my cock buried inside her.

I mentioned to her one night that things had changed and maybe we needed to restructure her job.

"Why?" she asked with a frown. "Am I not doing everything at the shop I should?"

"No, I have no complaints. But you're working there all day, then making dinner, looking after the house. It wasn't what we agreed on."

She shrugged, her eyes not meeting mine. "I don't count what I do here in the house as part of my job anymore, Maxx. I like looking after you."

Her words warmed my chest, melting the block around my heart. It was happening more and more. I cared about her more every day, but somehow seemed incapable of telling her. I could praise her work, give her a hard time, make her come harder than a freight train, but I couldn't tell her what I was feeling. I wasn't sure I ever could. It bothered me, but I wasn't certain how to get past it.

We had our first class, all three of us speaking. The women seemed hesitant to talk until Stefano asked one woman a direct question, listening as she hesitantly told him she felt stupid coming into a garage. "My last mechanic informed me I should know the PSI of my tires off the top of my head. I had no idea what that even meant, and when I told him, he rolled his eyes and walked away. I looked it up and tried to use an air machine, and I somehow added too much, and almost blew it out," she confessed.

Stefano shook his head. "Would never happen here. There are no stupid questions. It means you want to learn. And we'll listen."

That opened the floodgates. The hour turned into two, and when they left, all clutching the free oil change coupon Charly gave them, I sat down, shaking my head.

"That was something."

"I hope it worked," Brett muttered, sitting beside me. "It was actually fun."

Stefano chuckled. "It was. I'd be willing to do more. They were all great."

The next day, every woman called for an appointment. And the waiting list for the next class grew to over fifty.

Brett and Stefano agreed to change the class to twenty people and hold one every two weeks until the waiting list dwindled, then go back to the original idea of once a month. I would spell one of them off, so it was an easy addition to our schedule. Charly cackled over the idea of the waiting list dwindling. "Some of them are coming back every class just to see you three," she informed us. "Make sure to wear those tight shirts I ordered, with the coveralls loose around your waist." She popped her head around the door. "Ooh, start off with the coveralls on, then each of you peel them down slowly, nonchalantly, like you're hot. Not all at once, though. Don't make it obvious."

She was talking about the deep red coveralls with the logo on the back, our names embroidered on the front, that had arrived yesterday. She even got herself a pair, although hers were adorable and just for show. Ours were useful—or at least they were supposed to be.

We all laughed until we realized she was serious.

"She's selling us out," Brett said. "I feel like a piece of meat."

"Grade A prime beef, my friend!" Charly shouted from the office, making us all chuckle. At least she was honest about it.

She was beside herself with excitement and went back into planning mode. Between the classes, the ads she'd started running, and the first motorcycle I was waiting on delivery of for restoration, we were suddenly booked solid. She had a wait list for my services, an amazing chart of each request, the time needed, the pricing, what requirements and parts we had to order or find. It was laid out perfectly, and she spent a lot of time on each one, getting all the information from me and entering it so I could see it at a glance whenever I needed it.

She was brilliant. I never wanted to be without her. In the garage or in my personal life.

And still, I couldn't tell her.

CHAPTER 22

MAXX

I looked up from the schedule Saturday afternoon a couple of weeks later. "Another busy week ahead of us, guys."

Stefano glanced up with a laugh. "When isn't it these days? Business is booming. We don't even have time to look for a place."

Brett snorted. "Like you want to leave Mary's. You're spoiled there."

"Her cooking rivals my mama's, that's for sure. I'm not complaining."

Red walked in, wheeling her bicycle. I wiped my hands, thinking how pretty she looked in her summer outfit. I had gotten used to the skorts and frilly blouses she liked to wear after hours. "You off to Mary's?"

"Yep. Pie day. She picked up a mass of blueberries at the market."

I walked over and kissed her. "Okay. You sure you won't take the car?"

"Nope. I love riding the bike. And it's a gorgeous day."

"If you get into the wine, call and I'll pick you up."

"Or I'll stay the night."

"Call," I growled. I hated it if she wasn't in my bed.

She rolled her eyes. "Fine, bossy."

She waved as she pedaled down the driveway and rang the bell I had added to her handlebars. It had made her laugh, and she loved to ring it every time she used the driveway, announcing her arrival or departure.

I watched her go, her bright hair flowing behind her. She turned right on the road and disappeared, and I went inside.

Stefano grinned at me. "Whipped."

"Whatever. You do everything she says too." I smirked.

"I'm not stupid. I know who's really running the show."

Brett picked up the schedule and whistled. "Holy moly, how are we gonna handle all this?"

I picked up my wrench with a shrug. "Easy peasy. We just do."

Stefano stopped what he was doing. "Did you just hear yourself? Both of you? If Charly were here, she'd be chapping your ass over stealing her expressions."

Then he stopped. Realized what he had said and began to guffaw.

We all did.

Charly had gotten to us all.

My phone rang a while later, and I answered with a grin. "Mary? What's up? You need more sugar or something?"

"I need Charly to get here, Maxx. Quit hogging her to yourself. These pies aren't going to make themselves."

A cold shiver ran through me. "Mary, Charly left here well over ninety minutes ago. You're saying she hasn't arrived?"

"No. I've been waiting. I called her cell, but there was no answer. I thought she got busy with you in the garage."

Dread filled me. "I'm on my way."

I hung up and headed for the truck. Stefano and Brett were behind me. "We'll follow you."

I grabbed my keys. "No. Stefano go the opposite way and circle around. Maybe she remembered something she needed and headed toward Littleburn. Brett, you stay here in case she comes back."

"Maybe she got a flat tire and is walking."

"She'd answer her phone. Or she would call me." That, I knew for sure.

I climbed into the truck, yelling at Brett to put Rufus in the house as he tried to follow me. The gravel spun under my tires as I tore down the driveway. I drove to Mary's, keeping my eyes peeled for Charly, but the road was deserted. I only passed one car on my drive. Mary was in her driveway, looking worried. I opened the window. "Nothing?"

"No. I'll come look with you."

"No, stay here in case she shows up."

I drove back toward my house slowly, scanning the fields, desperate for the sight of bright red hair. I met up with Stefano when I arrived back at my house. He shook his head in response to my silent question.

"I'm coming with you," he said. "You drive and look on one side. I'll look on the other."

We began the drive back, me going slow as we scanned the road, fields, and endless trees. I slammed on the brakes. "You drive. I'm climbing in the back to get a higher visual."

"Good call."

I braced myself as the truck lurched forward. From this vantage point, I could see down more of the tree line and farther into the ditch. A short distance later, a flash caught my eye, and I pounded on the cab roof. "Stop!"

I rescanned the area, trying to figure out what I thought I saw. Once again, there was a flash of something shiny just behind us in the ditch. I jumped from the back and ran toward it, my stomach dropping when I saw Charly's bicycle, bent and broken, lying in the ditch, almost covered by the long grasses that grew along the edge of the road. Then I heard it. The faint sound of the bell I had put on the handlebars for her.

I took off running, yelling her name. "Charly! Red! Ring the bell, baby. I need to find you!"

I heard the tinkle of the chime and spotted her. She was on the ground, propped against a tree, obviously hurt.

I dropped to my knees in front of her, cradling her face. She was covered in mud and grass, blood seeping from a cut on her head, and her shoulder at a strange angle. Her cheeks were wet with tears, mixing in the blood and dirt. In one hand, she held the bell, ringing it until I found her.

"Charly, baby, what happened?" I asked, whipping off my shirt to staunch the flow of blood. Behind me, Stefano appeared and handed me a bottle of water. It was warm, but I held it to Charly's mouth.

"Drink," I ordered. Her eyes fluttered open and she sipped. "More," I said. "Take another sip."

She did, more tears beginning to flow down her cheeks. "I knew-I knew you'd find me."

"You fell off the bike?" I questioned, cursing as I looked at her ankle. It was swollen and bruised. I needed to get her to the hospital. "You lost your balance?"

She drew in a long stuttering breath. "It was lost for me."

I froze as her words sank in. My voice was ice when I spoke. "Someone forced you off the road?"

"Y-yes."

I carefully slid my hands under her, lifting her. She gasped in pain, her head falling to my shoulder. I walked slowly, trying not to jostle her. I saw Stefano ahead of me, lifting the bent bicycle into the back of the truck.

"Who?" I demanded quietly, already knowing the answer.

Her eyes were shut and she went limp, but I heard her response before she passed out.

"Donners."

I paced the waiting room, furious and intense. Brett arrived with Mary, and they were all silent and watchful, knowing I was about to explode. The staff wouldn't allow me in the room, taking Charly's limp form from my arms and rushing her away. I stood in the hallway, not moving until a doctor rushed past me. He glanced over his shoulder and stopped.

"Maxx?"

Jerry Harper was a customer of mine at the garage. I gripped his arm. "That girl in there. She's important. I need you to take good care of her."

He studied me, then nodded. "She's in good hands. I promise."

"You'll update me?"

"As soon as I can." He clapped my shoulder. "We need the space, Maxx. Go to the waiting room. I'll be out when I can."

I kept my eyes on the door that separated me from her, willing him to appear and tell me what was going on. She had slipped in and out of consciousness in the truck. Stefano drove as fast as he could, being careful to avoid as many potholes and dips in the road as possible. Every time we hit one, Red would whimper or groan, her body stiffening in my arms. All I could do was hold her, whispering quiet words of comfort in her ear, pressing kisses to her head, and promising her she'd be okay. Inside, I burned, planning on the punishment I would inflict on the Donner brothers once I made sure she was looked after. It wasn't going to end well for either of them.

Finally, Jerry came out, heading toward me. I stopped my pacing, facing him. The rest of my group joined me, all anxious for news.

"She's awake and talking. She has a lot of contusions and cuts, but luckily none of them need stitches. Her shoulder is dislocated, and her ankle is badly sprained. She has a slight concussion, so she needs to be woken up every two hours." He shook his head. "She's lucky. It could have been a lot worse."

I let out a long exhale of relief. "Can I see her?"

"We have to reset her shoulder." He met my eyes. "I need you to stay here and stay calm, Maxx. Once that's done, and we clean her up, you can see her."

"When can I take her home?"

"We want to keep her for a while. Her blood pressure is a little low—probably shock, but we want to be sure."

A strange feeling crept into my chest. It constricted my breathing, and I had to force myself to stay calm. Jerry must have noticed my struggle, because he patted my shoulder and his voice was soothing.

"It's quite a normal reaction, Maxx. She's hurt, and her body is adjusting. We'll monitor her closely."

I could barely acknowledge his statement.

"Is there someone to sit with her tonight?"

All four of us spoke at the same time. "Yes."

"Then I know she'll be in good hands." He looked behind me, addressing Mary. "Keep him here." He turned and disappeared into the room again.

She pulled on my arm. "Sit with me, Maxx."

I shook off her grip. "I'm fine—what the hell is going on?"

The sound of Red's anguished, pain-filled cry pierced my heart. My body locked down at the sound, and a noise I had never made escaped my throat. I needed to get to her. I pushed forward, but Mary stood in front of me, blocking my way, and both Stefano and Brett had a hand pressing down on my shoulder, not allowing me to move.

"It's done now," Mary assured me. "Her shoulder is back in place. It's very painful, but fast. She'll feel better."

"I should have been in there," I rasped.

She shook her head, a smile pulling at her lips. "I think Jerry was wise to keep you away. He knows you would have reacted and, no doubt, punched him in the face. He has a nice face. Shame to damage it." She cupped my cheek. "Relax. You need to relax. She is going to need you, Maxx."

I swallowed and forced my shoulders to drop. "She has me," I murmured.

Mary's eyes were tender. Understanding. "I know."

Jerry came from the room, looked over at us, and held up his hands. "We're giving her pain meds and strapping the ankle. You can go in soon. The worst is over."

He glanced toward Mary. "Good job. I didn't need the hulk appearing and breaking the place."

Mary laughed. "He has a little more control than that."

"Not much," Brett muttered. "Not when it comes to Charly."

I snapped my head in his direction, but he simply shrugged. "It's true, big guy. Give in and enjoy it. She's something special."

I looked toward the door that kept me from her.

He was right. She was.

It felt as if hours passed before I was allowed in to see her, although Mary told me it had only been forty-five minutes. I stepped into the room, pausing at the end of Charly's bed. I felt a strange lump in my throat looking at her. Tenderness and rage battled in my head. I wanted to hold her, comfort her. I wanted to go find the bastards and beat them until they were bloody.

Tenderness won out.

I moved to the chair beside her, sitting down and letting my gaze roam freely, assessing all the injuries I could see, and worried about the ones I couldn't.

Her face was wan, paler than I had ever seen her. Her freckles were drops of ink on the pallid skin. Her eyes were shut, her long lashes resting on her cheeks, and her matted hair was pulled away, leaving her face exposed. A huge bruise on her forehead and another on her cheek bloomed dark and angry. Abrasions were scattered everywhere. Her hands were resting on the blanket, more bruising and cuts marring her skin. Her ankle was propped up, a tensor bandage wrapped around it, the swelling evident. I was certain if I drew back the blanket on her I would see bruising and cuts on her legs.

Fury began to win out over the need to stay beside her, but before I could move, her eyes fluttered open, the mossy green almost gray with pain. Tenderness returned full force, and I learned a new lesson.

I hated to see this girl in pain. *My girl.*

She lifted her hand, seeking, and I carefully enclosed it within mine. "Hi," I managed to get out past the lump in my throat.

"Hi." She swallowed. "You found me."

I leaned closer, wanting to kiss her but worried about hurting her. I bumped the end of her nose with mine. "I'll always find you, Red."

A tear slid down her cheek.

"Are you in pain?"

"No. I think they have me on some good stuff."

"I told them only the best."

Her smile was wobbly, but there.

"Could I have some water?"

I poured the cold liquid into a cup and held the straw as she sipped.

"Better," she sighed.

There was a knock at the door, and a police officer walked in. I recognized him—another guy I'd gone to school with who came to the shop regularly with his wife's car. She had been at the class the other day, and I was certain she was coming to the next one.

Todd came forward. "Maxx."

I shook his hand, and he introduced himself to Charly. "I'd like to ask you some questions, if you're up to it, Miss Hooper."

"Charly," she insisted.

"My wife Bonnie, talked about you the other night. She loved the class."

Charly smiled, despite her discomfort. "Good."

"Why are you here?" I asked. I hadn't called yet, too preoccupied with Red.

"The doc called me. Said he had a patient run off the road. I came to file a report and see if we can find who did this."

"We know who it was," I snapped.

"Well, that will make it easier," he said, not reacting to my tone. "Can you tell me what happened, Charly? Take your time," he added gently.

I flipped my hand over on the bed, and she slipped hers onto it, holding my fingers. "I was on the bicycle going to Mary's. I saw a truck on the other side of the road. It slowed down, and I saw who was driving," she whispered.

"Who was it?"

"The Donner brothers."

"Who was the driver?"

"The younger one. Chase. Wes was in the passenger seat."

"Ugh," he muttered, so low I almost missed it. "Keep going," he said in a louder voice.

"The truck spun around and started following me. They kept coming abreast of me, making stupid remarks."

"Such as?"

"Asking me where my bodyguard was. Saying I wasn't so tough on a girly bike. Wes yelled he owed me some humiliation. I ignored them. They keep crowding me closer to the ditch, so I just stopped pedaling and let them go by. They kept driving, and I waited a few moments until the truck disappeared. I figured they'd had their fun and were gone, so I started going again."

She stopped, and I held out the straw so she could have another drink. She squeezed my fingers then continued.

"They were waiting ahead, at one of the crossroads. I saw them too late to stop, so I started pedaling harder. I decided I was going to pull over in the next break and call Maxx and tell him. I knew he'd come get me." Her eyes met mine, and I nodded.

I would always come if she needed me now. I knew that, with an utter certainty I couldn't explain.

"They came right alongside me, yelling and shouting insults." Her breathing picked up, and I moved close, holding her hand tighter.

"It's okay, baby. Just say it. They can't hurt you now."

"I was standing, pedaling as fast as I could. I was so close to the edge of the ditch, and I couldn't stop. I knew there was an intersection coming up—I only had to go about another ten feet and I'd be okay—I could veer away. But I suddenly felt a sting on the back of my legs. It was really painful, and it startled me. I lost control of the bike..." Her voice trailed off. "The next thing I knew, I was in the ditch, they were gone, and the bike was damaged and I couldn't move it. I crawled out of the ditch and the bell was lying there, so I grabbed it. I couldn't find my bag with my phone, and I was in so much pain, it was all I could do to crawl to the trees and collapse. I kept losing consciousness, and then suddenly I heard Maxx."

I took up the story, knowing she was exhausted. I told Todd how I found her, and when he asked about their history, I told him about Wes and the bar, and the other run-ins.

Todd was shaking his head. "I'm not surprised to hear the name Donner associated with this."

"What will happen if we file a report?" Charly asked.

"They'll be brought in and questioned." His voice was frustrated. "You know their daddy will have a lawyer there fast. It's going to be he said, she said. You didn't see another car, Charly? Anyone working in their field?"

"No."

He hung his head. "I guarantee you by the time the lawyer gets there, their father will have a witness that puts them in some other location at the time this happened."

My body shook with anger, because I knew he was right.

"They could have killed her," I snarled. "They need to be held accountable. This isn't some practical joke gone wrong. She is seriously hurt, and they are gonna get away with it?"

"I'll do what I can. You'll have to come to the station and sign a statement."

Charly looked positively ill. "Can we just leave it?"

"Leave it?" I roared. "Are you crazy?"

Todd held up his hand. "Calm down, Maxx. Why would you want to do that, Charly?"

"If they're going to get away with it, why make them angrier?"

"So, you want to do nothing?" I snapped, my anger taking over.

Mary's voice interrupted us. I hadn't heard her come in, but she must have been there for a while, listening. "You have to do this, child. Maxx is right—this goes beyond a prank. If we'd had rain in the last few days, there would have been water in the ditch. You would have been unconscious, and right now, you'd be in the morgue."

Charly gasped at Mary's frank appraisal, but she was right. That thought had been running through my head ever since I'd found Charly, making my stomach clench every time I thought about it. Todd nodded in silent agreement.

"Okay," Charley said faintly.

Todd stood. "I'm going to bring the boys in for questioning. You're certain it was Chase driving and Wes in the passenger seat?"

"Yes."

Todd fixed me a look. "Maxx, I know what you're thinking right now—what you're wanting to do. My advice—don't. Stay the hell away from them, and let me handle this." He paused meeting my eyes. "Don't jeopardize what I need to do to handle this legally. And don't do anything that will take you away from Charly. I don't want to have to throw you in jail for beating the shit outta those two lowlifes."

Mary spoke up. "I'll make sure he stays put."

I glared at her, but she ignored me.

Charly slipped her hand into mine. I looked at her, meeting her gaze. She was fragile and vulnerable, looking lost and in pain. "Please."

I couldn't refuse her.

"Okay," I promised.

CHAPTER 23

MAXX

Jerry finally agreed to let Charly come home in the early hours of the evening. Neither Stefano nor Brett would leave, and Mary only offered me a scathing look when I asked her, so it was a small group that escorted Red home. Stefano drove my truck so I could hold Charly. Brett followed us, and Mary went ahead to make sure the room was set up for when we arrived. Charly was more alert, and although she was acting brave, I knew she was hurting. Her shoulder was too sore to use the crutches they provided, so I carried her. It was easier on all of us, and I felt better holding her.

At home, Rufus howled at the sight of her in my arms, racing toward us, whining and barking. I stopped so he could sniff Charly, and she patted his head, then I went into the house, heading toward the bedroom. I settled her into bed, stripping off the hospital scrubs they let her borrow and sliding one of my T-shirts over her head. It would be far more comfortable. My rage grew when I saw the bright red welt high up on her thighs—the cause of her losing control of the bicycle. I had to inhale deeply not to react, knowing it would upset Charly, and I was careful not to touch the painful skin as I pulled the shirt down her legs.

I helped her lie back on the pillows, and Mary came in with a tray, containing some soup and toast. Charly ate a little, her eyes drifting shut, so I let her sleep, setting my watch for two hours.

I hated leaving her even for a short time, but Mary insisted, so I went downstairs and had a sandwich. Rufus remained by the bed, refusing to leave, so I allowed him to stay. I finished the sandwich and ran a hand through my hair.

"You don't all have to stay here. I'll look after Charly."

"And who will look after you?"

I scoffed. "I'm fine."

"You can't go after them, Maxx," Mary stated calmly.

"I swear, I won't—not tonight."

"Not at all. You need to let the police handle it."

"And if they don't?" I growled, fisting my hands on the table. "Wes whipped her with a reed or a branch—something thin and sharp. She's covered in bruises and cuts. If she hadn't landed in the ditch…" I trailed off, unable to finish the sentence. "They need to be held accountable."

For a moment, there was silence, then Stefano spoke up. "There are other ways of getting retribution without using your fists."

"Such as?" I asked.

He shrugged. "I can dismantle a truck in two hours with a socket wrench. Leave it in pieces scattered far and wide." His dark eyes twinkled. "Mercedes, too. They look great in pieces."

"Additives to gas lines can cause automobiles to break down —requiring expensive repairs," Brett muttered.

"A carefully placed cut on a tire could leave someone stranded on a country road. Heaven knows who might wander by," Stefano drawled.

"A pill slipped into a beer in a bar could make someone pretty damn sleepy. God knows how they ended up in the middle of the next province with no cell phone, keys, cash, or recollection of driving there," Brett offered.

"Handcuffed to their bumper," Mary added.

I glanced around the table. "Remind me not to make any of you angry."

Mary snorted. "Another good one would be a call to the tax department. That should cause some grief for their father. Unclaimed wages paid under the table would bring them trouble."

I held up my hands. "I get it. I'm not leaving her—not tonight, not tomorrow, not until she can get around again. I won't risk leaving her alone. Even though I want to feel his bones break under my hands for what he did to her."

"Wes is your target?"

I nodded. "He's the one who touched her. Frightened her into losing control. Chase used to be a good kid until the last few years. Then he started acting like Wes, but he's never been as... nasty. I think if he got away from Wes, he might act like a human being again. Wes has always been a little shit—right from the time we were kids."

"He went wild in his teens. His father did nothing to stop him, instead using his wealth to make the problems go away. Wes has never taken responsibility for his own actions," Brett agreed, having known him since we were all in school together.

"He is going to be accountable this time," I swore. "One way or another."

No one said anything but I felt the silent collective agreement from the group gathered around my table. All brought together by the little redhead upstairs.

Whom I had been away from for far too long.

I stood. "You all head home. Lock up behind you. I'm going upstairs."

"Make sure you give her something to drink every time you wake her," Mary instructed. "And keep ahead of her pain."

"On it," I said as I pulled a bottle of Charly's favorite cran-grape juice from the fridge. I filled a glass plus another of water, adding lots of ice since she preferred her drinks cold.

Upstairs, Charly was asleep, and I let her rest. I had another forty-five minutes until I had to wake her. I sat beside her, taking her hand in mine. It was unusual to see her silent. I missed her voice and the way her eyes danced as she told me off about something.

I pushed a heavy lock of hair away from her face. I loved her hair. It suited her personality. Wild and untamable. I watched her sleep, studying her. She was incredibly strong. Memories hit me. Seeing her in the bar. Kissing her for the first time and feeling that odd connection with her. My anger at finding out she was the person who answered the ad. Her refusal to back down.

I had to smile as I thought of the way she had simply refused to take no for an answer and the way she forged ahead, creating more chaos in my life even as she made it better.

She handled whatever attitude I gave her and dished it back tenfold.

And I loved her for it.

I stared at her, somehow not shocked as those words settled in my brain. I dropped my head as realization sank in.

I was completely in love with Charly.

"I know."

Her voice, low and raspy, broke the silence, and I snapped up my head, meeting her green gaze in the low light. She smiled and lifted my hand covering hers to her mouth and kissed my knuckles.

"I love you too, Maxx."

✗

CHARLY

Maxx looked startled when I spoke. I had woken, seeing his large figure looming over me, his head hanging down. He was holding my hand, his thumb gently stroking over the bruised skin. He was talking quietly, not aware, I was certain, that he was mumbling his thoughts out loud.

When the words "I love her," were breathed into the air, I heard his sincerity—and also his surprise.

The words didn't surprise me. It wasn't the first time he'd said them.

Our eyes met, his dark gaze intense.

"You know?" he asked, his voice a low hum in the room.

"Yes." I struggled to sit up, and he immediately stood, carefully lifting me until I was comfortable. He waited until I had some cold juice, then gingerly sat on the bed beside me.

"How?" he asked.

"Today," I explained. "When you found me. In the truck, you kept telling me everything was going to be all right. You held me so carefully…" I trailed off.

"I was terrified," he admitted. "You were so hurt. I wanted to take away your pain." He leaned close. "I had to concentrate on you to stop myself from going and finding those assholes and making them pay."

"You had your mouth against my ear." I demonstrated, touching my lobe. "You said 'I love you, Charly. Stay strong for me. I love you so much.' Over and over again."

He stared at me, gaping. He had no idea he'd said those words. His surprise made me smile.

"I-I don't remember what I said."

I held his hand between mine. "Do you want to take it back?"

His stern face softened, and he brushed my hands with a gentle kiss.

"No, Red—Charly—Charlynn. Whatever name you are at the moment, I love them all. I love you."

"And you hate that fact."

"I should. I swore I would never fall in love again, except now I realize I have never been in love before. Shannon was a catalyst for all the pain I felt. I traded the pain of losing my parents for the pain of a tumultuous relationship with her. I never loved her. I needed to be needed by someone, and she was there. She was no good for me."

"And I am?" I asked.

He cupped my face. "You are the best thing for me, Red. I love your feistiness and your stubbornness. The way you talk back to me. Challenge me. Defy me." His voice softened. "Insist on doing all those little things to take care of me. You show your love for me in a hundred and one ways."

"I thought I drove you crazy."

"You do. In the very best way possible. I adore everything about you, Red. Your sass, your funny little sayings, the way you flutter around like a bird when you get nervous or upset. I even love all the little dots on your skin. I want to trace them all with my tongue and see what they spell out."

I wrapped my hands around his wrists. "You really love me?"

He pressed his mouth to mine in a gentle, soft kiss, then rested his forehead to mine. "Yes, I really do."

"Me too."

I felt his smile. "I know. I was blind for too long, but my eyes are finally open. I see what everyone else already knew. You are perfect for me."

"Yes, I am," I replied tartly, then grimaced as the pain flared.

He stood with a frown. "Enough sentiment. You need more pills and rest."

"Will you stay?"

He indicated the chair beside the bed as he shook out some pills. "I'll be right there."

"I want you to lie beside me."

"I have to check on you every two hours."

"Set your alarm."

"Stop arguing, woman," he growled. "For god's sake, do what I tell you for once."

I took the pills and swallowed them, looking up at him. He was glowering and intense. Just the way I liked him.

"Whew," I sighed.

"What?"

"I was worried if you loved me, you'd start being all nice and sweet. I don't want that. I like you all growly."

He smirked and shook his head. "You don't have to worry, Red. I plan on being especially growly when it comes to you."

"Thank goodness. I will reward you amply for that."

He snorted, then lay down beside me, letting me rest on his chest. He wrapped his arm around me, holding me close. "Go to sleep, Red. I'll wake you in two hours."

There was silence for a few moments, and I felt the emotions of the day catching up with me and a few tears slip down my cheeks.

"Maxx?" I whispered.

"If you're talking, you're not sleeping," he pointed out dryly.

"Thank you for saving me."

He tightened his arm. "I always will."

More tears followed, and he pressed a tissue into my hand. "Come along, sweetheart. I got you," he crooned and rocked me. "Let the day go. Just let it go."

After a few moments, the tears eased and I relaxed. I slid my hand on his shirt and found purchase in the fabric. It hurt to hold it, but I bunched it loosely in my fingers.

"Maxx?" I whispered again.

He pressed a kiss to my head, his voice a gentle hum in the dark. "Right here, Red. I'm right here. Sleep, baby. I got you." He paused. "Love you."

Sometimes, not growly was nice too.

"I know," I replied.

With a sigh, I let the darkness wash over me.

I woke in the bright light of midday, the bed empty. Maxx had finally stopped waking me up every two hours early in the morning, allowing me to sleep. Gingerly, I sat up and swung my legs off the mattress. My body was sore, bruises scattered everywhere, cuts and abrasions littering my skin. I stared at my strapped ankle then at the crutches that were across the room. I stood, checking my balance, then began to hop. I made it to the end of the bed, wondering how I was possibly going to get clear across the room when the sound of heavy footsteps met my ears and a frowning Maxx appeared in the doorway.

"What the hell are you doing?"

"I have to pee."

He glowered. "You could have called." He strode over and lifted me in his arms, his gentle embrace at direct odds with his frowning face and terse words. He carried me to the bathroom and set me on my feet, then crossed his arms.

"Um—privacy please."

"Not sure I can trust you alone."

"I am not peeing with you in the room."

"I'll be right outside, then."

"No. You need to go to the hall. Otherwise, I'll have performance anxiety and won't be able to go."

He lifted one eyebrow, a grin playing on his lips. "Performance anxiety?"

"Just go," I demanded, pointing to the door.

He walked out, and I heard him cross the room, muttering about stubborn redheads.

I quickly went about my business, then hopped to the sink, washed my face, and brushed my teeth. I wanted a shower but was pretty sure I'd be vetoed on that. The door opened, and Maxx glared at me.

"You never listen."

"Would you have me any other way?"

His face softened, and he pressed a kiss to my head. "No."

He fussed but helped me slip on a pair of loose pants and a fresh shirt of his, then carried me downstairs. Mary was there, sitting at the dining room table, and she smiled as Maxx slid me onto the chair beside her.

"How are you?" she asked, patting my hand.

"Stubborn," Maxx muttered at the same time I assured her I was fine.

"The boys are waiting for you to wake up."

"Stefano and Brett are here?"

Maxx snorted, placing a cup of coffee in front of me. "They've all been here since eight. We had breakfast, and they're grilling lunch." He sat beside me, sliding his hand over my thigh, his touch possessive and firm. "Your favorite. We hoped you'd be awake enough to eat with us."

"I'm hungry," I admitted.

"Good," he grunted.

I sipped my coffee, closing my eyes as the first hit of dark, rich flavor exploded in my mouth. Mary must have brewed it. Maxx's coffee always tasted like burned tar.

The boys came in, carrying a platter of grilled teriyaki chicken. Mary placed a bowl of salad on the table as they each hugged me carefully before sitting down. Maxx filled my plate, setting it in front of me, and I dug in, famished. As we ate, I noticed them all watching Maxx and me. He never took his hand off me for any length of time, and he stared at me as if I were going to disappear any second. I knew I hadn't been myself yesterday, the scare and emotion of the day making me needy, but I was feeling much better.

I smiled at him. "I'm fine, I promise," I whispered in his ear. He pressed his lips against my cheek.

"Good."

I turned and met three sets of curious eyes.

"We love each other," I said simply. "I mean, who could resist me?"

That broke the tension, and they laughed.

"Who, indeed," Maxx teased. "I didn't have a snowball's hope in hell."

"Nope," Mary agreed. "I knew it."

"Shut up, old woman."

She simply grinned.

Brett looked at Maxx. "Did you tell her?"

Maxx frowned. "I was going to wait until after lunch."

I shoved the last bite of chicken into my mouth and chewed. "All done."

He rolled his eyes and rested his elbows on the table.

"The Donner brothers are in jail."

"Their father out of town or something?" I asked.

He shook his head. "Todd said Chase showed up before he could go get them. Wes showed up before Todd could talk to Chase, demanding to see his brother. Todd put him in a separate room and went to talk to Chase. Chase confessed. Broke down, Todd said. Told him everything, demanding it be put on tape. He also informed Todd about a bunch of other things Wes has done. Apparently, Chase single-handedly solved a host of small crimes that have occurred lately."

"Wow," I said.

"Wes denied everything, saying they'd seen you on the other side of the road, but you looked wobbly on the bike. Claimed they never went near you or touched you."

"Of course," I stated dryly.

"He lost it when he found out what Chase had done."

"Why did Chase do it? What on earth prompted him to go against his brother?"

Maxx scrubbed his face, a small frown on his mouth. "It seems Chase has been seeing a girl in Lomand. Wes isn't happy about it since he is losing his sidekick, and Chase is realizing the error of his ways. He told Todd he wants to be worthy of this girl and decided to come clean. He thought Wes was just going to tease you a little. Instead, he spent the day thinking he'd killed you. This girl convinced him to do the right thing."

"Oh."

"The pain you felt, Charly? That odd mark on the back of your thighs? Wes had a thin branch. He basically whipped your legs, which, of course, startled you. Caused you to fall."

Maxx sat back. "With Chase's signed confession, not even his father could talk his way out with money. He's facing jail time."

"And Chase?"

"No idea. I am sure his lawyer will use his confession to make his sentence lighter. Maybe time served. Wes, though, is facing time for assault, petty theft, vandalism, and a few other charges."

"He's been a busy boy," Mary mused.

"Are you okay with this?" I asked Maxx.

He sighed. "I'm grateful he'll finally stop harassing people. He's been getting more out of control for a long time. Maybe some jail time and counseling will do some good. I only wish he hadn't hurt you for it to happen."

"I'm fine," I assured him. "I'll heal."

He only nodded.

I sat in silence for a moment. "So, Chase fell in love and

found his conscience. He chose a chance at a life with her over his family."

Mary smirked. "Isn't it amazing what love can do?"

I met Maxx's eyes. Despite the downturn of his mouth, his dark stare was filled with tenderness as he looked me. I felt his love and intensity in his presence beside me. His protectiveness and need to care for me, as deep as my need to look after him. His grip on my leg tightened as our gazes locked.

"Isn't love grand?" I quipped.

"Isn't it just," he muttered darkly.

But I saw his smile. And I winked at him.

"I know."

CHAPTER 24

CHARLY

I stared into the closet, looking at my choices, planning.

Maxx was an amazing caregiver. Attentive, patient, and gentle.

Far too gentle.

It had been ten days since the accident, and I was fine. My ankle got tired easily, but as long as I kept it wrapped, it was good. The bruises were fading, the cuts healing, and my shoulder in perfect working order.

Maxx had yet to touch me, other than to hold me at night, kiss me sweetly, or cup my face on occasion.

I was going crazy. I tried everything but present myself to him naked. At this point, I doubted even that would work. He would pick up a blanket and tuck it around me, admonishing me not to get cold.

A small voice in my head told me he regretted saying the words "I love you." Except his eyes said it every day. The way he treated me screamed it. There was something stopping him, and I couldn't figure out what it was.

Frustrated, I told Mary, who laughed.

"He's being male, Charly. Overthinking this."

"I don't understand."

"He keeps thinking of you lying and broken on the ground. He's afraid of hurting you."

"But I'm fine."

"Then show him."

"How?"

She smirked. "Oh, child. You know exactly how."

She was right. There was only one thing left to do.

I grabbed a T-shirt, a denim miniskirt I never wore, and a pair of scissors.

Desperate times called for desperate measures.

I could hardly wait to see his reaction.

MAXX

I stood in the garage door, staring over the yard. It was still early, the sun barely up. I hadn't slept much, too keyed up to do so. I was tired, grumpy, and short-tempered. A bad combination. Even Charly was subdued around me, which was unusual.

I couldn't seem to get past what happened to her. How close I'd come to losing her. A little rain, or another few feet where her head would have met concrete and not grass—the possibilities of "what if" seemed to haunt me. I wasn't sure how to move on from it. I was afraid to touch her with anything but gentleness, afraid to admit to the fear I had felt that day. Afraid to give in and make love to her in case I hurt her in some way. She had been distant herself, and I wondered what was going through her mind. Wondered if she regretted admitting her feelings.

I wondered how long we'd be at this impasse.

I saw the lights on upstairs in the house, and I knew Charly was awake. I was sure she'd be down soon enough. I took a draw on my coffee, knowing she'd throw out the pot I'd made and make fresh for everyone. She'd be sweet and organized, staying busy and on top of things. Pushing herself needlessly.

I swallowed as the door to the porch opened and she walked out of the house. For a moment, I didn't notice anything except her gait. Her footing was solid, indicating her ankle was better.

As she drew closer, it hit me.

Her outfit.

She was wearing a denim miniskirt, cut so small, it barely covered her thighs. The T-shirt she wore had a jagged neckline as if she'd taken a pair of scissors to it, exposing one shoulder. It was tied up in a knot under her breasts, hugging her torso and flashing the skin of her stomach. The new logo screaming "Hard as Steel" rested right under her bouncing breasts. Her hair was up in pigtails that sat high on her head. And those damn sparkly sneakers were on her feet.

As she drew nearer, it became evident she wasn't wearing a bra. Her nipples were hard and showed through the tight T-shirt. I glared at her as she approached. I braced my arm across the door, preventing her from entering the garage.

"I don't think so," I snarled.

She looked up at me, innocent. "I'm working in the store-room today. It's going to be hot. I'm dressed appropriately for the weather." Then she ducked under my arm and kept walking. With a low growl, I spun on my heel and followed her, stopping her halfway through the garage.

"That outfit isn't appropriate for anywhere but the bedroom."

"Is that an invitation?"

"No," I spat. "Change."

"No, I don't think I will," she retorted, shook off my grip, and beelined for the office.

Before I could move and stop her again, she dropped something and bent over to pick it up, giving me a full view of what else she wasn't wearing.

She was naked. Fucking naked under that miniskirt.

My cock, which was already pressing against my jeans, lengthened further, almost choking itself in my pants. With a low roar, I was on her in an instant, forgetting everything except the need to be buried inside her. I flung her over my shoulder, smacking her bare ass, berating her as I strode outside and toward the house.

"You asked for this, Red."

She clung to my ass.

"You had to push me, didn't you?"

She pinched me, giggling in her throat.

"You want to be fucked?" I snarled. "You're going to be fucked."

"Thank god," she breathed, tapping out a rhythm on my ass. "Hurry up, then, Grump."

I smacked her again, listening to her little gasps, feeling the way she was squirming on my shoulder. I ran my hand up her thigh and groaned.

"Feel how wet you are," I hissed. "You want this, baby?"

She grabbed my ass, squeezing.

"Can't you move any faster, old man?"

Inside, I kicked the door shut and headed upstairs. I dropped her on the bed, and in ten seconds, tore the miniskirt from her body, and ripped the T-shirt off her torso.

"You are not wearing that again," I growled, kicking out of my boots and yanking my jeans down. My cock jutted out, erect and angry, wanting inside her. I pulled off my shirt and looked at her. She was smiling, mischievousness dancing in her eyes. I hesitated one second, and she frowned.

"Don't get all touchy feely again, Maxx. Take me." She opened her legs. "Hard."

I was on her in a second. Kissing, licking, biting—any and all doubts gone from my mind. She was here. With me. Wanting me as much as I wanted her. I needed to let go of my fear. To let myself go.

We were wild, moving across the bed, our tongues and mouths searching for all the spots we knew best, learning new ones. I lapped at her heat, and she stroked my length, teasing the crown and cupping my balls.

I pushed her back to the bed, sucking her breasts, scoring over the sensitive nipples with my teeth. She cried out and arched against me. I teased her with my fingers, stroking her wetness, pumping them into her until she gripped at my shoulders.

"Inside, Maxx. I want you inside."

I buried myself with one hard snap of my hips.

We both cried out with pleasure. I didn't wait for her to get used to me. I began to move in long, deep strokes, lifting myself up on my knees, dragging her ass up my thighs and holding her hips tight as I drove inside her. She wrapped her legs around my waist, her low moans and whimpered gasps of my name burning into my brain.

I ignored the marks that lingered on her skin. I concentrated on the pleasure on her face, the flush in her cheeks. Her impassioned cries. The sounds our bodies made as they moved together. The feel of her muscles clutching at me.

She stiffened and cried out, screaming her release, gripping at the sheets. Sweat covered my brow, beading down my back as I held her tighter, lifted her higher, sank deeper.

The small lamp beside the bed hit the floor. A pillow fell from the bed. The headboard creaked, the mattress shifted, and my orgasm hit me like a tsunami, washing over my body in a long, sucking wave that obliterated everything in its path, leaving a blank, weightless darkness before throwing me back to earth.

I collapsed on her chest, spent. She wrapped me in her arms as I nuzzled at her damp skin.

"I think I made my point," she murmured.

"You did. Quite thoroughly."

"No more, Maxx. I'm fine." She hugged me harder. "Shake that day off. Stay with me."

I covered her mouth with mine and kissed her. "I'm right here, Red. I always will be."

She pulled me back down. "Good."

"The garage," I mumbled, feeling exhaustion bear down on me.

"The guys will handle it. Go to sleep."

I tried to fight it, but I felt it pulling me under.

I had to tell her before I succumbed to sleep. I had to say the words.

"I love you, Red."

She pressed a kiss to my head.

"I know."

EPILOGUE

Three months later

R ed came barreling out of the office, heading straight toward me. I stopped in the middle of a conversation with Brett, frowning at her.

"What?"

"I need the rest of the day off." She took in a deep breath. "And your truck."

"Oh boy," Brett muttered and moved away.

I scratched my chin with a grimace. "Not happening, Red. The one time I let you drive it, you almost took out the oak tree beside the garage. It's too big for you."

"But I have to go!"

Her voice quavered, and I moved closer. "Go where?"

"Solemn Ridge."

I gaped at her. "That's three hours away. What the hell is in Solemn Ridge that you have to go today?"

"The storage place I have my boxes in. I forgot to pay the bill, and if it's not paid today, I lose everything, Maxx! All my dad's things, all my..." She trailed off, her voice cracking. "I have to go."

I yanked her into my arms. "I'll drive you, Red. It's okay."

I met Brett's eyes, and he nodded. I knew he and Stefano would cover the garage for me.

"I have to go to the bank, then get there and pay him. If I want to keep the boxes there, I need to pay six months in advance."

"I'll pay with my credit card, and you bring your boxes here. Put them in the barn. You should have said something. We could have gone anytime and gotten them."

"I forgot," she admitted. "I was thinking of a recipe and remembered it was in a cookbook of my mom's and realized that it was in the storage place and I hadn't paid since I've been here. I called to make arrangements and the man told me the locker would be repossessed if I didn't pay."

I pulled her into my arms and stroked her back. "Okay. It's okay. I'll pay it, and you'll get your stuff. You won't lose anything, Red. I promise."

Three hours later, I was dealing with the manager of the storage place. He was short and stout, with a bad comb-over, and reminded me of Danny DeVito. He was lecturing Charly until I walked in to see what was taking so long. His eyes widened as I slipped my arm around her waist.

"Problem?"

"The credit card isn't in her name," he informed me.

"No, it's mine. I was on the phone outside."

"I told you that," Charly huffed. "And I already apologized. I sent you a change of address and my phone number. You never called."

"I never got it."

I interrupted him. "Just put the charge through—" I glanced

at his name tag "—Arnie, and give her the new key. We'll unload the locker and be out of here." I tapped on the counter. "Now."

He slid a key toward Charly. I kissed her forehead. "Go open the locker. I'll bring the cart. Don't lift anything."

She left, and I glared at the manager. "You could be a little more polite."

"Listen, you know how often I get stiffed? She's lucky I gave her a couple extra weeks." Arnie grumbled, fumbling with the credit card machine. "Damn lines are down. I gotta try again."

It took over ten minutes, and I finally went around the counter to help him. He had pulled the cable loose with all his fussing. He bitched about dealing with problem customers and payments all day. He finally put the payment through, and I went to the truck to get the handcart. I had just pulled it off the truck when Charly came tearing out of the building, her hair streaming behind her and her face pale. I dropped the cart at the look of utter panic on her face.

"What?" I grabbed her arms. "Red, what happened?" If that bastard had touched her, I was going to kill him.

"Maxx," she gasped. "It's-it's here."

"What's here, Charly?"

"Your bike."

I frowned in confusion. "My bike?"

"Your Indian motorcycle. I think I just saw it."

I strode down the hall, my heart beating a hundred miles an hour, anger burning in my gut. Charly explained that as she went toward her locker, there was a couple arguing loudly in the aisle next to hers. She heard them talking about moving the contents of the locker somewhere else since they were out of money and couldn't pay the rent anymore.

"It's time to sell it," the woman hissed. "It's worth a ton of cash."

"It's too soon."

"No, we'll sell it out of province. Indian motorcycles are huge in the States."

At the mention of an Indian, Charly had headed toward the aisle and strolled down it as if looking for her locker. She glanced toward the open door and saw my bike, recognizing the color and custom-made saddlebags and seat, then kept walking so as not to cause suspicion. She described the couple, leaving me no doubt it was Shannon and Billy.

Outside Unit 2221, I looked at Charly, who nodded in assurance. The door was partially closed, and I could hear them arguing about how to get the bike out and where to store it. At the sound of their voices, I knew Red was right. It was them. I shoved open the door and stepped inside.

"Back in my garage is the best place," I snarled.

Two shocked sets of eyes looked at me. Two mouths gaped open.

Then all hell broke loose. Shannon started shrieking it was all Billy's idea and she was just biding her time until she could get the bike back to me. Billy protested loudly it was Shannon who came up with the idea. Shannon shoved Billy, who stumbled backward, and then she lunged at me, trying to get past. I gripped her arms, shaking my head.

"I don't think so, bitch."

Charly spoke. "I'll call the police now, Maxx?"

"Yeah, baby, do that."

Shannon's eyes grew round. "Baby? You're cheating on me?"

I barked out a laugh. "You fucked my best friend, robbed me, and took off with my bike, and you thought, what? I'd forgive and be waiting for you after all this time? After everything you did? Holy moly, are you barking mad?"

Billy scrambled off the floor. "What the hell, Shannon?"

"What's going on here?" Arnie appeared, and Shannon's expression changed.

"Oh thank goodness," she exclaimed, laying her hand on her chest. "This man is trying to rob us."

I snorted. "You have that the wrong way around. You robbed me. This——" I indicated the bike, dusty from sitting in a locker "——is my Indian motorcycle. These two stole it from me over a year ago."

"I have all the paperwork to verify it at the office," Charly spoke up. "I'll send it to the police."

Arnie cleared his throat. "I don't want any trouble here. I have rules, and I'll enforce them."

I wanted to snort. Enforce them? With what? The grease from his comb-over? Even Red could take him with one hand tied behind her back. He barely came up to her shoulder.

"The police will sort it out," Charly said, lifting her phone to her ear, her ring catching the light.

Shannon shrieked again. "You're engaged?"

I winked at Charly, loving how she lifted her chin and narrowed her eyes. She almost looked scary.

"That's right. We are. You have something to say about it?"

Shannon peered at the ring, a smug grimace curling her lips.

"Oh god, you gave her your mother's ring? Still a mama's boy, Maxx, I see," she said snidely. "Too cheap to spring for a new one."

Before I could say anything, Charly stepped in front of her, snarling and defiant.

"Listen, you heartless shrew. You know nothing about this man. What you scoff at and make fun of is his beautiful soul. Something which you don't have. And if you think your words will bother us, you're wrong. You're a thief, a liar, and a horrible person. So, your opinion means nothing to us. By giving me his mother's ring, he shows how much he loves me. He trusts me with something important to him." She paused. "Which is why you never got your greedy hands on it."

Shannon blinked at her, and Charly stepped back and looked her up and down. "Good luck in prison though. I hear hair dye isn't allowed, so your roots are gonna grow out. I'm sure you'll still be, ah, *popular* with the prison population, though."

Holding back my laughter, I wrapped my arm around her waist and kissed her head. "Call the police, Charly."

Billy held up his hands. "No, Maxx, please, man. Don't do that."

"Why the hell not? You stole from me." I looked around the locker. "Where's the Ducati?"

"Um, we sold it for parts."

My grip on Charly tightened, and she patted my arm. I had liked that bike, but I was grateful if they stripped one, it was the Ducati, not the Indian.

"But look, man, your tools are back there, and your dad's bike is safe. Take it. Take it all and let us go."

Shannon cursed at him, and he shook his head. "For once, Shannon, shut the hell up. I'm tired of listening to you. Ever since we started, my life has been a living hell."

She gaped at him. I doubted he had ever spoken to her that way. Billy didn't have much of a backbone. For a while, I had lost mine as well, and she took advantage of that. In retrospect, losing the bike had been a blessing since she went with it.

I studied Billy. He was gaunt and drawn-looking. Unhappy. Shannon looked the same as I remembered. But I noticed for the first time how hard she looked. Her eyes were cold and vacant. Her expression dissatisfied. Had she always looked that way, or had I gotten used to the sweetness of Charly's face?

Whichever it was, they deserved each other, and I was glad

Shannon was gone. I had to admit, though, I felt more pity for Billy than her. He had to put up with her.

"You know, he's right," drawled Arnie. I had forgotten he was even there. "If you involve the cops, they'll seize the bike and everything for evidence. God knows when you'll get it back."

Billy nodded furiously. "Take it. Let us go. We'll never bother you again. You'll never see us again."

"As if I could trust anything you say. You'll double-cross me and try to steal it again."

He shook his head. "No, I won't. I'm done. With all of this. I am sick and tired of it all." He looked at Shannon. "Especially you."

That caused a string of curses and accusations from Shannon. Charly peeked up at me, her eyes round as Shannon threw a major temper tantrum, including stomping her feet and flinging her arms around.

What the hell had I ever seen in her?

Finally, I reached my limit, and I whistled. Loudly. The piercing noise stopped Shannon mid-tirade.

"Enough," I commanded. "Just do what Billy said and shut the hell up, Shannon. Jesus, you chap my ass."

She opened her mouth, and I held up my hand. "One more word. One. And I'm calling the cops." She closed her mouth, glaring daggers at me instead.

"You have three minutes to get out of my sight before I change my mind. And here's a word of advice. Your pictures are up all over Lomand and Littleburn, and there is a warrant out for your arrest. Do not try to come back. You do, and I will have you arrested. Regardless of getting the bike back, you still stole the Ducati and a whole pile of cash, so there's more than enough to convict you."

Neither said a word. I focused on Billy. "I trusted you. You were my friend. You made the choice of her over me. I never want to see you again. Ever. Do you understand?"

"I get it. You won't."

"Then get out of here."

He moved past us, Shannon starting to follow. He looked over his shoulder. "I'm done with you too. Don't follow me."

He walked out, moving fast, and after a moment, she followed, arguing and pleading. The sounds of their voices faded away, and I sighed. Arnie hurried behind them, muttering about them stealing something from the office.

Charly looked up at me. "Your motorcycle," she whispered. "You got your motorcycle back."

I smiled and drew my fingers down her cheek. "Because of you, I did."

"I guess forgetting to make the payment was a blessing."

"You're the blessing, Red."

She looped her arms around my waist. "I liked you all tough and gruff. Telling her off."

"That felt good," I admitted. "I have to say, I feel sorry for Billy. He looks like shit."

She grinned. "I think Shannon is going to have to find her next victim." She paused. "I never knew you could whistle like that."

I smirked and whistled under my breath. "You were damn sexy defending me to her, Red. All tough and gruff," I repeated her words and bent down to kiss her. "Sexy as hell."

"We're a good team."

"We are."

She beamed up at me. "Let's load up your bike and my boxes and go home."

"Sounds like a plan."

✕

TWO YEARS LATER

I stood back and admired the two bikes in front of me. "Amazing job, Stefano," I praised. "This detail is stunning."

He grinned. "It was fun. What a great couple they are—and easy to work with."

I had to agree. In their late fifties, Teddy and Rose were avid riders. They had come to us with their matching Harleys, wanting them detailed and decked out. We sat with them, listening to what they wanted, and I was certain we had surpassed expectations.

Teddy was simple. He wanted black on black, lots of chrome and some silver airbrushing. His one request—a small rose somewhere he could see it on his bike for his wife.

Rose was harder to pin down. She loved feminine things, and her favorite color was purple. But she didn't want a simple, one-color bike. We ended up with a unique paint effect that started silver at the front, gradually darkening to gray and lavender, finishing with a rich vibrant purple at the back. Stefano had airbrushed an effect on the bike that looked like lace edging and added delicate lavender roses in places to highlight the beautiful finish. In the same place he added the rose for Teddy, he put a small teddy bear for Rose. We added other touches to the bike, the purple-edged seat and matching leather bags that would give her lots of storage. His bike had the same additions since they loved touring on the weekends.

Both bikes were works of art and would bring the garage more acclaim.

I clapped him on the shoulder. "You get to unveil them. You deserve the recognition."

He grinned. "Thanks, Maxx."

I strode through the restoration area—a new addition to the garage last year. Business was booming. I had to expand the garage to four bays, plus add the area for our restorations. Stefano worked only in the restoration area now, and we had expanded to cars as well as motorcycles. Three of us were working there full time, and we brought in a couple of extra people as needed. My eye caught the gleam of red paint, and as usual, I stopped and cast my eyes over the Indian motorcycle displayed in the corner. It was complete with the emblem finally added and another touch I never expected.

Charly was in the garage sorting through the boxes we'd brought from the storage locker. I insisted she unpack them and use her dad's things as further embellishments in the garage—he had an amazing collection of tools and car memorabilia. The pieces would be a great addition to the walls. I wanted her to add the personal items to the house so it would feel like her home—not just mine.

I heard my name being shouted. I looked up from the bike that I was inspecting carefully and stood as Charly came barreling out of the barn, holding something aloft.

"I found it! I found it! It was there, Maxx!"

I had no idea what she was talking about until she placed the Indian figurehead in my hand. I was struck silent as I studied it. They were rare, especially in this condition.

"I knew my dad had one a long time ago. I thought it was gone, but it was in the boxes! You can add it to the bike!" she exclaimed, dancing around in her excitement.

I had no response other than to lift her off her feet and kiss her. She was constantly full of unexpected surprises. This was a particularly good one.

Now, it graced the front of the bike, shining and epic. I rarely rode the bike anymore, instead using it as a display and taking it on occasion when I appeared at events to talk about restorations. It was a crowd-pleaser, but I only did it rarely. The bike had too much sentimental value to risk it being damaged or stolen.

Brett ran the garage, and our reputation was top-notch. I had made Stefano and Brett both part owners, and they were as diligent as I was about our status. Brett was a born leader, and the staff respected him. The garage was now renamed Reynolds & Co. Restorations and Repairs.

In the garage, the newly expanded area was busy. I raised my hand as I went through, pleased with what I saw. All bays full, all hands on deck, and a full schedule for the day. I passed Chase Donner, who greeted me with a grin. "Hey, Maxx."

I tilted my chin. "How's it going?"

"Great. On my way for another pickup."

"Safe trip."

He smiled and picked up the keys to the truck, walking out of the garage, whistling. I could recall the day he had shown up at the garage. I was busy working on a bike when Brett interrupted me.

"You might want to go out front."

"Problem?"

"Chase Donner is talking to Charly."

I was outside in five seconds flat. I headed toward Charly, already growling. What the hell was he doing here? And why was she even speaking to him?

Chase saw me and backed up, holding up his hands. His brother was in jail, their father apparently finally washing his hands of his sons. Chase was given a light sentence and had come home a few weeks ago.

"I'm not here to make trouble."

"Why are you here, then?" I snarled.

Charly put a hand on my arm. "Chase came to apologize to me, Maxx."

That gave me pause.

"I see."

Chase stepped forward. "I'm sorry for everything. All the trouble Wes caused, the fact that I was driving that day when Charly got hurt. I want to do something to make up for it."

I grunted. "You said your piece. You can leave now."

Charly frowned at me. "No, he wants to do something, Maxx. He's trying to find his feet." She gazed at him with a sad smile. *"No one will give him a chance."*

"Hardly surprising," I snorted.

He didn't react. *"I deserve that. But I've had some counseling, and I know what I did was wrong. I'm trying to move forward."* His hands gripped the baseball cap he was holding, his fingers moving restlessly. *"I wanted to offer my services if there was anything I could do to help you. To make up for what I did."*

"First off," I snapped, *"you can't make up for it. Second, if you think I would let you anywhere near this place or my wife, you—"*

"Maxx!" Charly snapped, interrupting me.

I stared at her, and she pulled me to the side. *"He needs a chance. He's trying to make a fresh start."*

I gaped at her. *"You expect me to help him?"*

She crossed her arms, glaring. *"You gave me a chance once."*

"Totally different."

She tilted her head, tapping her foot. *"If I can forgive him, then you should too. After all, he is the one who put his own brother behind bars because of how terrible he felt. That says a lot about his character."*

I knew that stance. The tapping of her foot and the inflection of her voice. She wasn't going to back down on this. *"What do you want, Red?"*

"We're getting busier all the time. We need someone to shuttle customers when they drop off their cars. Pick up parts. Wash cars. Run errands for me."

"You expect me to give him keys to a company truck?" I asked, incredulous.

"Yes. It's called trust. He needs a place to live and something to do. He needs help. The room in the garage is vacant. He has a parole officer willing to vouch for him," she insisted.

Jesus, she not only wanted me to let him work here but live here too.

"It's menial work," I pointed out.

"I'd do it," Chase spoke up. *"I would do anything, Mr. Reynolds. Please give me a chance."*

I looked in his eyes and saw nothing but honesty and desperation. I looked at Charly, who gazed back at me, her eyes pleading. "Please," she whispered. "I'm asking for me."

I could never say no to her anymore

"You take your meals in your room. I'll pay you minimum wage and deduct board."

"That's fair."

"Hardly," Red snipped.

I ignored her.

"You answer to Brett. He says you're out of here, and that's it. You fuck this up, I'm taking you down," I said to Chase.

"You won't regret it," he assured me.

And to this day, I hadn't. In the year he'd been with us, I'd seen the changes in him. He'd worked hard to fit in, and now he was simply one of us. Meals weren't boring—I never knew who was going to be at the dinner table anymore, and the bottom line was, it didn't matter. He had proven himself to me and everyone else. Brett had started teaching him how to work on cars, and the kid was a natural.

As usual, my wife had been right.

Not that I admitted it. Charly already had enough power over me.

I shook my head and returned to the present. I was looking for Charly. She wasn't in the garage much these days, although she snuck in more than she was supposed to.

I headed out the side door and toward the side of the house, smiling at the sight of the gazebo I had built in the yard. We had gotten married in it, one bright fall day. It was simple and perfect. A few friends, Red in a pretty dress and me in a suit. Vows that meant something were exchanged—rich and special to each of us. Food prepared by Stefano's family, who had taken us into their fold and treated us like their own. Our wedding cake was a pie. Lots of pies. It was a day of laughter and happiness.

And at the end of it, Charly was my wife.

It was all I needed.

I entered the house, grinning at the smell. It was pie day. Fillings were bubbling away on the top of the stove, and I knew Mary would be here shortly. Soon, an abundance of pies would appear. It was one of my favorite days of them all. I hadn't been sure it was going to happen this month, given Charly's condition, but she had insisted.

She was seated at the table, a glass of water in front of her, her feet propped up on a chair. I crossed the room and bent over, kissing her head. She looked tired.

"Why the hell are you not resting?" I demanded.

She opened her eyes, smiling as she rubbed her hand over her swollen belly. "Someone is far too active for me to do that."

I dropped to my knees and pressed a kiss to her tummy. "Hey, little man, give Mommy a break."

She patted her belly. "I think he wants pie as much as you do."

I shook my head. "You're eight months pregnant, Red. You shouldn't be doing a pie marathon day."

"Mary will be here soon. I did everything slowly. Once I roll out the crusts, she'll fill and bake them. I won't do any lifting or bending."

"Stubborn woman," I grumbled.

"Fussy husband."

I narrowed my eyes at her and growled. She chuckled and fanned herself.

"Don't go getting all growly and sexy, Maxx. You know what happens when you do that." She rubbed her stomach again. "I end up pregnant."

I had to chuckle. "It was your outfit that caused that to happen if I recall right."

She sighed. "My leather vest didn't last long."

"Neither did your skirt."

The day we were opening the new restoration area, she came downstairs and asked my opinion about her outfit. She had been sex on legs, wearing a tight leather vest with nothing else under it and a matching skirt. Leather boots completed the look.

"I thought it was perfect for the opening. Biker-chick-ish." She smiled widely, already knowing what my reaction would be. I gaped at her, unable to believe she really thought I would allow her out in public wearing next to nothing, when it dawned on me. I had been so busy with all the details, I had been neglecting her. Stressing over other things. It had been days since I had made love to her. She wanted me back in the moment.

And I was right there with her.

I stalked toward her, shaking my head. "I don't think so, Red."

The sexy, no-one-is-ever-seeing-that-outfit ended up on the dining room floor a few moments later, torn to shreds. I chased her into the living room and took her over the sofa, growling and showing her exactly what my opinion was on the subject. The leather boots stayed on, though.

A few weeks later, the morning sickness started, and I found out I was going to be a dad. She'd handed me a little wrench, tied with a yellow ribbon. It took a moment to sink in before I reacted. I was dumbfounded, excited, and scared all at once. Then I kissed her until she was breathless. Until she knew how much her news meant to me. How much she meant to me.

She had given me yet another dream I'd never thought I would have.

The wrench now hung over my workbench, framed and displayed proudly.

Next to my wedding day, it was the greatest day of my life.

"You still shouldn't be doing this. You look tired."

She waved her hand. "It will pass. My back was a little achy, but it feels better now."

I heard the sound of Mary's truck, and I stood, going to the door. Mary waved as I opened it, but before I could step out to help Mary carry a box she was holding, the sound of Charly's panicked voice made me turn my head.

"Maxx?"

She was standing, holding her stomach. A puddle of water was at her feet. She met my shocked eyes.

"Not an ache. A contraction."

"Holy moly," I muttered.

"No pies," she said in a shaky voice. "Today is now baby day."

Thomas Sean Reynolds arrived only four hours later, apparently anxious to make his presence known. At eight pounds, he was a good-sized baby, especially given he was early. He also possessed a great pair of lungs, which he liked to use to show his displeasure. Named after my dad and her brother, he was long and healthy, with a head full of hair that looked suspiciously dark red. He liked to hold my finger from the moment they put him in my arms. The first time he did that and blinked up at me with his wide eyes, I fell more in love than I had thought possible. The intense feelings I'd had all through Charly's pregnancy seemed insignificant to the massive emotion that now swelled through my body.

I was fascinated by him. Infatuated. I could barely put him down. I held him in one arm, and grasped Charly's hand, staring between the two people I loved the most in the world.

She had been amazing. Labor had progressed so fast there was no time for an epidural, and watching her bring my son into the world was one of the most profound experiences of my life. She amazed me before—now I was in complete awe of her strength.

The hospital was quiet, Charly finally resting. Tomorrow, visitors would come, and I knew the room would be buzzing with people and gifts for the new arrival. I wondered if it was rude to refuse to let anyone else hold my son. I could probably glower enough that they wouldn't ask. Charly might have something to say on the matter, though.

Stefano texted me to tell me his mother and sisters had been to the house, finished the pies and filled the freezer with enough food, we were set for weeks. Kelly had texted, saying she would arrive home next week and would be making a trip out to see Charly. She still flitted around the globe, taking her photographs, but she and Charly saw each other when they could and remained close.

Then the next day, I could take my family home. My feisty, beautiful wife and my son.

How my life had changed.

All because of the sleeping redhead who still kept me on my toes and loved me with a fiery passion that amazed me. She made my world brighter. Her spirit filled our home and the garage. She was adored by many, and her funny little expressions were now commonplace by all who knew her. Easy peasy, holy moly, chap my ass, were bandied about as normal parts of conversation. But they still made me smile hardest when she used them—especially thrown at me.

Her sassy mouth made me fall for her. The way she handled my grumpy ass and never backed down. The way she demanded that I never change. That she loved me exactly the way she found me.

My Red.

She stirred, and I leaned over and kissed her. "Love you," I murmured.

That sassy mouth curved into a smile before she drifted back into sleep.

"I know."

X

Thank you so much for reading REVVED TO THE MAXX. If you are so inclined, reviews are always welcome by me at your book retailer.

This was a fun story to write. Charly was just the type of heroine I love - gives the hero *just* enough of a hard time.

Want more men of Reynolds Restoration?

A car in trouble and a woman who is someone he get into far too much trouble with! Stefano Borelli is getting his HEA in BREAKING THE SPEED LIMIT.

Can he get her to stay in Littleburn? Brett Conner is hoping to tame her restless need to wander in SHIFTING GEARS.

If you'd like another glimpse into Maxx and Charly's future, click below to grab a little more time with them - Extended Epilogue Revved To The Maxx available at Bookfunnel: https://BookHip.com/MZJSX

Enjoy meeting other readers? Lots of fun, with upcoming book talk and giveaways! Check out Melanie Moreland's Minions on Facebook.

Join my newsletter for up-to-date news, sales, book announcements and excerpts (no spam). Click here to sign up Melanie Moreland's newsletter
or visit https://bit.ly/MMorelandNewsletter

Visit my website www.melaniemoreland.com

Enjoy reading! Melanie

ACKNOWLEDGMENTS

As always, I have some people to thank. The ones behind the words that encourage and support. The people who make my books possible for so many reasons.

Lisa, the owner of the mighty red pen and the lover of your commas, hater of mine.
Good job.
LOL
Many thanks for your continued efforts. One day I shall learn— but it is not this day.

Beth, Trina, Melissa, Peggy, and Deb—thank you for your feedback and support.
Your comments make the story better—always.

Karen, my faithful sidekick and keeper of passwords. You rock my world, keep me on my toes, and chap my ass on a regular basis. I would be lost without you.
I claim you for the next fifty years.
Mine.

To all the bloggers, readers, and especially my promo team. Thank you for everything you do. Shouting your love of books— of my work, posting, sharing—your recommendations keep my

TBR list full, and the support you have shown me is deeply appreciated.

To my fellow authors who have shown me such kindness, thank you. I will follow your example and pay it forward.

Stephanie Rose—your kind words and support have meant so much to me lately. Thank you.

My reader group, Melanie's Minions—love you all.

ABOUT THE AUTHOR

NYT/WSJ/USAT international bestselling author Melanie Moreland, lives a happy and content life in a quiet area of Ontario with her beloved husband of thirty-plus years and their rescue cat, Amber. Nothing means more to her than her friends and family, and she cherishes every moment spent with them.

While seriously addicted to coffee, and highly challenged with all things computer-related and technical, she relishes baking, cooking, and trying new recipes for people to sample. She loves to throw dinner parties, and enjoys traveling, here and abroad, but finds coming home is always the best part of any trip.

Melanie loves stories, especially paired with a good wine, and enjoys skydiving (free falling over a fleck of dust) extreme snowboarding (falling down stairs) and piloting her own helicopter (tripping over her own feet.) She's learned happily ever afters, even bumpy ones, are all in how you tell the story.

Melanie is represented by Flavia Viotti at Bookcase Literary Agency. For any questions regarding subsidiary or translation rights please contact her at flavia@bookcaseagency.com

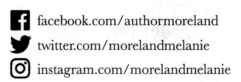

facebook.com/authormoreland

twitter.com/morelandmelanie

instagram.com/morelandmelanie

Printed in the USA
CPSIA information can be obtained
at www.ICGtesting.com
LVHW020552200823
755496LV00016B/944

9 781988 610948